OCEANSWEPT

OCEANSWEPT

Lara Hays

Book One of the Oceanswept Trilogy

Haze Publishing

ISBN-13: 978-0615928265
ISBN-10:0615928269

Acknowledgements

This book would not exist without the inexhaustible faith of my best friend and editor Jamie Boyd. Thank you.

Ryan Brijs, your visual creations made this work breathe with life. I am so lucky to have such talent in my corner.

A sincere thanks to Tisa Woolf, Jeromy Caballero, J. Clark Gardner, Meagan Spaulding, Jessica Zetterquist, Julie Groff, Stephanie Frederick, and Normandie Hays for their support and assistance.

Justin, you've helped a dreamer become a doer. Thanks for your sacrifice and countless soda runs.

Thank you to every single one of my readers. This book has been a work of passion, a trial of faith—a true pleasure to bring to life. I hope you enjoyed reading it half as much as I enjoyed writing it.

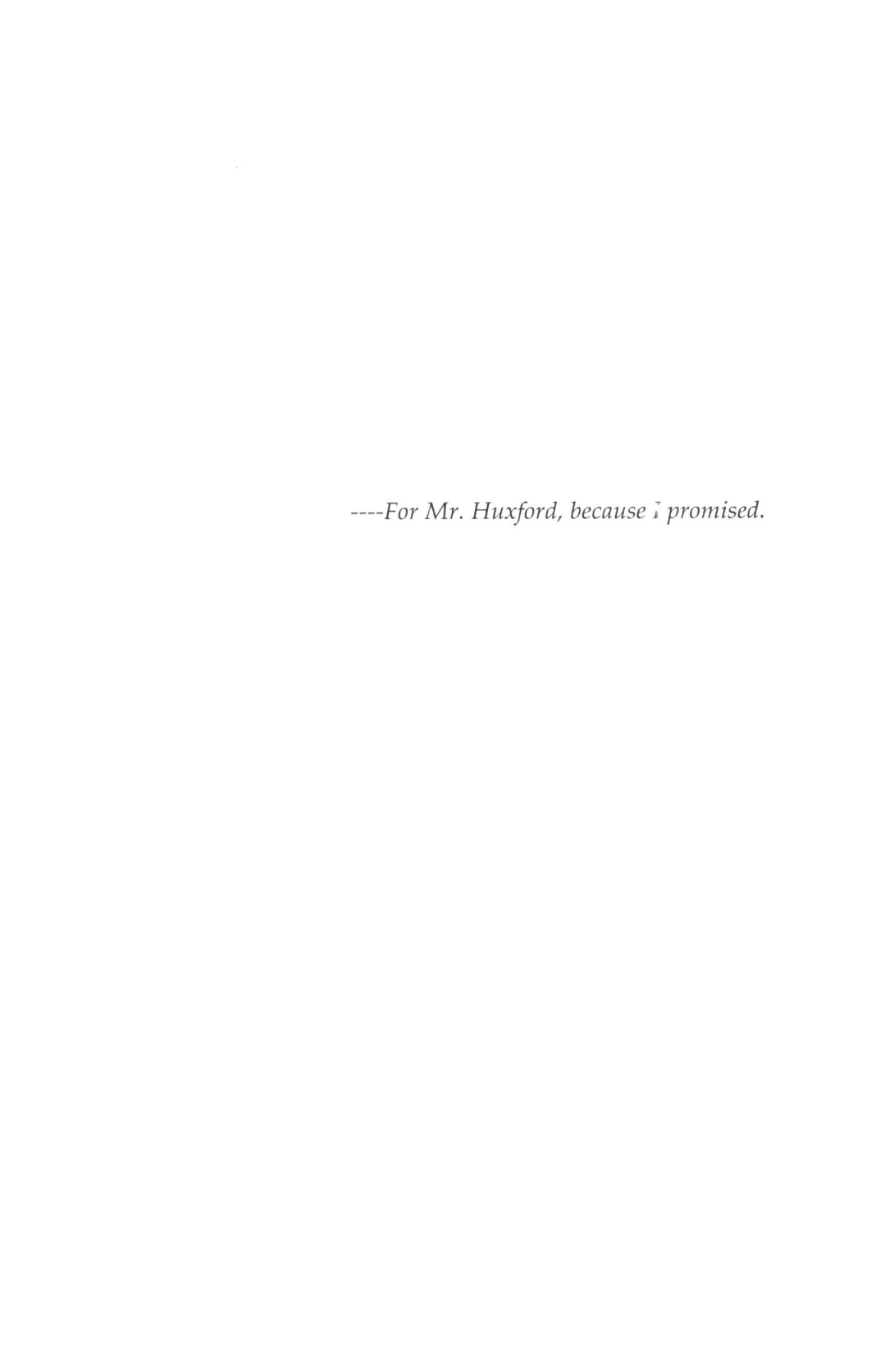

----*For Mr. Huxford, because i promised.*

PROLOGUE

THE AIR HUNG TREACHEROUSLY still, as if calculating its next violent outburst.

With a trembling hand, I pushed my sopping hair from my face and looked up at the boiling green clouds. I had never seen a sky that color. It was the shade of illness.

We were in a hurricane.

And from the quickly dying wind and the glimpses of blue sky fighting to break through overhead, I knew we were skirting the eye of the storm.

Braced in a corner of the main deck with a death grip on a line of rigging, I sat frozen with terror. Storms like this sank ships.

A man wearing the uniform of a naval admiral ran frantically about the deck of the ship shouting at every person he saw.

My father was looking for me.

"Here!" I called, waving an arm over my head.

A nearby sailor heard my cry. "Admiral Monroe!" he

hollered as he pointed in my direction, "Your daughter's over there."

My father ran across the waterlogged deck as I staggered to my feet. His thick hands pulled me into his chest. We were both dripping wet.

"Are you hurt, Tessa?"

I shook my head. "Is everyone all right?" I asked.

"I believe so."

In the eerie stillness, we surveyed the ship. The main deck was flooded, debris floating around us. From bow to stern, sailors scurried about, preparing the ship for the storm's next onslaught.

"There's so much water. Can the ship hold?"

"God willing. The men are at the pumps now."

My father's trained eyes scanned the sails. His mouth tightened into a concerned line.

"Go to my quarters," he dismissed me. "You can wait out the storm there."

He hurried to the captain, pointing at the fore-topsail. The sail had blown free and become entangled in the shrouds. The wind was picking up, its chaotic patterns blowing into the jammed sail. The captain relayed the message to the first mate, who hollered orders to cut the sail loose. Two sailors climbed the ratlines, their deft figures shrinking in the distance overhead. My head grew dizzy watching them climb to such heights.

A deafening groan pierced the air.

Whirling in confusion, I pressed my palms against my ears and looked to my father.

"The mast!" he cried.

Wooden shards as big as swords rained down on me as the massive spar in the middle of the ship tipped in my direction, as if bowing before a dance partner.

My father rushed to my side. "Run!" He pushed me starboard, one step behind me.

I covered my head with my arms in a weak attempt to shield myself from the plummeting splinters.

The groan ended with an explosive crack and the mast plummeted towards us.

"Jump over!" my father yelled, steering me to the rail.

"Over?"

Before I could protest, he hoisted me by my waist and tossed me over the rail. I barely had time to close my mouth before the black water swallowed me whole. Kicking my legs, I shot to the surface in time to see my father splash beside me.

I fought against the giant swells and swam towards my father, our fingers finally linking.

"Just keep swimming," my father panted. "They'll send a boat."

The sailors on board scrambled in the aftermath. They released jollyboats to fetch us and the handful of sailors who had fallen overboard with the mast.

I looked at my father. His face was gaunt and his eyes dark as he looked at the surrounding storm. When he caught my gaze he tried to smile in reassurance, but the smile did not reach his eyes.

Large swells attacked me, and I barely bobbed above water long enough to take a quick breath before another wave tackled me.

"Papa, I can't—" A wave smacked me in the face, stopping my words with a mouthful of brine.

"They're coming," my father managed between onslaughts of water.

My legs stiffened with every kick. My energy was draining fast and I was spending more time below the water than above it.

I panicked. I thrashed. I swallowed ocean water.

Forcing me to look into his eyes, my father steadied me

with his steely gaze. "Tessa. Keep swimming. The boat is nearly here."

I tried to do as he ordered, but my body refused. My head went under again. My father pulled me above the waves and cinched me close to his chest.

"Don't you give up, Tessa," he grunted fiercely. "Don't you give up."

The broken ship bobbed precariously on the horizon, the fallen mast looking like a dismembered limb. A sudden sheet of rain pelted the surface of the water and the green-black clouds roiled in the heavens. Going through a hurricane was dangerous for anyone, but for two people in the clutches of the ocean, exhausted from treading water, it was a death sentence.

I willed my legs to kick. They refused. I slipped under the water.

Everything went dark.

CHAPTER ONE

I AWOKE TO THE sound of waves breaking against the hull, their rhythm keeping time with the ship's fluid dance. Soothing and serene, it was a sound I had grown to know well over the past few weeks of my voyage across the Atlantic.

The blackness of the ocean at night pervaded my cabin like a heavy vapor. It was so thick that I felt as if I could touch it, send ripples through it with a flick of my finger.

I felt like I had been asleep too long. My head pounded. My body felt wooden. I struggled to remember the previous night. My memories were a blur. I must have taken ill.

I sat up slowly. My stomach lurched. I closed my eyes and breathed deeply, suppressing my urge to vomit. It was a familiar practice. I had been battling the nag of nausea since we'd been at sea. My father reassured me I would find my sea legs, but that obviously had not happened yet. He had also promised me the voyage would last only six or seven weeks. We had been sailing for nine.

My father, Archibald Monroe, was recently promoted to admiral in the British Navy. Along with his promotion came an assignment to relocate to the West Indies and secure the trade port at St. Christopher—commonly called St. Kitts. With the influx of Spaniard privateers and independent raiders, it was a task as dangerous as it was critical to the Empire.

Despite the dangers, I was thrilled by the idea of life in the West Indies. Good riddance to the filth of London, the dreadful moors, the bone-chilling fog. I was ready to embrace the constant heat, the graceful palms, and the fledgling society of St. Kitts. The colony was certainly buzzing about the imminent arrival of a revered admiral and his genteel daughter. A dozen invitations to balls would be waiting when I disembarked. I had every intention of playing the coquette. After vetting suitable matches, I would settle for no less than the most eminent suitor, perhaps even a governor's son. I would secure a position in society that would have been out of reach in the motherland.

But after nine weeks of sailing, it seemed we'd never drop anchor. I was frustrated by the long, dull days with no companions, the cramped quarters, and the bland food. A brief stop in the Canaries a month ago rekindled my excitement, but my eagerness quickly turned to impatience. Would my new life in St. Kitts never begin?

I ran my fingers through my long, chestnut-colored hair—or rather, I *tried* to run my fingers through my hair. It was so full of mats and tangles that I hardly recognized it. It felt more like frayed rope. I tugged and straightened my stiff clothing, suddenly realizing I was not wearing my usual nightshift, but only my undergarments. Startled, I tried to think why I was in such dress, especially in so public of circumstances.

Something was wrong. I tried to focus in on the feeling

nagging at the back of my mind, but I was too confused to make much sense of anything.

I staggered around my room, with my arms stretched before me, palms splayed wide, feeling for my dressing gown that I had hung on a hook by my bed.

I did not find it.

I dropped to the floor and explored my small cabin in search of my trunk.

I did not find it.

"Lucia!" I called. How dare my maid move my belongings? "Lucia!"

When she hadn't responded within two full minutes—a generous courtesy—I made my way to the door. My father would hear about this. My fingers fumbled against a wooden latch instead of the brass handle I expected. I gasped.

And then I remembered.

The mud-colored sky. The guttural groan of the breaking mast.

I closed my eyes against the memories, only to find them more vivid.

My things weren't here because this was not my cabin. This was not my ship.

We had obviously been rescued. This thought should have put me at ease, but I still felt agitated. I needed my father.

Because I had no dressing robe, I resorted to pulling the linens off the small bed and wrapping the undersized sheet around my shoulders. It barely offered any decency, but it was the best I could manage.

Taking a deep breath to steady my nerves, I swung the cabin door open and peered into the darkness.

To my left, the corridor disappeared into blackness. To my right, the moonlight illuminated the end of the corridor leading to the deck. There was another door across from mine. I quietly pressed my ear against it. A thunderous snoring came from within. I stepped back quickly. That was definitely not my father.

My eyes strayed down the corridor. I could either seek the aid of a sailor on deck or wait in my cabin for someone to come to me. I sneered at the thought of venturing out on my own. I returned to my cabin.

I tried to fall asleep to no avail. After at least forty minutes, I garnered the nerve to seek the aid of a night watchman.

I clutched my sheet with both fists and stealthily walked to the end of the corridor. I stopped at the edge of the deck to take in my surroundings.

An overcast sky glowed silver with the backlighting of a full moon, illuminating the ship before me. My eyes wandered to the two masts towering into the night. The yards crossed each mast like the spindly arms of a scarecrow. I easily identified them all—from the main yard closest to the deck to the distant royal yard that marked the top of the mast. The heavy canvas sails were taut with a strong wind, stretching against the silvery sky. For a moment, the tranquility of the night stilled all my anxieties.

Approaching footsteps broke the moonlight's spell. I whirled around, trying to see who was closing in. I saw nothing.

I was suddenly afraid of what I might find on this deck, though I couldn't say why. These seamen were my rescuers, I reminded myself, and I was deliberately seeking the aid of one. I had no reason to fear them. Still, I began to consider vanishing into my cabin and waiting for my father to come to me.

I was slowly backing into the shadows of the corridor, intent on doing just that, when a voice cut through the breezy night.

"Don't be frightened, miss."

My heart pounded as I waited for the man to show himself. I clutched even more tightly at my insufficient sheet, though it billowed and blew about, exposing my pantalooned legs.

Though I had been brought up at sea, I had never been comfortable with sailors. They were base creatures lacking morals and decency, ready to seize any hedonistic opportunity. No doubt a lady like me would be considered such a prospect.

A man emerged from the darkness, though shadows still cloaked his features. He stood tall and lean, the posture of a strong young man.

"Don't say a word. Just follow me," the man said in a low voice.

"Excuse me?"

"You best do as I say."

"How dare you—"

"Shh!" He hissed.

The man closed the distance between us. I felt his face inches away from mine.

"I will not be threatened into submission." I sounded bolder than I felt. "I demand you take me to your superior this instant or—"

The sailor glued a hand across my mouth, pressing me against the wall of the corridor. He turned his head nervously towards the sound of a shuffle in the distance.

Taking advantage of his split attention, I let out the loudest, shrillest scream I could muster. His hand pressed tighter against my mouth, all but muffling the sound.

"Do you have no value for your own head?" Fury rumbled through his dark whisper.

Grabbing my arm with his free hand, he steered me into the cabin from which I had come.

"You need to know two things," said the sailor. "One:

you are not safe on this ship. Two: I will do my best to keep you safe, but if you don't trust me, you'll wish you were dead by sunrise."

Stunned, I stopped fighting him.

"I am going to let go of you now. Do not scream. Understand?"

I nodded my head, knowing I would make a fuss the second I could. The man released his grip. I sucked in a breath, ready to scream again.

"Please," the man whispered desperately.

His pleading surprised me. I let my breath out in a huff.

I wanted to get as far from him as I could, and I took a step back only to be met by the bulkhead. The cabin was so small and the sailor filled half of it.

We stood awkwardly in the cramped cabin, each staring at the other. The sailor broke the silence.

"What's your name?"

I withheld my answer. This man wanted my silence and he would get it.

"Are you injured?"

I remained silent.

"Does it hurt to move?" he pressed as if talking to an idiot. "Are you in physical pain of any kind?"

I looked away.

"You don't have to cooperate. But if you won't answer my questions, I'll have the medic examine you personally."

My eyebrows shot up. "You would not dare."

"So, are you hurt then?"

I glared a bit but decided I had better answer or he truly would call a medic. I shook my head brusquely.

"Tell me your name."

All these demands! "Miss Monroe to you," I sneered.

"I'm Nicholas. Now, stay here in your cabin. I'll be back for you later."

I was inclined to do the opposite of what this man said. But part of me wondered whether he was right. Was this ship as dangerous as he said?

"Can you at least send my father to me?"

"Your father?"

"It would be a considerable kindness," I pressed.

The young man shifted his weight. "Your ship was lost at sea."

"The hurricane. I remember."

"We pulled you from the wreckage." There was a hesitation in the sailor's voice. I didn't like it.

"Yes, how very noble of you. I'm sure my father will reward you handsomely. Now if you'd just send him to me."

"Miss Monroe, there was no one else."

Pieces of a puzzle fit together now. The memories of the compromised ship. The pull of the stormy ocean. Waking up alone without my overprotective father nearby.

"My father?" I faintly asked.

"Lost at sea, I imagine. I offer my condolences"

The trill of a bell echoed through the night, signaling the end of the first watch. Nicholas poked his head out of the cabin, peering both ways down the corridor. Pausing in the doorway, he issued another cryptic warning. "I know you have no reason to trust me. But believe me when I say that leaving this cabin is certain death."

Nicholas tipped his head and backed out of the room, closing the door behind him, leaving me alone in the cabin that would either be a haven or a prison—I knew not which.

I threw myself on the bed and cried against the pillow.

CHAPTER TWO

I CRIED UNTIL I vomited in the chamber pot and then I cried some more. My father was dead.

After the second bell of the middle watch, a soft rap sounded at the door. I stifled my sobs and waited for an indication of danger.

"Miss Monroe? Please open the door."

I ambled to my feet, despite the stiffness in my legs, and wiped my eyes before opening the door.

The silhouette of Nicholas stood in the doorway. "Are you hungry?"

My stomach growled in response. "I suppose so."

"Let's get you something to eat then."

I rummaged through the bed linens and found the sheet I had used as a cover before and draped it over my shoulders.

Nicholas scanned me from head to toe. "That's hardly effective."

"I suppose you think I should go without?"

With an amused smile, Nicholas shrugged off his canvas jacket and handed it to me.

Instinctively, I took the jacket and put it on. It still held the sailor's warmth. The hem hit me below the knees and the sleeves swallowed my arms. It hadn't been properly laundered in ages—at one time it was probably white but now the canvas was a sodden grey. I wrapped it around my torso, feeling surprisingly safe. It smelled of heady musk and ocean brine—a scent I found oddly pleasing.

Nicholas offered his arm to me. I hesitated, but took it. It was too dark for me to make my way alone on an unfamiliar ship.

He hurried me out of the corridor, across the main deck, down a steep ladder into a pitch-black room, and then released my arm. I stood as still as a statue, afraid of what I might run into if I tried to follow his footsteps in the darkness.

A moment later, a lantern blazed with life, flooding the ship's galley with light. The perimeter of the room was dotted with mismatched cabinets and oversized barrels. A heavy, worn table filled its center.

Nicholas lifted the lantern and turned towards me. I stifled a gasp.

He was beautiful.

The firelight danced on high cheekbones, emphasizing the chiseled angles of his face. His jaw was strong, his lips full. Tawny skin was offset by dark curls tied at the nape of his neck with a red bandanna. The sun had lightened several tendrils to the color of honey. His raw features were so unlike the pasty British gentlemen I was accustomed to.

Realizing I was staring at him slack-jawed, I broke my trance and shuffled forward a few awkward steps.

"Hang the lantern, will you? Right there?" Nicholas gestured to a hook above the table.

Was I his maid now? Before I could refuse, he pressed the lantern into my hand. A sudden charge surged through me when our fingers touched. I turned away quickly and hung the lantern as I had been asked.

Nicholas lit several tallow candles and busied himself in the kitchen. "Not much in the way of fine dining, but a full stomach will help some," he said with a warm smile.

I sat on a barrel and watched.

Confident that the shadows of the lantern hid my eyes, I stared unabashedly at the stranger as he fished around the cupboards and drawers. His every movement was fluid and lissome, like a choreographed dance. He was tall and muscular, with a wide chest that narrowed into a taut waist. He wore the traditional uniform of a sailor: bare feet, dark canvas breeches, a leather belt, and a white linen shirt with billowing sleeves.

Nicholas wore two things I did not expect. The first was a leather baldric that hung over one shoulder, crossing his chest and securing a pistol and sword at the hip. Ornate carvings, metal rivets, and a series of gilded buckles conveyed its value. It surprised me to see a common sailor with such a beautiful piece of finery. Beyond that, his weaponry concerned me. What need would a common sailor have to be armed as such? The other surprising item Nicholas wore was a crucifix on long, golden chain around his neck. Though unassuming, the value of such a thing was undeniable.

As I examined Nicholas's necklace, I found my eyes tracing his collarbone and the curve of his muscles as they disappeared under the thin fabric. Blood pumped into my cheeks. I looked away quickly.

While lighting a fire in the rickety stove, Nicholas said, "How about a proper introduction, Miss Monroe? Tell me your Christian name."

I still had not decided whether I liked this man, and I debated if I should answer him. Under normal circumstances, I would not. He was vulgar and familiar.

But as I caught my eyes wandering the planes of his chest yet again, I wondered if I was more irritated at his manners or at my own lack of offense at them.

"My name is Tessa," I finally answered.

"Tessa," he repeated to himself. "It fits. And you are from England." It was not a question.

I nodded.

"Age?"

"Seventeen."

"And what possessed you to journey to these blistering islands?"

A sting of untapped grief taunted me as I thought of my father. I answered carefully, defying the lump rising in my throat. "My father...we're sailing to St. Kitts. He is an admiral in the British Navy and was reassigned."

The sailor said nothing as he prepared a stew in a large pot.

I sat as straight as I could and asked the question I had been dreading, "What happened?"

"Hurricane," he said simply. After a beat, he continued, "We nigh missed it ourselves. North up, near Grand Bahama. Got a strong wind out of that one. When the rains stopped, we saw shredded planks floating all over, and there you were, drifting along in a jollyboat. Thought we had us a corpse when first caught hold of you."

I pictured how I must have looked drifting lazily in a jollyboat amidst all the wreckage, amidst all the drowning men. What a fantastical image.

"You found just me?" I asked, not wanting to believe my father, Lucia, or any of the crew with whom I had become acquainted had all perished

"Aye, lass. Just you, a lot of broken wood, and several barrels of rum."

"You must send out a search party. Search for survivors."

Nicholas shook his head. "Would be worthless to search. No survivors."

I recoiled at his indifference. "Well, I survived, didn't I? Did you even bother to look?"

"Of course we looked," replied Nicholas hotly. "We scavenged the entire wreckage for anything of value."

"Barrels of rum, you mean."

"Human life, I mean." He gave me a condescending scowl.

I hated this man. He was rash and rude and I didn't believe a word he said.

"Go back," I demanded. "Search again."

Nicholas ignored me.

"I said, go back. I survived. Others probably did too."

"It's been four days. There is no one else. Going back would be a waste of time."

I crossed my arms in protest. "How can you be so cruel? Indulge me. Please, sir. Turn back."

Nicholas turned from the stove and slammed his hands down on the table. I jumped at the noise. "First—*you* are not the captain. I do not take orders from a foolish girl. Second—*I* am not the captain so the choice is not mine. And third—it's been too long. Accept the reality. You are the *only* survivor."

I looked away, tears filling my eyes at the sting of his words.

He stared at me stupidly as my trickle of tears turned in to sobbing. His hardened face melted with a sigh.

"Don't cry," he stammered. "I shouldn't have been so harsh. So cruel, as you say. I'm sorry, Tessa."

"Call me Miss Monroe," I demanded.

Nicholas shrugged. "I have no use for propriety."

"And I have no use for you." I stood up and marched towards the ladder.

Nicholas rushed forward and caught my elbow. "You can't go up there."

I whirled at him. "You are not the captain. I do not take orders from foolish sailors."

Laughter erupted from the hardened sailor. I stood dumbfounded, watching as he struggled to catch his breath.

"Tessa, I like you. I really, really like you. Won't be long until I fall in love with you. I'm halfway there already."

My eyebrows knit into an incredulous scowl. Was he serious?

Nicholas chuckled at my expression. "You will fall for me, too. It won't be one-sided, I promise."

My jaw dropped. This man belonged in a madhouse. I inwardly vowed that would never happen.

"Easy now, luv. Time will prove it. For now, sit back down. The night is young.

CHAPTER THREE

I SANK BACK INTO my chair uneasily.

Nicholas placed two wooden cups on the table. I sniffed at the contents. The alcoholic stench of rum burned my nostrils. I pushed the cup away in disgust. Rum was not an appropriate drink for a lady.

The sailor took a hearty swig from the cup in front of him. He wiped his mouth on the back of his arm. "Fairly fresh."

"Is there anything…else? Perhaps tea?"

"Tea?" he smirked. "A high demand for the middle of the ocean. Ain't nothing but rum here."

I nodded once and willed myself to take a sip. My throat burned and my eyes watered. An involuntary cough escaped my lips. Nicholas chuckled softly.

He crossed to the stove and ladled stew into two tin bowls.

He was relaxed enough in the silence, but I was uncomfortable beyond measure. I did not know how to conduct myself. This man—this *sailor*—had no sense of

on

propriety whatsoever. Yet an alliance with him was proving paramount. I forced myself to continue our conversation.

"Would you please tell me your full name?"

"Nicholas Holladay." He spoke with a slight sailor brogue that made everything he said sound poetic. "But around here, everyone calls me Marks on account of me being such a good marksman," he patted the pistol dangling from his baldric.

"What's your position?"

"I am an officer here. I guess you'd call me the first mate." He met my eyes and puffed his chest.

Second-in-command of the ship. Though lacking the attitude of a gentleman, he was far above the station of working-class sailors. I esteemed him more.

Nicholas placed the bowls of cloudy liquid and a plate of flattened rolls on the table. "A feast for a sailor. Eat up."

I reached for one of the flattened rolls first because it was the most recognizable thing before me. It was crusty to the touch, and when I tried to take a bite from it, the roll resisted my teeth and a mist of chalky crumbs fell into my stew. It was entirely inedible.

"What? You've never had hardtack before?"

"I…uh…"

"And you call yourself an admiral's daughter. Tsk, tsk. I'm sure you had a constant supply of tea and crumpets. Puddings and pastries, too."

His lips curled into a boyish grin as he picked up an identical rock-hard roll and dipped it in his stew, letting it absorb the liquid. He bit off the soggy corner.

Copying Nicholas, I soaked my hardtack in my stew. The result, if not palatable, was at least edible.

Nicholas watched me eat. "I suppose somethin' as common as hardtack is far beneath your status."

I pushed away my food. "You think I'm somehow less than you because you eat hardtack every day? Because I am thousands of miles away from the only home I've ever known and I am orphaned?"

I tried to hold back the tears that welled in my eyes.

Memories of my final moments with my father replayed themselves. He had been so composed in the face of death just to reassure me. I must have gone under the water. He pulled me out, kept my head above the waves. As his last act, he used all his strength to roll his unconscious daughter into the rescue boat meant for him. Exhausted, he succumbed to the pull of the ocean.

And now I was wholly alone. Alive, yes. But barely. What would come next? Where would I go? Who would watch after me? What was I to do?

Too many questions and not a single answer.

My world had once consisted of a loving father, devoted servants, a beautiful home, and any opportunity I could dream of. And now my world comprised the dank galley of a strange ship, food barely fit for swine, and the flimsy comfort of a filthy jacket.

I gave in to the tears and buried my head in my arms on the tabletop. If I was aware that Nicholas was watching me, I did not care. He was an intruder in my very small world. No pride or sense of decency compelled me to harness my emotions. I refused to listen as Nicholas called to me, trying to pull me out of my hysteria.

"Tessa," Nicholas gently prodded.

I would not let myself stop crying, for then I might lose the only thing that had given me reprieve from my new and painful existence.

"Please, Tessa," Nicholas tried again. He draped his arm across my shaking shoulders. Without further invitation I fell into his embrace, craving the warmth and comfort that only another human could provide. My face pressed against the smooth skin of his neck and my arms found solace against his chest.

If I had been coherent, I would have recognized the sailor's slight stiffening at my very forward move. I would have been embarrassed by his awkward hesitation. But all I knew was that within a moment his uncomfortable stature softened and he wound his arms around me into a protective cocoon. I cried against his shoulder for longer than I knew, coughing on sobs I could not control.

Finally, the sobs subsided into pathetic whimpers. My eyes burned with sorrow but were out of tears. As I calmed myself, the nature of my surroundings rushed back into my chaotic consciousness. I was suddenly aware of Nicholas's airy, marine scent, and the feel of my skin on his. Awkwardly, I noticed how thin his shirt was. I could feel every line of his body beneath the fabric.

I had forgotten myself. How had I let myself get so familiar with a stranger? Here I was, in the arms of a man—a sailor—almost sitting on his lap and crying into his shoulder. I was wearing his coat!

I pulled away from Nicholas's warmth with my head down and reoriented myself on my stool. My fluttering hands quickly dabbed at my eyes and nose, wiping all traces of moisture away. I attempted to smooth my hair, but it was a futile task. I dared not think of what I must look like. I stole a quick glance at my companion. His eyes were wide with a sort of surprised worry. Feminine hysterics were not something he was used to dealing with.

I straightened my posture and turned my attention to my meal, avoiding any further eye contact.

As I finished my last bites of stale broth, Nicholas broke the silence. "The watch ends soon. Let's get you back to my room."

Stunned out of my embarrassment, I looked at him wide-eyed. This had gone too far. I had allowed this heathen to become too familiar with me. "Sir, I know I have been anything but proper tonight, but I doubt I have made any impression whatsoever that would elicit such an offer!"

A look of confusion creased Nicholas's brow, then an apologetic grin flashed across his beautiful lips. He let out a low chuckle. "No. Not like that. The room where you have been sleeping, well, that's the first mate's quarters. My room. I've been staying in the fo'c'sle with the rest of the crew. I did not mean …" he trailed off.

As his words sunk in, humiliation replaced my alarm. My face flushed.

Nicholas looked for my understanding then continued, "I meant that you can go back to that room, *alone*, and rest up."

I nodded in concession and braved another swallow of rum. Although I had already slept for four days, the exhaustion from my sobbing coupled with the soothing effects of the alcohol made me feel as if I could sleep for four more. I was eager to be alone. I wanted as little as possible to do with any of the sailors on the ship—including Nicholas.

Suddenly, Nicholas leaned in close to me and took my hands in his. Before I could pull them away, I felt the same rush of electricity I felt when our fingers brushed before.

"Listen, lass, you have no reason to believe a word I say. Asking you to trust me is asking more than I deserve. But I need you to…just try to trust me on this one thing. These sailors are not…gentlemen." He chose his words cautiously. "They will be…unsavory once they learn that you are awake. Best to avoid the lot of them. Just stay in the cabin and sleep."

It was a warning I did not need. My father had made certain I was well aware of the distasteful habits of sailors.

They were a breed apart, he cautioned, and only lived for pleasure. I clearly understood that a young woman such as myself could be used for pleasure in the most unpleasant of ways.

"What should I do if I need something?"

"That is where I come in," he said, flashing a dazzling smile. "I will check in and make sure you have everything you need. Tomorrow night, I'll come to you when it is safe to come out."

I rolled my eyes. He obviously relished acting as my savior.

Nicholas stood, still holding my hand, and pulled me until I was standing next to him. I pulled my hand back but he didn't let go. Before I knew it, he extinguished the lantern and candles and we were left in utter blackness. I feebly admitted to myself that I was glad for his solid grip. He stole up the ladder and peeked across the main deck before leading me across the ship in the wan light of the early morning.

As we stepped into the corridor, I pointed to the door across from mine and started to ask who slept there. Nicholas anticipated my question and pressed his salty forefinger across my parted lips, shushing me. He leaned close into my ear and barely whispered, "Captain's quarters."

Nicholas guided me across the cabin threshold without crossing it himself. He let go of my hand and began to close the door.

I blocked the door from closing and Nicholas looked at me quizzically.

"Mr. Holladay, what will happen next?"

He fixed my gaze for a moment, then replied simply, "I will get you somewhere safe."

It was a vague answer, but it was an answer I wanted

to hear, needed to hear. His eyes never wavered from mine and I was transfixed by his stare. The pealing of a bell broke the moment and Nicholas closed the door quickly, leaving me alone in my prison.

CHAPTER FOUR

DAWN STRAINED TO BREAK and its faint glow made it easier to assess the cabin I had been banished to. When I stretched both my arms out, my fingertips barely brushed both walls of the narrow room. A thin, straw-filled mattress on a wooden shelf served as the bed. No window. No touch of design. It was simply a wooden box. A coffin.

My blankets were heaped in disarray on the floor, thanks to my attempt to use my sheet as a covering. As I remade the bed, I felt a strange, stiff lump of fabric mixed in with the blankets. Smoothing it out and straining to see its shape in the dim light, I recognized it as my dress. My corset was there too.

I tried not to think about who had undressed me and laid me to bed, but the thought was difficult to ignore. Was it done by a gruff and hungry sailor who took a little too much pleasure in the task? Perhaps it had been Nicholas. This idea was only slightly less offensive.

I touched the fabric, now rough with dried seawater, thinking on the last time I wore it. My maid Lucia had dressed me with care then styled my long hair to withstand the wind. I took tea with my father as the sun rose. A sudden wind pitched the ship and the hurricane was upon us before I finished breakfast.

Tears sprang into my eyes. I didn't bother to blink them back. I fell into the hard bed and let them flow freely. It wasn't long until the sedation of the rum took over and I drifted into a restless sleep filled with fitful dreams.

The faces of my father, my maid, and Nicholas swam through my tangled mind. Obscure noises from the deck made their way to my consciousness. A bell rang periodically, marking the onset of various shifts. I heard the familiar cadence of human speech, but no discernible conversations. I learned to tune out the constant rhythm of raucous sea chanteys.

Night fell. Anticipating my chaperone's arrival, I decided to slip on my gown. Dressing myself for the first time in my entire existence would have been a chore under any circumstance, but it was a particular challenge in such cramped quarters. The corset was impossible. I fumbled with the laces, twisting my arms behind me and hobbling about the room. Frustrated with the blasted thing, I eventually kicked it under the bed and regretted that my willowy figure could not fill out the dress on its own.

The dress was easier to slip into, though fastening the buttons was almost as frustrating as trying to tie the corset. I buttoned the dress halfway before giving up.

Heavy with salt—and lacking the aid of a corset—my gown hung limply against my bony figure. It was the best I could do. At least I was dressed.

My heart raced at the sound of approaching footsteps. I was eager to get out of the cabin but hated the idea of another long night being judged by the arrogant sailor. As if *he* had the right to judge *me*! It would serve him right if I refused him my company tonight.

I sighed and slouched against the door. I was too bored, too hungry, and too anxious to see that through.

A tap sounded on the door.

My hands fluttered as I smoothed my disheveled hair. I quickly pinched my cheeks.

Why was I so worried about my appearance?

"Miss Monroe?"

The door creaked as I gingerly opened it. I winced at the sound. Nicholas stood before me wearing a broad smile. My breath caught in my throat.

"Found your dress," he noticed.

I looked down at the tattered gown and shrugged.

"Ready for your nightly recess?"

"My nightly recess?" I repeated indignantly.

"Shh!" He hissed, throwing a stealthy glance over his shoulder.

"Why are you acting so suspicious?"

"I told you. I am protecting you. Now, c'mon. Supper's ready in the galley."

I crossed my arms. "No. This isn't normal. I refuse to leave this cabin until you tell me what you're hiding from me."

"All right, luv. If that's what you want, I won't force my company on you." Nicholas began to walk away, his sinewy figure disappearing in the darkness.

I sighed in exasperation and scurried after him.

"First," I said, "I am not your *luv*. Second, I am only coming with you because I am famished. And finally, I will discover what you're hiding from me, even if I have to go to the captain himself."

Nicholas stopped abruptly. "Don't do that," he said darkly without bothering to look at me.

"The idea worries you," I said proudly. "You know you'll be punished. Chided, at least. Finally, I have some leverage over you."

"Listen here, *luv*," he emphasized the pet name deliberately as he looked into my eyes, "go to the captain. Be my bloody guest. It'll actually improve my standing with that codger. I told you once and I'll tell you again—if you do that, you'll wish you were dead by morning."

The warning was so bombastic, I nearly laughed aloud. Nicholas didn't laugh, though. I stared at him through narrowed eyes, trying to sense a joke. Or at least derision. But I only sensed sincere passion.

"I won't go to the captain," I said.

"Thank you," Nicholas answered with a slight curl of his lip.

"Yet," I added. "I *will* find out what you're hiding from me. You can tell me yourself, or I will find out on my own."

Nicholas shrugged. "You're treading in dangerous waters, lass. But do what you must. For now, let's eat."

CHAPTER FIVE

NICHOLAS OFFERED HIS ARM, which I hesitantly accepted. A rush of warmth ran through me the moment our skin touched. My stomach danced. I looked at him in alarm, wondering if he had felt it too. He was staring back at me as if he had.

I swallowed hard and let Nicholas lead me across the deck.

It was eerily still. There was no trace of the night crew. Not even a breeze ruffled the sails. I thought it odd that not a single soul manned the deck. Perhaps Nicholas had arranged it that way.

The sky was clearer than the night before. Countless stars twinkled down upon the endless black ocean and a silver moon stared down at me. I felt even smaller, even more lost than I had before.

In the moonlight, I took keener notice of the ship. The deck was littered with tangles of sailing line, barrels, and other clutter. Loose belaying pins rolled sloppily around. This certainly was not a military ship.

When we approached the hatch to the galley, Nicholas

released my arm. I felt cold and alone again and secretly wanted to be near him. I carefully made my way down the narrow ladder and sat at the table.

A lantern was already blazing over the table. Nicholas filled two bowls with steaming soup and poured two cups of rum. As a treat, he served me a spoonful of pickled vegetables. The taste of vinegar was strong, but it was invigorating compared with the rest of the meal.

"How was your day?" Nicholas asked me.

I shrugged. "Very long."

"Yes, it would be. I apologize for that."

"No need for apologies," I countered politely, though I wondered what he was really apologizing for—my boredom or my confinement.

We ate in silence for a while.

"I think it's time we become acquainted. Since you're sleeping in my bed," Nicholas said with a wicked wink.

I stiffened at his affront. "We don't have to talk."

Nicholas barked a laugh, then covered his mouth with his hand. "Pardon me for supposing that you wouldn't mind a bit of conversation after your *very long* day. I may as well treat you like a sheep out to pasture—watch you eat and send you back to the barn."

I glared at him. "That's exactly what this is, despite the…*conversation*."

"Come on, Tessa—"

"*Miss Monroe*," I corrected.

"If you say so. Let's be civil. It will make the time pass easier. Play along."

"What would you like to know?" I asked curtly.

"Tell me everything."

"That may take all night."

He smiled broadly and said, "I think we have all night."

I felt myself blushing, though I didn't know why.

"You're no stranger to the sea," Nicholas stated. "Did you sail with your father often?"

I nodded. "Occasionally. On short voyages."

"The whole family would join in the fun, then?"

"Just me," I said as I absentmindedly stirred my stew. I glanced up and saw that Nicholas was confused. "I meant that I am the whole family. Just my father and me."

"Your mother?"

"She died giving birth to me," I said indifferently.

Nicholas's brow furrowed. "Both parents gone," he muttered to himself, but not quietly enough.

"Yes, both parents gone," I repeated. "Thank you so much for bringing up the topic."

"I'm sorry. I lost my parents at a young age too."

He almost sounded sincere.

I glowered at him. "Do not pretend we are anything alike."

Nicholas sneered in return. "With your fancy tutors and nannies, your private menagerie, your hired playmates…you don't have to tell me that we are nothing alike."

"I did not have a private menagerie!"

Nicholas scoffed and swigged his drink. "Tell me, then, what was your life like?"

I rolled my eyes. "I was a spoiled brat. I never wanted for a thing."

"Which surely leaves you wanting for something."

"After insisting how privileged I am, you're now questioning it?" This man was insulting.

He shrugged. "Nobody can have everything. And the more you try to get it all, the more you realize what you can never have. Just something I've learned."

"You presume too much, Mr. Holladay," I bristled. "You do not know me at all."

Nicholas sensed he had jarred a personal nerve. His

eyes were pleading when I looked at him. He hadn't meant to offend me with his philosophical waxing. I didn't know why I felt the need to ease his discomfort. I had no reason to care of his thoughts or feelings. But something inside me softened and I felt compelled to pardon the offense.

In an offering of peace, I rekindled the conversation. "Tell me about this ship."

Nicholas's eyes grew bright. He rattled off the ship's details. "She's a two-masted brigantine, as you saw. Fast as the four winds. Survived three hurricanes without so much as a ripped sail. Decent tonnage. Holds over a dozen cannons and is populated with nearly one-hundred men. She's called the *Banshee*."

"The *Banshee*? As in the evil Irish specter that calls to you before death?"

"Aye. That *Banshee*, indeed."

I shuddered. "Such an ominous name."

"Can't hurt in these waters."

"What do you mean?"

He grappled with his thoughts before answering. "The balance of power in the Spanish Main is unsteady. Broken treaties and battles, not to mention those out for themselves."

"Pirates, you mean." My father had warned me of those too. It was one of his gravest concerns about his new position in St. Kitts.

Nicholas shifted. He caught my eye for a brief moment, then looked away. "Aye. So, it doesn't hurt to have an ominous name, as you call it."

"Is that why there are so many cannons on deck? Self-defense?"

Nicholas stared at me blankly for a full minute. "Aye," he finally answered. "Dangerous waters and all."

His answer was unsettling, though I didn't know why.

"I take it this is not a passenger ship. What does the *Banshee* do?"

Nicholas smiled wryly, laughing softly to himself. "Transports goods, mostly."

He was oddly uncomfortable. Nicholas had no problem bragging about the ship itself or his duties as the first mate earlier, so why was he acting so evasive now?

"How did you become a sailor?" I asked, steering the conversation away from the ship. He was hiding something, and I would find it out eventually. But I did not want to rouse his suspicions.

"Ah, now that is a story worth telling."

He downed the remains of his drink and sat back in his chair with a grace I envied and began his tale.

"It is rare for a lad to grow up wishing to be—" he paused abruptly and started over. "I never knew I would grow up to make my living this way. As a lad, I was apprenticed to a carpenter—a respectable trade in anyone's book. I loved it. I loved taking virgin wood in my hands and making something beautiful. I was uncommonly good at it, especially for a young boy."

"Then why did you stop?"

"My mum died. I had no father. I could not afford to live off my apprenticeship, and I was far too young and poor to start a shop of my own. I couldn't join the military—too young for that too."

"How old were you?"

"Twelve, thirteen? Somewhere in there."

Though several years older than he had been, I, too, was now an orphan with no way to provide for myself. I pushed away the comparison, reminding myself that many children were orphans. We were nothing alike.

"So what did you do?" I asked.

"I stayed alive," Nicholas shrugged. "I slept in alleyways, performed odd jobs for scraps, and tried to stay warm, but I was starving. So I started stealing things. Bread, coin purses, whatever I could use. I lived like that for a year. Sneaking from town to town, trying not to get caught."

I would never have thought I would have compassion for a thief. But suddenly I did. I understood the pride Nicholas took in his vocation. He had made something of himself—even as a sailor—in a very hard world.

"Once, as I was trying to avoid an angry constable, I found the best hiding spot ever—as a stowaway on a ship. It was only a matter of days before I was discovered pilfering food from the galley. I could've been hanged right then."

"Hanged? For stealing food?"

He nodded.

"You were only a child. That seems extreme."

"Maybe, but that's how it is. At sea, law is everything. One sign of weakness and enemies will capitalize on it."

I shuddered.

"But this captain, he was a good man. He knew I did not have the heart of a criminal. I was just surviving. And when he learned I was trained as a carpenter, he offered me a pardon so long as I worked on the ship. So, at fourteen, I became the ship's carpenter and I've been sailing since."

"How old are you now?"

Nicholas paused. "Twenty-one, I guess. It's easy to lose count."

I smiled. "Do you ever wish you were still a carpenter? That you did not have to sail for a living?"

A huge grin split his face, "Tough question, luv. From the first day as one of the crew, I knew I had a calling here. The surf. The sun. I'd bet against sevens that God made the ocean just for me. But there are times when I wish things were different. I wish I weren't bound to this ship or this particular company. But I could never leave the ocean. Sailing was made for me—and I for it."

"It sounds like it. You are awfully young for an officer, aren't you?"

He nodded. "A natural sea dog, indeed. I'm strong, I guess. Good balance. I can climb the rigging faster than anyone on this ship. I'm particularly good with weapons. I learned to fence, to throw knives, but I am a natural crack shot with a pistol. A marksman."

"And so they call you Marks," I remembered. "But I always heard that pistols are of no use at sea."

"Aye, in general. They take time to reload and they are difficult to aim in an emergency. But if you can take one shot and make it count, it's an asset to any crew."

"But does a merchant ship really have need of such precision in an emergency?"

"The Caribbean is a treacherous place for any ship."

Though I had been practically raised upon the ocean and familiar with every aspect of sailing, it was evident that life on the Caribbean was a world away from the cold waters of the English Channel.

"Have you ever shot anybody?" I asked curiously.

Nicholas cleared his throat but did not answer. I searched his face, but he refused to meet my eyes. The silence grew heavier with each passing second. Finally, Nicholas stood, collected our dishes, and put them on the counter.

"Time to go back."

I looked at the hatch. It was still pitch black. There was no sign of dawn, no ringing of bells to announce the early watch.

Suddenly I was distraught by the thought of the small, lonely cabin. "But it's not morning yet."

Nicholas walked to the ladder and gestured for me to follow him.

"It was wrong for me to ask that, Mr. Holladay. Please don't think I meant something by it, because I didn't. My father is an admiral. I understand life at sea."

"Do not pretend we are anything alike."

Nicholas turned and climbed the ladder. I had no choice but to follow.

At the threshold of my cabin, Nicholas gruffly commanded me to stay inside.

As he turned to leave, I caught his elbow and motioned for him to lean in close. "In truth, Mr. Holladay, I think I should present myself to the captain," I whispered.

Glancing up and down the corridor, Nicholas stepped into the cabin, pulling the door closed behind him. My heart thumped at his proximity.

"I understand you trust me very little and respect me even less. But I am begging you, do not talk to the captain."

Confused by his sudden candor, I tried to explain myself. "But couldn't the captain help me—"

"No," Nicholas whispered sharply. "Do not talk to him. Do not go near him. Do you understand?"

"Y-yes," I whispered.

"Do I have your word?"

"I-I…"

"Tessa, give me your word that you will not attempt to talk to the captain or anyone else on this ship besides me."

The force of his words alarmed me. I was reluctant to swear to anything, but under the power of his stare I eked out my promise. "You have my word."

CHAPTER SIX

THE NEXT DAY WAS as long and torturous as the day before. I dared not think how many more days like this I would endure.

As promised, Nicholas placed a plate of hardtack in my room while I was sleeping. I forced myself to eat the entire roll. I curled up on the bed again, tracing the wooden grain of the walls with my fingers.

A sound like angry thunder shattered my anguish. A strong vibration kicked against the ship and nearly tossed me to the floor. Another booming noise followed. I sat up, rigid as a board, and clutched the sheets to my chin. Shouting punctuated each deafening rumble. The ship lurched again.

The last time the ocean was this choppy and the thunder was this loud, my ship sank. My stomach twisted with fear.

A fist banged on the captain's door, directly across from mine.

My breathing stopped.

I heard the sound of the door opening and a rushed

conversation followed. I strained to hear the exchange. Two words clearly cut through the chaos. Two words that made me numb, "...*under attack*..."

Sounds escalated. The booming thunder and lurching continued at varied intervals. No. Not thunder. Cannon fire. Voices barked all around. The sound of running feet was so pervasive that it was impossible to distinguish one set of footsteps from another. Crashing, banging, screeching, and thumping. Sounds of violence surrounded me.

There were only two reasons we would be attacked. Either we were in the midst of a naval battle—which made no sense because the *Banshee* was not a military vessel—or we'd become a target for pirates.

Nicholas had reminded me repeatedly how dangerous these waters were. I'd been so naïve, thinking he was exaggerating. Nicholas also said this ship transported goods. Perhaps it was carrying tobacco, rum, or newly minted money. Plenty of treasures for any pirate to loot.

My hands began shaking.

Pirates were cruel and merciless. Survivors were rare and were often sold into slavery or kept captive. Everyone aboard this vessel would be killed or maimed. Then, after every valuable item had been taken, they would sink this ship. Would I be drowned or hoarded away with the booty? Neither alternative was particularly appealing.

A primal terror overcame me. I could not wait for imminent death in this wooden cage. I would run. Hide. Wait out the attack. Then as the ship was sinking, I could clutch to a floating piece of wreckage and hope to be rescued at sea for a second time. It was an impossible escape, but it was the only way to avoid what would come to a young woman in the hands of pirates—torture, slavery, and only the glimmering possibility of death.

A volley of footsteps pounded on the deck above my cabin, spurring me to action. I had to escape while I could.

A chilling scream echoed from the deck. My blood ran cold.

I didn't have time to dress. Without wasting a moment, I threw Nicholas's jacket over my underclothes—perhaps I would look like a man—and swung my door open.

Bracing myself against the hallway bulkhead, I hurried towards the deck. If I could cross unseen and dash downstairs to the galley, I knew I could make my way into the bottom of the ship and hide in the bilge with the ship's seepage.

The battle on the deck was worse than I imagined. A blood-soaked man brandishing an axe froze me in my tracks. He was pure evil. He towered over me like a hulking predator, his twisted face dripping with blood.

A series of piercing screams reverberated through the air, and a horror like I'd never known filled my soul. The bloodied pirate looked down at me, a curious expression on his face. I willed my legs to move, to take me anywhere. I broke my frozen terror and ran.

The screaming stopped.

It had been mine.

Everywhere I turned was a scene of chaos as grisly as the last. Filthy pirates wielding all kinds of weapons overtook the bulwarks and crawled across the deck like ants.

I backed myself against the portside railing, unsure of what to do. Any moment, I could be taken hostage or cut in to bloody bits.

My presence did not go unnoticed. A wiry man with long, stringy grey hair and a wicked scar on his forehead pointed in my direction, grunting at his large companion. The two pirates advanced slowly and deliberately, like wolves toying with a rabbit so weak that there was no need for cunning, no need for speed. Their jeering smiles dripped with venom.

My only escape was just behind me in the depths of the merciless ocean. A watery grave was a welcome reprieve from the violence surrounding me.

My hands desperately fumbled along the caprailing behind me. Without turning my back on the approaching monsters, I tried to launch myself over the side of the ship but I could not get enough leverage.

My terrified eyes met their stalking gazes. I couldn't look away. I shrank harder and harder against the bulwarks as if I could melt into the wood.

With nothing else to do, I screamed.

A figure flew from a rope in the sky and landed directly between the two pirates and me. His back was towards me, but I instantly recognized the red scarf tying back the honey-colored curls and the powerful form of his posture.

It was Nicholas.

But I felt no relief. This rescue was futile. The hunger in the pirates' eyes did not diminish. One defender would not stop them. What Nicholas had meant as a rescue mission was nothing more than suicide.

Drawing a cutlass from the scabbard at his hip, Nicholas leveled it at the pirates and proclaimed, "She is not for you." His voice rang with authority.

"C'mon, Marks, just a little fun," the small pirate said.

"Spoils o' war, and all that," the burly one echoed.

They continued to advance, barely noting the sailor blocking their way.

"You can have at her too. No reason not to share." The wiry man's eyes never left mine.

"Black won't hold kindly with his things being

touched." Nicholas stood even taller and withdrew his pistol.

The men halted under this greater threat. They broke their gaze from me and glared at Nicholas now, their eyes narrowing into slits. I did not understand Nicholas's words and how they pertained to me. I just knew that whatever he said seemed to be working.

The stalemate between the pirates and my rescuer lasted several excruciating heartbeats. Nicholas held his stance without moving a muscle. The angry pirates looked from Nicholas to me then back to Nicholas again, muttering indiscernible grunts to each other. They pressed on.

Nicholas aimed his pistol at the small man and cocked it. A shot cracked and the small pirate jumped back, yelping. The bullet missed his foot by a mere inch.

"Next time it's your knee," Nicholas darkly promised.

The pirates cursed Nicholas and left us.

Nicholas harnessed his pistol and turned to me. Instead of taking my hand and dashing for safety, he grabbed my upper arm and shook me from my post at the rail. Fury boiled in his eyes and a snarl formed on his lips.

"What the bloody hell are you doing?" he boomed. "You promised to stay in your room!" He punctuated his words with angry gestures, waving his cutlass wildly. I cringed at his brutal reprieve, afraid of his wrath and the weapon he so carelessly brandished.

"Do you have any idea of what you have done?" he bellowed, shaking me. His eyes were hard, his expression fierce.

"I-I am s-s-sorry," I stammered.

Still clenching my arm, he brusquely shoved me in the direction of the small hallway, meaning to escort me physically, I was sure, back to my cabin. My shaking legs could not keep up with Nicholas's forceful gait and I fell, breaking his grip on me. I looked up to his face in supplication, terrified by his temper. His angry features were framed by the billowing sails of the ship.

It was then that I noticed a flag atop the mainmast that I had never seen before in the dark of the night. It billowed black against the pale sky.

A dark realization made its way into my muddled thoughts.

The pirates had called Nicholas *Marks*, the name he said his shipmates called him…

A large explosion off the port side of the ship ripped my attention away from my disturbing thoughts. Another ship, larger than the *Banshee*—oh, I should have known just by the wicked name of this cursed vessel!—exploded into flames. With my back pressed against the portside bulwarks, I had failed to see it before.

I gaped at the orange flames and rolling black smoke. Countless pirates swung from ropes, leaving the burning vessel and dropping onto the quarterdeck of the *Banshee*. Several frantic victims tried to do the same, only to be tossed to the waves or bludgeoned to death.

I had not been entirely mistaken. A ship *was* under attack, but it was not this ship.

My eyes strayed again to the black flag flying on the mainmast. A gust of wind unfurled the flag in all its terrifying majesty. Against a black background, the image of two white swords piercing a skull let all who saw it know that this was a pirate ship.

Nicholas followed my gaze to the burning ship beside us and to the telltale ensign, waving overhead.

He knew that I knew.

When Nicholas looked at me again, all trace of fury was gone. The anger had been replaced by a flat, stoic look that frightened me even more.

Another man approached the scene. Nicholas's eyes flicked in his direction then continued searching my face.

"The prisoner's awake, eh?" the approaching pirate asked Nicholas cheerfully.

Nicholas grunted.

Prisoner? Had he called me *the prisoner*? The situation was graver than I dared consider.

My only route of escape was to dive over the ship's edge. I eyed the distance to the chest-high gunwale, wondering if I would have enough time to launch myself into the ocean. I was trembling all over. Would my legs even work? I had to try. I scrambled to my feet.

Nicholas raised his cutlass, leveling it at my throat. All thoughts of running dissolved instantly. With the threat of the sword rooting my feet to the deck, he addressed the approaching pirate. "This filthy wench has insulted me. Lock her in the brig."

CHAPTER SEVEN

MY WRETCHED CRIES ECHOED in the hollow belly of the ship. I lay curled in the corner of the brig, sobbing loudly. I did not care who heard me, who I bothered.

If I thought my cabin was a cage, I now knew better. Iron bars crusted with rust and dripping with moisture surrounded me on all four sides. It was larger than my quarters upstairs, roughly eight feet by eight feet square. The only furnishings were a wooden chair, a small stool for sitting, a tin plate for food, and a bucket for relieving oneself.

I had been crying in the ship's prison for hours now, the memory of the morning's atrocities still strong. Of all the horrors I had experienced today, the worst by far was Nicholas's betrayal.

Angry tears burned my eyes. He had lied to me.

Why had he put on a charade? Courting me nightly then locking me away like an animal during the days, just a novelty for his entertainment. And what else? What else did he have planned? What would he have eventually done with me? Or *to* me? And now that I knew the truth, my execution was certain.

Sobs of hatred seethed between my teeth. I angrily tore off Nicholas's jacket and threw it across the brig. It caught on the chair, pulling it over. The violence was liberating. In three wide steps I reached the wooden chair, raised it over my head and threw it across the tiny room into the metal bars. It clattered noisily.

This outburst meant nothing, really, but I felt in control for the first time. I could not control what happened in the world—hurricanes or murdering pirates—but I could control the life of this stupid chair. I threw it again. And again. I picked up the tin dish and hurled it against the bars. The din echoed throughout the belly of the ship and the bars left scars on the thin plate. I laughed loudly. Standing in the middle of the brig, I threw everything— the bucket, stool, the chair, and the noisy dish. My sorry cries had turned in to screams of rage. If Nicholas had no use for propriety, then neither did I.

A square of light appeared at the top of a steep staircase that led from the main deck into the ship's hold. Two men shimmied through the hatch and hurried down the ladder.

My tantrum did not lessen. If anything, its intensity only increased with the promise of an audience. I screamed, the burning on the back of my throat matching the burning of hot tears in my eyes.

"Miss Monroe!" a voice exclaimed in disdain from the ladder. It was Nicholas. Illuminated by a lantern, he marched solidly behind a round, ruddy pirate with hair like straw and a beard to match.

The tin dish slammed noisily into the bars separating

me from the pirates. They flinched. I grabbed the chair and threw it as hard as I could in their direction.

"Tessa, now!" Nicholas bellowed approaching me, his posture angry, his eyes smoldering.

I stopped in my tracks and faced the men, my chest rising and falling dramatically with each heavy breath. "Oh, *now* is it?" I sneered, stepping closer to them. "If you want me to stop *now* then I better stop *now*! I suppose I owe you an apology. Is that what you came for?" The boiling hatred within me spilled over, lending a dangerous edge to my voice that I did not recognize. "Oh, I am sorry, *sir*. I am *sorry* for my temper. I am *sorry* my lack of manners has disrupted your pillaging. I am *sorry* your charade is up! What more do you want? A curtsy?"

Nicholas passed the lantern to the other man and approached the brig door. He held a ring of keys.

I shrank back, fear eclipsing my anger. No longer was I looking at the face of a friend who had lied to me. I was staring into the eyes of a trained killer.

Nicholas opened the door and crossed the threshold.

To back down from him now would reveal how vulnerable I was. And he was the one who told me that an enemy would capitalize on any sign of weakness. With my pulse thundering in my ears, I forced myself to stand tall and take a step forward. "Don't you come near me," I hissed with a bravado I did not feel.

Nicholas stopped and eyed me cautiously. "You need to trust—" Nicholas started.

"How dare you speak to me of trust?" I interrupted, fanning the flame of anger still burning in the back of my mind. I was cornered. But even the meekest cornered animal lashes out. "You murder for money. You lied to me for gain. I will *never* trust you. Never."

Nicholas stepped closer to me. I backed up. I could sense the bars just inches behind me.

"I stopped them from killing you," stated Nicholas matter-of-factly, as if this explained away everything.

"You should have let me die. It would have been easier than killing me now." I jutted my chin in defiance, my last show of strength before he slaughtered me.

Nicholas stepped hesitantly forward, holding his palms up, "I am not going to kill you."

My entire body trembled. My eyes flickered to his sword, waiting for him to draw it. Hoping to die with a little dignity, I steadied my shaking voice. "You already have. I will die in this cage."

"Come here," said Nicholas. He closed in on me and placed a hand on my shoulder. I recoiled from his touch like it was a branding iron, and skittered against the back of the brig.

Nicholas reached for me again. I slapped him hard across the face, the sound ricocheting through the hollow belly of the ship. I had not planned it. I instantly regretted it. His retaliation would be fierce.

"You will not touch me!" I seethed, taking advantage of Nicholas's stunned silence. "You will not speak to me. You will not even remove my bones from this cursed prison. I'd rather the rats bury me in their stomachs than you touch my rotting flesh!"

My strength was spent. I sank against the bars, terrified of what would happen next. My eyes stayed focused on Nicholas's sword.

He massaged his cheek where I had hit him, flexing his jaw. His nostrils flared slightly and I tensed, waiting for a blow. Instead, Nicholas stormed out of the brig. I flinched as the metal door clanged shut.

I cowered in my cage, shaking uncontrollably. What had I done? Had I won my life? Or a slow and agonizing death?

A shiver of panic took root as I watched the two sailors

ascend the ladder. They were leaving me to die, just as I asked. The ruddy sailor disappeared into the square of light. Nicholas paused on the ladder, turned, and looked at me.

It was too dark to see his expression but his posture was tense.

I wanted to call him back. I wanted to know if any of the comfort and warmth he had shown me before was real. If he had ever been my ally at all. But I held my tongue and he said nothing more to me. He turned and continued up the ladder.

Revulsion welled within me. I hated Nicholas for being a pirate. I hated him for lying to me. But more than anything, I hated him for leaving me.

"You're a monster," I whispered. The words were not intended for him, but the acoustics of the ship amplified them. Nicholas froze, exhaled angrily, and then vanished into the daylight.

* * * * *

My wish for solitude was granted. Aside from quietly placing a hardtack roll beside the brig twice a day, no one disturbed me. I never bothered to see who brought the food. I was afraid it might be Nicholas, and I never wanted to see him again. Still, I couldn't help but wonder why he hadn't come down again. Was it so easy for him to give up on me?

I refused the hardtack, leaving it for the unidentified creatures that scurried in the shadows. I vowed to starve. That was the only way out of this prison.

There was little to do but sulk, and I became remarkably good at it. I was angry with my father for making me leave England. I was angry with the captain of my ship for sailing us into a hurricane. I was angry with the pirates for rescuing me from a promising death at sea. But mostly, I was angry with Nicholas.

I focused on him constantly, screaming in frustration at times, cursing under my breath at others. Everything bad was because of him. It was his fault that I was imprisoned in the damp, putrid brig. It was his fault that I was slowly starving to death. It was his fault I was alive at all. And because he was the one who had told me my father was dead, that became his fault too.

I knew there was something unnatural about the way he treated me. I knew there were devastating secrets. I had suspected it all along. Still, how could I have missed all the signs that I was aboard a rogue ship?

Nicholas had expertly explained away my doubts. I had even started to trust him. And he knew that.

But it was all a façade. He was a pirate and I was his plunder. It was nothing more than that. The only reason I was down here was so no one could help me. His power as an officer prevented the other sailors from coming to my rescue. If only I had gone to the captain as I had wanted to, I would not be here now.

I thought about his efforts at kindness. He acted as though he was responsible for me and wanted to protect me. He acted as if he had affections for me.

Was any of that genuine? Was there any part of him missing me now?

His absence was my answer.

CHAPTER EIGHT

I HAD BEEN IN the brig for four days when someone quietly approached with another loaf of hardtack. I was sitting on the floor, knees pulled up to my chest, with my back to the approaching man. As usual, I didn't move a muscle or acknowledge his presence. It would be Nicholas, I thought. It was not enough for him to leave me to my misery. He would insist on degrading me more. He was just waiting for my moment of weakness when I would beg him for mercy. He would wait forever.

As I continued to brood in the silence, I realized I had not heard the man retreat. Angrily, I turned my head, prepared to confront Nicholas, but to my surprise I saw a pitiful pirate standing behind me wringing his tar-covered hat in his hands. It was the ruddy pirate with the straw hair who had come down with Nicholas the first day.

I stared directly at him, challenging him for existing in my space. He looked down at his busy hands, then motioned awkwardly to the growing pile of hardtack.

"Beggin' yer pardon, miss, but you'll lose yer strength if ye don't eat," he said meekly.

I turned my head back around and stared at my knees. My pantaloons were covered in filth. Ignoring him was harder than I thought. "That's the idea."

"If'n I sneaked ye a bit o' meat, would you eat that?"

"No," I said flatly. As if on cue, my stomach grumbled audibly in protest.

"You're Miss Monroe, aye?" he asked.

I said nothing.

"Me name's Skidmore."

I traced a black stain on the knee of my drawers. The silence lasted a long time. I thought he must have left when I heard a labored sigh and a soft scuffling noise. I looked over my shoulder at him again. He had hardly moved at all.

"What?" I demanded.

He met my eyes, pleased that he had elicited a response from me. "Pardon the idea, miss, but maybe ye could use a friend."

This was too much. Too weak to stand, I shifted around so I could to face him. "I am a prisoner in the custody of pirates," I spat out the word like dirty water. "I have no need of friends."

His eyes wide, he shuffled uncomfortably, still not leaving.

Suddenly, an idea came to me. "There is something you could do for me," I stated, trying to keep the malice in my voice to a minimum.

Skidmore's expression lifted.

"I would like to speak to the captain."

Skidmore stepped back, shaking his head almost imperceptibly.

"I demand to see the captain!"

"That can't be done, miss," Skidmore said under his breath.

"Of course not," I said snidely, "Mr. Holladay would

never allow that. A prisoner would never be allowed to plead his case with someone who actually might help. Does the captain even know I am here? He would never allow this. And Mr. Holladay knows that. He knows that the captain would never stand for his second-in-command to usurp power the way Mr. Holladay has. It's despicable."

The pirate continued to stand before me self-consciously, wringing his hands. He didn't want to be here, and I didn't know why he was.

"Take your leave. Some friend you are. You're completely useless."

* * * * *

The next day the man called Skidmore returned. He carried a large wooden crate and set it on the floor within my reach. He pulled a flat, wooden plate from the crate and set it next to the pile of hardtack. Next he pulled an orange and a small piece of salted meat from the crate and set them on the plate.

The excitement of seeing the plump, fresh orange overtook my vow of starvation. I grabbed it and hungrily tore into the rind. I sunk my teeth into its moist flesh before I had even finished peeling it, letting the juice dribble down my chin.

Skidmore smiled triumphantly.

He gestured to the crate he had brought with him. "Ye can have anything in there ya like." He was so soft-spoken I strained to hear every word he said.

Inquisitively, I peered into the crate. In the dim light of the ship's underbelly, I couldn't see what the box contained. Just a mass of black.

"Mostly clothes. But you'll find a book and a candle, too."

The past five days had been miserable, sitting for endless hours with nothing but my hatred to entertain me. I was as determined as ever to die in this forsaken pit, but I did not see how passing the time with a book would interfere. I reached a shaky hand into the crate and fumbled around.

Skidmore knelt by the box. Frightened, I instantly pulled my hand back. He fished out a tallow candle and a small tin box. He opened it to reveal flint and steel and showed me how to use them to light the candle.

"Open flames aren't generally allowed below deck, what with the risk of fire and all. But seein' how you're not a drunkard like the lot of us, I reckon you'll handle it fine. Mind it carefully. A toppled flame will send us all to the devil."

I nodded, tempted to light the Banshee on fire right then.

When I held the lighted candle, Skidmore stepped back, giving me the freedom to search the box myself. I pulled a silken dress of Wedgwood blue through the bars. I stood, lifting it with me. It was an elegant day dress, something I would have wished to own in my past life. With little ornamentation, the dress was exquisite simply because of quality workmanship and luxurious fabric. I knew just how this color of blue would complement my chestnut hair and brown eyes. Still grasping the candle in one hand, I held the dress against my frame and was pleased to see it would fit. It would be a bit long—it had been meant for someone taller than I—but that was workable.

I draped the dress across my chair in the corner, making sure it would not touch the damp planks or the rusty bars. Reaching again into the box I pulled out a book of Shakespearean plays. My heart leapt. Familiar stories would be so welcome during the long days ahead.

Next, I pulled out a black quilted dressing robe. It was always damp in the brig and my clothes were constantly wet. I had refused to touch Nicholas's coat since my first day down here when I'd torn it off. This would be welcome during the cool, drafty nights.

The box contained a lumpy pillow and a tattered brown blanket—it suspiciously resembled the blanket from Nicholas's cabin, though all blankets on board were probably quite similar. I could spread it on the floor to keep the wetness away. There was another dress; a fancy ball gown of canary yellow taffeta. It looked as though it would fit as well, although I did not have the petticoats needed to fill out the skirt. My fingers lingered on the intricate lace that edged the sleeves and the black satin sash tied around the waist. How strange it was to be holding such a lovely gown in the brig of a pirate ship. I smiled at the irony as I draped the dress across the blue one on the chair in the corner.

The last items I fished out of the crate were a hairbrush and a handheld looking glass. Holding the candle in one hand, I lifted the mirror and looked at my reflection. A tiny gasp escaped my lips.

"I look half dead," I muttered to myself in amazement.

Skidmore laughed quietly, "No offense, Miss Monroe, but I must agree."

I flashed an impertinent glare at him before examining my reflection more closely. My face was thin and pinched. My large brown eyes—normally flashing with intelligence and good humor—were sunken into gaping sockets. Purple moons underlined my eyes. I examined my face closer, hoping it was just shadows from the candle light I was seeing. No. The dark rings were truly there. My normally fair skin was sallow and grey. My reddish-brown hair hung limply, dull and tangled.

Why was I surprised? I had hardly eaten anything for a

week and sleeping was next to impossible. Besides, I was a prisoner on my way to death. It was only fair that I look the part. I could not expect myself to look rosy and charming.

I set down the mirror gently, no longer able to look at the corpse who stared back at me. "Where did you find these things?" I wondered aloud. On a ship full of ferocious men, it seemed impossible that such lovely female fineries were just lying about.

Skidmore fidgeted, avoiding my peering gaze.

"Oh."

The sweetness of the orange I had devoured churned in my stomach and I rushed to the pail. The candle slipped from my grasp and the light extinguished. I retched into the pail, tears squeezing from the corners of my eyes. When I was done, I quietly folded the exquisite dresses, the warm dressing gown, and the blanket. With the stack in my arms, I slowly turned to face Skidmore.

"How could you?"

He blanched at my words, his face falling. I could see he was confused and it was difficult to be angry at his attempted kindness. His cruelty had been unintentional.

"These things…they came from that ship you ransacked last week, didn't they?" I held out the stack of items in question.

He shuffled uncomfortably. It was all the answer I needed.

I gently placed each item back into the crate, including the candle. When I was done, I carefully pushed the crate out of my reach.

"Please take these back. I do not want them."

"But, miss," he argued, "they are of no use to anyone but you."

"No," I insisted, my voice growing stern. "I will have nothing to do with your contemptible raids."

I crossed my arms and stared at Skidmore. He continued to look at his feet.

"Did he send these things?" I asked with contempt. "Did he think it would be funny?"

Skidmore didn't answer.

I crossed the brig and retrieved Nicholas's coat from the corner. I tossed it through the bars to Skidmore. He caught it smartly.

"Give that to your first mate with my regards," I said icily.

"He's no first mate, miss," Skidmore corrected.

I scoffed. "Surprise, surprise. He lied about that too."

"No, but he is the quartermaster."

"Quartermaster?"

"In ships such as this—"

"Pirate ships," I corrected.

"Aye, pirate ships. You see, us pirates don't take kindly to the notion of an all-powerful captain like you see in navies and on merchant ships, seein' as we're not fond of the law and all. A quartermaster is appointed by the crew to represent the crew and holds nearly as much power as the captain himself. He leads boardin' parties, pays the crew, delegates work, lays on punishment, and the like. Can veto much of the cap'n's commands too. Except in times of battle. He's a lot more important than a first mate."

"It makes no difference to me," I retorted. "Please return his coat to him. And do not bring me any more gifts."

In a single swift movement, I spun around and sat with my back to the pirate. He shuffled quietly away, leaving the crate of goods and the ghosts that came with it.

CHAPTER NINE

EVERY DAY I EXPECTED Nicholas to come to the brig. I expected him to gloat over me, to torture me, to attempt to win my affections…something. I knew the time would come when I would have to confront him. I looked forward to that moment with equal parts of dread and welcome. I deserved answers. He was the only one who had them. But each day passed without an appearance.

Skidmore returned several times each day. We engaged in brief conversation, and although I loathed admitting it, I liked his visits. I began eating again. Hardtack was the usual fare, but occasionally salted meat or dried beans made their way onto the menu. I would eat these small luxuries, knowing they had come from the *Banshee*'s galley and not from the pillaged ship.

When I asked Skidmore to remove the crate a second time, he informed me that he had been ordered to leave it within my reach.

"Mr. Skidmore, what am I doing here?"

"On the *Banshee*?"

"In this brig. Will I ever be let out?"

Skidmore hitched his breath. "I cannot say."

"You cannot say or you do not know?" I watched the pirate closely to see if I had uncovered the truth. It was difficult to tell with Skidmore. He always seemed nervous no matter what I said.

He didn't answer.

"Please, Mr. Skidmore, I deserve to know my sentence. How long will I be imprisoned? What happens next? Will I be killed? Trained to work the ship?"

Skidmore's blue eyes crinkled with a pleasant smile. "There be no plans for your death, Miss Monroe."

"I suppose that's a relief. Still…tell me something."

I wanted to ask about Nicholas and his intentions with me, but my pride would not allow it.

Skidmore nervously mussed his hair, his eyes darting around the hold. "I'm just following orders, miss."

"Please, Skidmore," my fingers grasped the bars in desperation, "can't you ask…someone?" I couldn't bring myself to mention the quartermaster's name. "I can't stay in here forever."

I could tell that I would get nowhere with Skidmore. He bumbled uneasily, too kind to be cruel to me, yet too loyal to offer me anything relevant.

Finally, Skidmore stopped his shuffling long enough to look at me. "You ought to be content where you're at."

I wasn't sure whether it was a threat or a reassurance. Either way, Skidmore offered me no more information and was as unsettled as ever.

* * * * *

On a particularly cold night, a storm tossed the ship to and fro and the eerie creaking of reluctant wood filled the air. I huddled into a corner of the brig, supporting myself against the bars. The brig's few furnishings tumbled back and forth across the floor as the ship rocked in the strong gale. More water than usual dripped down the iron bars, soaking my clothing and hair. When I was shivering so severely that I could I hardly move, I remembered the blanket in the crate.

I peered through the blackness and reached towards the crate. It wasn't there. The ship rolled, and I rolled with it, tumbling into the back corner of the brig. The chair and bucket rolled with me. I heard the crate bump into the bars. Before I could reach it, the ship rocked again, tossing me headfirst into the bars I was headed for. The pail and the chair knocked into me and I heard the crate slide away.

This time I anticipated the ship's bucking and clung to the bars as the ship rocked in the opposite direction. I heard the crate skidding towards me and grabbed its edge as it banged into the brig. With one arm securing the crate and myself, I used my free hand to rifle through the contents. I pulled out the pillow and the scratchy blanket. As the ship rocked again, a puddle of water splashed on me, causing my teeth to chatter even more ferociously. Without a second thought, I pulled the quilted dressing robe through the bars.

I removed my wet clothing and put the robe on. I was instantly warmer, though I felt strangely vulnerable without my usual undergarments. I knotted them around the bars of the brig to keep them off the floor. Placing the blanket between the wet floor and my bottom, I huddled back into the corner of the brig to brace myself against the ship's movement, bunching the pillow behind my head for comfort.

With the warm robe wrapped around me, my shivering finally subsided and I was able to rest, though I was frequently jolted awake by the sound of the scooting chair. When I did sleep, my dreams were as tumultuous as the restless ocean.

After that night, I found the contents of the crate more and more tempting. I lit the candle and read *Hamlet*, my favorite. The idea of putting my undergarments back on—grey with filth—repulsed me, so I continued to wear the black robe. Skidmore was happy to see that I had made use of the items. Once, he caught me brushing my hair and offered to bring me a bucket of seawater and a lump of soap so I could wash myself and my underclothes. He made good on his word and brought a bucket the next day.

Bathing was more than a bit awkward with only a small bucket, especially since I had never bathed myself in my life. I managed somehow, even kneeling over and dunking my head to wash my hair. It felt wonderful to scrub out the weeks of filth. It took me over an hour to brush through all the tangles in my hair. At times I wondered if I had pulled out more hair than remained on my head, but finally it was smooth and tangle-free. Once I was clean, I scrubbed my undergarments. Even in the dim light I could see the grime floating off the clothing.

Once my undergarments were dry, I was tempted to put them back and try on one of the beautiful dresses in the crate. But every time I thought of the dresses, I imagined their previous owner and how she must have died. Did it happen when the ship exploded? Was she ruthlessly hewn down to a bloody corpse by a relentless pirate? Did she perhaps throw herself into the sea as a last resort as I had hoped to do? When I thought of her, I had no desire to wear those dresses.

Skidmore supplied me with extra candles as needed. With his gentle nature, I had difficulty thinking of him as a pirate. I came to recognize him as a friend, and I valued him for that.

I wished to ask him about Nicholas, but persuaded myself not to. Why should I care about Nicholas anyway? Judging by the amount of time I spent thinking about him, it was clear that I did. There was something about him. It was more than the way my heart had fluttered every time I saw him or the way I had lost all words when his eyes found mine. He had meant something to me, after all. As counterfeit as it had been, Nicholas had been my protector. My rescuer. My friend. I thought by now Nicholas would have come to see me, even if in mocking derision. But with Skidmore looking after me now, apparently Nicholas was done with me. And that bothered me more than I liked.

* * * * *

Searing wax spattered across the pages of my book. I tried to wipe the droplets away but only succeeded in spreading a fine film of wax across "Sonnet 29." I scraped at the wax, my fingernail rasping against the paper.

I heard the creak of the hatch door opening and the rhythm of slow footsteps.

"Morning watch already? It feels too early for that."

No one answered, but the footsteps grew nearer.

"Skidmore?"

I strained to remember the last bell I heard. I could have sworn it was still midnight watch. Skidmore worked the midnight watch and only came down after he was off duty. A visit from him this time of night was unprecedented.

I put the book down and stood, stretching the candle out beyond the bars and squinted into the blackness. I could see nothing. For a moment I thought to blow out the flame in order to see better, but decided against it. It would take my eyes minutes to adjust. Besides, I wanted to see who my strange visitor was.

He was nimble. Nearly silent. I remembered the way Nicholas moved with such easy grace. My heart thudded. It had to be him. His ridicule was past due.

"Mr. Holladay?"

All that answered me was a dim echo.

"If you're here to humiliate me, let's get on with it."

Still no answer.

My palms grew damp. A sour rot spread in my stomach.

I tried to provoke a response. "If you're not here to mock me, then you must be here to apologize. Well, I accept. No hard feelings. In fact, don't even bother to say you are sorry. Let's forget the whole sordid incident and enjoy a lovely conversation over a cup of rum."

Still no answer. There was something unnerving in the sly, steady approach of the stranger.

"I know you are there. Show yourself."

I was now positive that whoever was approaching was not Nicholas. He would have answered me. I was sure of that. The air grew thicker, heavier somehow. It felt wet in my lungs as if it were drowning me. My eyes widened as they stared into the darkness, my ears strained to hear every small noise.

A sharp jingle of metal sounded just beyond the pool of my candlelight. My brave façade faltered. I had not forgotten that I was locked on a ship with a hundred lawless barbarians.

Footsteps shuffled towards me and a figure materialized. A bald head ringed by a mop of stringy grey hair. Scraggly grey brows over sunken eyes. A hooked nose, crooked from some past damage. A spattering of pock marks. A thin, silver scar marking the man's forehead. Thin, cracked lips turned up in a smile.

With a sudden intake of breath, I recognized him as the small, wiry pirate that had threatened me on the deck during the attack. He couldn't get at me then, with Nicholas pointing a sword at his throat, but now, in the stillness of the night, this man had come for what he wanted.

CHAPTER TEN

MY STOMACH TIGHTENED AS the unwanted visitor approached. There was a resolve in his eyes that caused the hair on the back of my neck to prickle.

One of his arms was entwined around a large, ceramic jug. In his other hand he playfully jingled a ring of keys. I swallowed hard. His threatening smile grew wider as he saw the fear in my eyes. His eyes probed every last inch of me, lingering on the bit of bare skin that showed at the top of my robe.

My hand flew to the lapels, and I covered my exposed skin as if it would help at this point. My thoughts raced as I tried to find a way out, a way to fight back. Obviously, running was not an option. I would have to face him. That left me with only two courses of action—beg for mercy and hope to soften his heart or put on an air of bravado in hope of intimidating him. He hardly seemed sympathetic enough to listen to any measure of begging. Remembering how my strength and temper had scared Nicholas and Skidmore my first day in the brig, I decided to try intimidation.

I took a deliberate step towards the man. "What do you want?" I demanded, hoping my tone was as harsh as I meant it to be.

His sallow eyes still lingered at my neck. Was he staring at my skin or noticing my frightened hand clutching tightly at my robe? I forced my fist to unclench and I pulled my hand to my side. He couldn't know just how vulnerable I was.

But he already knew. It was why he was here.

He held up the jug. "Skidmore sent me. Said ye might enjoy a little *refreshment*." The jeering smile never left his face.

"Rum, is it? Leave it in that crate. I will get it when I want it."

He continued to advance. "Nay, it's too big to fit through those bars." He jingled the keys. "It's best I deliver it personally."

"I do not want your rum. I do not want anything to do with you. Just turn around and leave." Although I tried my hardest to sound threatening, a shrill edge of panic sounded in my voice.

Sneering, the man held out a key and dragged it against the bars walking the length of the brig, then back again.

My one chance to flee would be when he opened the gate. I could dash out quickly and hide in the darkness of the ship's hold.

He stopped his pacing in front of the gate. Slowly, deliberately, without ever taking an eye off me, he positioned the key in the lock.

"Leave now or I'll scream," I threatened, stepping back.

"Please do," he beckoned, turning the key.

I tried to summon a scream, but my breath caught in my throat. My mouth was dry. I was frozen with terror. I wondered whether screaming would even help. I was a prisoner here, a *nothing*. No one could possibly care if I lived or died. Would anyone even respond? Worse yet, would my screaming only signal other pirates to come and join in the games? Perhaps they were already waiting, and this man was only the first in a long line.

The pirate slowly opened the gate of the brig, breaching the protection of my iron bars. I watched for my chance to run but he opened the door just wide enough to slide through into the brig with me, blocking my escape. If he wasn't going to let me out, I would force my way out.

As he was slipping through the gate, I rushed directly at him, grabbing the gate with both hands and slamming it into him with all my might. The edge of the iron gate cracked into his face, smashing the back of his head into the sharp metal door frame.

He cried out in agony. Blood spurted from his nose. With more force than I thought the scrawny man had, he pushed back the gate and swung the heavy jug at me, hitting me squarely on the jaw. I flew through the air and crashed into a heap against the back of the brig.

"You cheap hussy!" he swore, slamming the door shut behind him. We were locked in the brig together. Only the keys would unlock the gate and he no longer had those. He must've dropped them somewhere in the darkness when I slammed into him.

The pirate threw the jug onto me. It hit me in the ribs, knocking the breath from my lungs.

Although I had dropped my candle, it stayed lit as it rolled into a corner of the brig. In the distorted shadows, the sailor looked horribly demented. Blood covered the bottom half of his face and stained his shirt. His features twisted with rage. A low noise hissed through his clenched teeth.

In two large steps he crossed the brig and knelt over me. I screamed with all my might.

His hand grabbed my throat and bashed my head

against the floor. "Quiet. You take what's comin' to ya."

With one hand still on my throat, his other hand roughly stroked my leg.

"Please," I whimpered, unable to hide my fear.

He tightened his grasp on my throat and slammed my head against the floor once more. Brilliant stars flashed across my sight. I kicked as he grappled at my legs. Without relaxing his hold on my neck, he climbed on top of me, using his weight to immobilize me.

Silent cries wracked my body. Tears poured from my eyes.

I clawed at his face, threw my knees into his back. Try as I did to escape, the struggle was fruitless. He leaned down and pressed his face into the crook of my neck. The stench of rum on his hot breath mingled with the metallic scent of blood. My stomach threatened to retch. I screamed again. He panted heavily against my shivering skin.

The ship swayed gently, but enough that the candle rolled directly towards us. Without hesitating, I snatched the still-burning candle and shoved the flaming stick into the man's eye. He reacted just as I hoped he would, reeling back and releasing his grip on me to protect his face. I punched his neck, making him choke for air. With all the strength I could muster, I rolled the man off me. He stumbled to his feet, ready to fight back.

I could not let that happen. I bent down quickly and grabbed the handle of the jug of rum with both hands, swinging it up with all my might as I stood. The heavy jug hit him directly under the chin, and he toppled onto the floor.

In the darkness I could barely see his figure moving on the floor of the brig. He was righting himself, preparing for battle. This would not end well. One of us would wind up dead. I wanted it to be him.

I crossed quickly to him and dropped the jug on top of his head before he could stand, never letting go if its handle. It was the best weapon I had. Screaming with fury, I swung it at the man again; this time it slammed into his shoulder. Scrambling clumsily on the floor, he reached into his boot and pulled something out.

A plane of cool silver glinted in the darkness. A dirk.

Preparing to crush him before he could use the dirk, I raised the jug over my head with both hands, stretching as high as I could to get as much momentum as possible. A swift kick landed directly in my stomach and I doubled over. The ceramic jug slipped from my hands and shattered on the deck. Rum splashed my legs, its odor filling the night. The pirate pounced on me. I tried to dodge him, but the man grabbed my hair, yanking me back against him. I felt a cold blade against my throat.

"Yer a saucy little vixen," he crooned. A spatter of blood showered me as he spoke.

I gagged at the reek of his breath.

He maneuvered me until I was cornered against the bars. With deliberate measure, he ran his tongue up the side of my face. I cried out quietly, tears streaming down my cheeks. He pressed his lips against mine in a perverse sort of kiss, stabbing at me with his blood-soaked tongue. His teeth found my bottom lip and bit down on it hard, drawing my own blood.

He pressed the point of the dirk into the hollow of my neck. The pain was so sharp I was sure he had pierced the skin. The tickling sensation of blood on dripping on my throat confirmed my fears.

"We do this right now. You fight me, you die."

He yanked me to the deck by my hair and kicked me with all his might in my back. I writhed in pain. Laughing, he kicked me again, this time in the side of the head. My ears rang and flashes of red light exploded in the dark. I curled up defensively, unable to move, unable to cry out, my arms cradling my head. His hands unhinged his belt and I knew this was it. I couldn't fight anymore, though I wished I could. If I could fight for just a bit longer, he would be forced to stab me, to kill me.

Then this nightmare would finally be over.

CHAPTER ELEVEN

A SPARK OF BLINDING light filled the darkness and a deafening crack left my ears ringing.

The last kick to my head must have been causing hallucinations. An eerie silence engulfed me and I felt myself slipping deeply into the calm.

"Wrack!" a voice boomed. "Leave her alone!"

That voice was no hallucination. Someone was here to stop this.

Paying no heed to the demand, my attacker—Wrack—forced me from my protected ball and knelt on top of me, the dirk grazing my cheek. Between my sobs I choked for air.

A new light appeared. Softer. More constant. It grew brighter, closer. I shifted my head slightly and through blurred vision I saw who pounded down the ladder.

Nicholas.

I blinked, sure my mind was playing tricks on me. Yes, it was Nicholas. Skidmore followed closely behind him, holding a lantern high.

Despite the violent trembling that shuddered through

me, I couldn't move. There wasn't any fight left in me, and I had no way to buy Nicholas the time he needed to find the keys and stop this man.

"Get out of the brig, now!" Nicholas's deafening demand caused me to shudder. "That is an order!" His urgent steps crashed across the floor.

Nicholas's threats didn't stop the pirate. He pulled my robe up, exposing my legs. An earsplitting explosion sounded, and the door of the brig swung open. Nicholas was standing there, holding a smoking pistol. Skidmore hurried behind Nicholas, the lantern in one hand and a sword in the other.

In one swift motion, Nicholas pulled Wrack off me and cracked the butt of his pistol across Wrack's face. My attacker crumpled to the deck, unconscious.

"Get him out of here," Nicholas growled.

Skidmore set the lantern down in the brig, and flung the unconscious pirate over his shoulder like a bag of cargo.

I felt the warmth of Nicholas's touch on my face, and soft though it was, I couldn't help but wince. I balled my fists and swung at him, landing feeble punches against his chest.

"No! No!" I screamed, flailing my fists violently, though I knew I was too weak to protect myself.

"It's me, Tessa, it's me. It's Nicholas. He's gone. He's gone."

"Don't touch me. I hate you! I hate you!"

Nicholas lifted me onto his lap, cradling me in a tender embrace.

My flailing punches melted into uncontrollable shaking, my screaming into sobs. I wept, stuffing my fists into my eyes.

Nicholas soothed me gently, speaking words so softly that I could not understand them. He held me securely, his arms around me, his head bent over mine, pressing his lips against my ear.

My violent sobbing settled into soft cries. Exhausted, I finally lay limp in Nicholas's arms.

He softly stroked my hair. "Can you hear me?" he quietly asked.

I tried to respond but could only manage a pathetic moan. My entire body burned with fiery pain.

He sighed deeply. "What did he do to you?" he whispered to himself. His fingers—light as a butterfly's touch—grazed my swollen face. "Can you move at all?"

I shook my head ever so slightly. Even this small movement sent shocks of pain through me.

"I'm just going to look at you closer, Tessa. Don't be scared." Nicholas laid me down, tucking my robe around me. He grabbed the lantern and held it overhead. He examined my face, gingerly touching the spreading bruise on my jaw where Wrack struck me with the jug. He touched my bloodied lip. I heard him gasp when he saw the pool of drying blood on my neck and shoulder where Wrack's nose had bled on me. After a moment of closer examination, Nicholas seemed satisfied that the blood was not mine.

"Your neck is bruised," he observed. I coughed as he gently stroked the tender muscles where I had been throttled.

"Nicholas?" I rasped, finally finding my voice.

"I'm here." His voice was husky.

Struggling for strength, I coughed out the only question that was on my mind, "Is he gone?"

"Aye, he's gone. You will never see him again," promised Nicholas. "Where did he hurt you?"

I swallowed hard, hoping to get some moisture in my dry throat. "My neck," I croaked, cupping my throat to demonstrate how I'd been strangled. "He kicked my head and my back and in the stomach." My voice was a barely audible whisper.

"And here?" he asked, stroking my jaw.

"A jug of rum."

"That explains the broken clay. It looks like you were cut from that too."

He was holding my left hand. It was covered in lacerations I'd not noticed before.

"Did he…?"

"No," I whispered. "You arrived just in time."

He solemnly examined my wounds again. "We need to watch for bruisin' where he kicked you, but I don't think anything is broken. Tessa, I'm going to carry you up to my cabin. You'll be safe there." With a hot fury in his voice, he added, "I promise no one will hurt you again."

"Nicholas?" I asked again.

"Yes?"

"Why are you here?"

"To take care of you, of course," he said like it was blatantly obvious.

"But you put me here."

He quickly sucked in his breath.

"Tessa," murmured Nicholas, "you do know that I never meant you any pain, don't you?"

His eyes shone with concern.

I struggled to slow my racing thoughts, to make sense of what had happened, of Nicholas's abandonment, and his tender actions now. Finally, I whispered, "But everything you've done has caused me pain."

Nicholas scooped me into his arms, wrapping me in a soft embrace. I felt a sob ripple through his chest. I cried with him.

CHAPTER TWELVE

NICHOLAS CARRIED ME TO his cabin and tenderly laid me on the wooden bed. He piled several blankets on me, trying to stop the quivering that tore through me. I couldn't stop shaking. I couldn't stop crying.

When Skidmore came to offer help, Nicholas described my injuries then sent him for supplies. He returned quickly with canvas rags and a jug of rum identical to the one Wrack had brought to the brig.

I trembled at the sight of it.

"Don't be frightened," Nicholas reassured. "It's just for medicine."

After pouring a splash of rum in a cup, he coaxed me to drink. "Take small sips. You'll feel better and the pain will ease."

My shaky hands could barely hold the cup. Nicholas helped me guide it to my lips, but the smell brought back horrible images from the attack and I could not drink it. I shook my head feebly. "I can't."

Kneeling beside the bed, Nicholas poured the rum on a canvas rag, then delicately dabbed at my wounds. The sting of alcohol sent stabbing pain through me. I cried out.

"It hurts too much," I whimpered.

"It stops infection. I'm so sorry. Just a little more."

I clenched my teeth as he ran the cloth over my cuts.

"There. Finished."

He peered at me, a grave look clouding his features. For the first time, I noticed the color of his eyes. During our dimly-lit conversations in the galley, I had always assumed they were brown, because the rest of his coloring was so tawny. But they were a captivating shade of grey, their lightness emphasized by his tan skin, thick lashes, and black eyebrows.

"Your eyes are grey," I found myself saying, reaching as if to touch his cheek, but stopping before my fingers found him.

He pulled my hand against his face and smiled kindly, a look of relief washing over him. "Well, at least you can see straight."

My stomach fluttered and I smiled at the building infatuation. A painful breath was all it took to remind me that this was not a man I should fall for—he was the one who caused all my pain.

I pulled my hand back and looked away.

Nicholas cleared his throat uncomfortably then bandaged my cuts. An occasional sting caused me to cringe.

"Tell me everything that happened," Nicholas prompted stoically.

Gravely, I relayed how Wrack let himself into the brig and attacked me. I told the events plainly and without embellishment, crushing any emotion I felt. I hardly believed the words I uttered.

Nicholas did not look at me the entire time I recounted the story. He was so quiet I wondered if he had stopped listening. The heavy stillness continued after I finished.

I could not stand the weight of the quiet. I had to break the silence. "How did you know?"

Nicholas was silent for a moment more, still refusing to meet my eyes. "My keys went missing about thirty minutes prior. I searched all over for them, and then I went to the men to see if any of them had seen them. I discovered that Wrack was missin' too—he'd left his watch early. When I heard you scream, I realized where he must be. I called for Skidmore and loaded my gun."

His eyes finally found mine. The sadness in them was undeniable. "I was too late." He sank back against the wall, elbows resting on his knees, looking like a broken child. His hands covered his face, his fingers pushing into his hair. "I should never have put you in that brig."

"Then why did you?" It was a question I wanted answered since my first moments in that prison.

"I thought you would be safer." He sighed and went on. "It is a dangerous time to be on this ship. The crew is ready for mutiny, ready for violence. The way the men talked about you when we fished you out of the water—I knew there would be trouble. The captain called you for his own and demanded everyone else leave you be. There was a time when the captain's orders would've been enough, but not now. I argued that it would be wrong to harass you before you awoke and most of the men agreed. A kind of sanctity for the unconscious," he scoffed bitterly. "I was so glad it was me who found you the night you awoke. There's no telling what would've happened if...I thought things would be better if the men still thought you were unconscious."

"Then I showed myself to everyone," I said quietly, understanding Nicholas's response on the deck that day.

"Of course you did. How could I expect you to stay in your room amidst that commotion? You must've been terrified. I should've gone to you, explained everything."

Nicholas laid his head back against the wall and stared at the ceiling. "Never mind that we were in the middle of a raid—something the boys had been wanting for weeks. As soon as they saw you, they wanted you. Forbidden treasure and all that. And when I saw the way Wrack eyed you…" he closed his eyes and shook his head against the thought. His hands clenched into white-knuckled fists. He exhaled slowly, deliberately uncoiling his hands. "And when you realized that we were nothin' more than a load of marauders—you were ready to throw yourself overboard. The look in your eyes…I had to act swiftly to keep you safe. Safe from yourself. Safe from the crew. The brig was the only thing I could think of."

"But you left me there. *For weeks.*" My voice faltered. "You never even bothered with an explanation."

Nicholas's grey eyes hardened. "I tried. Remember?"

"You should have come back," I argued weakly.

"You told me not to." He sighed heavily and lightly pounded his head against the wall behind him and cursed under his breath. "But I should've. I did the absolute worst thing possible. I barricaded you in with a shark."

He was anguished with guilt. I couldn't help the sympathy I felt for him. "You did what you thought was best. What more could you have done?"

"I should've kept guard. Stayed with you day and night."

"You couldn't have done that."

"Well, I could've done more," he growled.

My head swam from the pain. My chest ached with every breath and I still quaked from the trauma. I needed to rest, but I was hungry for this conversation. Until now, I had not realized how much I had missed Nicholas during the previous weeks. He was finally here, telling me everything I needed to hear. Ignoring the agony within my body, I pushed to keep the conversation flowing.

"You sent Skidmore."

"Aye," he nodded, staring at the ceiling.

"To be my friend."

He nodded again. "He's a good man. I trust him."

"And you sent me that crate." Though the gifts had upset me, I saw now that Nicholas had not meant to mock me with them, but that he honestly wanted to improve my circumstances.

"I thought of you," he said simply, still staring at the ceiling. "I couldn't keep away from you. I came to watch you."

"You did?"

Finally, Nicholas looked at me.

He nodded. "Not every day, but as often as I could. Sometimes I'd sneak in behind Skidmore. But sometimes I would go down alone and watch you mope, watch you cry, watch you read."

"And you never said anything?"

I felt betrayed all over again. Betrayed that he had ignored my request for solitude and betrayed that he let me think he had abandoned me. No matter that these seeming betrayals were completely contradictory. I couldn't help but feel both at the same time.

He should have said something. All this time I had thought he had deceived me, forsaken me. Things would have been much more bearable if I had known he was there keeping watch, protecting me from a far worse fate.

He held his hands up in defense, "I thought you'd slap me."

We both laughed, but my laughter was cut short by a groan of pain, and I wrapped my arms around my torso.

Nicholas immediately knelt over me, his hands fumbling helplessly over my injuries.

"You need to rest," he insisted. He tucked the blankets tighter around me.

"I'm all right," I said in a broken whisper, struggling to make my breathing return to normal.

"I'll go and let you sleep. But I won't be far."

The thought of him leaving was unbearable. I needed him with me now. And not just because I didn't want to be alone. "Don't leave me," I whispered, my breathing turning erratic once more. I winced as I fought back the pain that threatened to consume me, "Please stay."

His eyes danced. "I'll stay," he reassured me.

I closed my eyes and breathed shallowly, willing the agony to stop.

"It pains me so to see you hurting so."

I opened my eyes and forced a smile. "I'm getting better by the moment."

Nicholas cocked his head and peered at me, as if he knew I was lying. He smiled a little then sat back down.

"When I would watch you in the brig, I wanted nothing more than to help you. I couldn't stand to see you crying. I wanted so much to go to you and hold you. But I thought I'd just bring you more pain. You were so angry. I was a helpless voyeur, watching you cry, watching your nightmares."

"I had nightmares?" I did not remember dreaming at all.

"Aye. You called for your father every night. One time, you even called for me." He looked away. It was hard to tell with only the light of the lantern in the room, but it looked like Nicholas was blushing. I could feel blood rushing to my own cheeks.

"I called for you?" I asked, embarrassed.

He shrugged, but a soft smile tugged at his lips. "Aye. Just once. Mostly you cursed my name, but once, just once, you called for me. I was down there, watching you. I thought then would be the time to go to you, to try again. But I was so scared of hurting you more. I still cannot forget the look in your eyes. You called me a monster."

My previous flush of embarrassment turned in to a flush of shame. "I-I didn't mean it—"

"Yes, you did." He played gently with a strand of my hair near my face.

That was fair. "All right, I did. I meant it. But only because I thought you were a double-crossing murderer who was going to kill me."

He laughed at that. "Did you really think that of me? That I was going to hurt you?"

My eyes were grave as I nodded. "That's what you do. You are a pirate. I still don't know what to think of you."

He lifted his hand away from my face. "What do you mean?" His eyes tightened noticeably.

"It's this exactly," I sighed. "Right now, you seem kind and warm. But I can't trust that. You've turned on me before. It could happen again. After all, you *are* a pirate."

"Piracy is what I do, not who I am," he defended.

"Well, yes, but it isn't like you're deceiving people into buying a tonic to make them beautiful. You make your living through bloodshed and terror."

The heavy silence between us resumed. Nicholas shook his head and started to stand.

I was not sure what I wanted from him, but I did not want him to leave.

"I cannot condone what you do," I offered, "and I never will. But that doesn't mean I want you to go."

His eyes lit up.

"I am...confused," I admitted. It was an understatement.

Nicholas settled back down. He wasn't going to leave.

"If it makes you feel better," he said, "I am the quartermaster. I mete out punishment, I divide plunder, I navigate, and I concoct strategy. But I rarely engage in it."

"I suppose you earned your rank sitting on the

sidelines?" I mocked. "I am not a fool." Hurt flashed across his features.

"You speak the truth." He stared intently at his hands, as if they had all the answers he needed. "I'm not happy with what I have become, Tessa. It's not as though I sought this life. Everything I told you before is true. I was a kid starving on the streets. I got a job on a ship helping with the carpentry. But that ship was sacked by pirates. I watched as my crewmates were disemboweled, beheaded, and keelhauled. I was kept alive only because of my skill. It was either sign on or be killed. I was fourteen. And so without really meaning to, I became a pirate."

He sat closer to me now. I could feel the warmth of his breath on my clammy skin. My heart raced. "I always wanted another life," said Nicholas. "I guess I just never had a reason to find one before now."

His grey eyes searched mine. He ran his fingers through my hair, careful to touch me in only the gentlest ways. Though I held his gaze steadily, my breathing grew shallow. No one had ever looked at me this way before, with such intensity.

His touch was electrifying. I found myself craving it, wanting more of that warmth. He smelled like the wind-tossed sea—clean and fresh and slightly salty. He inched closer, his thumb brushing my bottom lip. I parted my lips slightly, our eyes searching each other's.

Nicholas leaned in slightly. I lifted my chin to him and closed my eyes, waiting. His hand caressed my cheek, then I sensed him pull away. I opened my eyes. He drew back slowly, looking at me apologetically.

"You need your rest."

I stared blankly at him, confused by his actions and my own emotions.

"I won't leave you," Nicholas added, misinterpreting my expression. "I will stay right here while you sleep."

I breathed deeply, trying to mask my disappointment. My head swirled.

"Close your eyes," he commanded.

I obeyed but it was long time before sleep finally found me.

CHAPTER THIRTEEN

COMPLETELY EXHAUSTED, I SLEPT soundly. Nicholas woke me periodically to monitor my wounds and feed me warm broth. I was so tired and this constant waking frustrated me, but he insisted it was necessary to keep me from losing consciousness.

I felt much safer with Nicholas nearby. He comforted me as much as he knew how, with reassuring conversation or additional blankets and pillows. His compassion never wavered and I began to believe his story—that everything he had done was to protect me. I craved his touch—that touch that I had once thought too brazen and presumptuous.

I was rarely alone. Nicholas stayed with me every moment he could, even sleeping in a cramped ball on the floor. If he could not personally watch over me, Skidmore stood guard outside the cabin.

I longed for Nicholas every moment he was away. I found it harder to breathe when he wasn't there, which fortunately was not often. I craved his conversation and hungered for his occasional caress. Though broken, wounded, and confined to a hard, wooden bed, I found a welcome sense of calm when he was near.

"I must look horrible," I said as Nicholas dabbed at my wounds with a cool, damp cloth on the third day after the assault.

"You're healing smartly," Nicholas reassured.

I touched my face gingerly, feeling the puffiness of my bruised jaw and the tender lumps on my head.

"Tell the truth…how bad is it?"

Nicholas pursed his lips, deciding to be honest. "I can see that you are healing. Your bruises are turning purple and yellow. And your cuts are closing. But I hurt every time I look at you."

"I must be completely disfigured."

"No, no," Nicholas smiled softly. "You will be fine. You're as pretty as ever. I just meant that I will never forgive myself for what happened."

"You cannot hold yourself responsible for another man's actions."

He scowled at me, his beautiful face glorious in its anger.

"You *can't*," I stressed.

"You'll never convince me of that," he murmured.

* * * * *

Later that day, a pounding at the cabin door startled me awake. Nicholas sprang to his feet as the door flew open, his hand at his scabbard.

The doorway framed a terrifying creature that I could only assume was a man. He was tall. Very tall. He wore a wide-brimmed black hat and a sweeping black jacket that nearly brushed the deck. Stringy white hair hung about his shoulders. His skin was paper white and nearly translucent. His face was thin and bony, his nose a long, sharp line. Everything about him looked severe. But the most shocking thing about the man in the doorway was his blood-red eyes. If demons existed, he might be one.

I pushed myself into a sitting position and glanced quickly at Nicholas, gauging his response to this demon.

Nicholas made no reaction whatsoever. "Captain Black," he said simply.

So this was the pirate captain. It was as if he stepped out of my nightmares.

"Wrack is dead," the captain said without introduction. His fearsome eyes darted between Nicholas and me.

Nicholas took a step towards the captain. "Dead? What happened?"

The captain's crimson eyes bore into me, his stare unwavering. I trembled and pulled the blankets up to my chin. Without shifting his gaze, he said, "He caught a fever last night. Isn't that right, Miss Monroe?"

I looked to Nicholas for reassurance. He looked at me, his eyes pinched with confusion, then back at the captain.

"I-I'm sorry?" I stammered, confused at this man's meaning.

"Fever started last night. Then he died within twelve hours. Never heard o' anythin' like that."

His words were pregnant with a meaning I could not grasp. Although I had no sympathetic feelings for the dead pirate, I imagined that one fewer man on board could prove burdensome for the captain and crew. But there was something more ominous than that in his words. Nicholas seemed as dumbfounded as I was.

"Beggin' your pardon, sir," Nicholas started, "but Mr. Wrack was hurt somewhat badly during his attack on Miss Monroe."

"Aye," the captain nodded, an unusually pink lip curling over his teeth into a devious smile, "she dealt a bit o' damage, that wee one, didn't she?" He turned his red eyes to Nicholas. "But the strange thing is, he died of a fever, not from any bloodied nose or bashed in head."

"I'll call the crew and make arrangements to cover his work," Nicholas said, moving to do just that.

Captain Black held up a papery white hand, halting Nicholas. "The crew ain't worried about the workload, Marks." The red eyes focused on me. "They are more concerned with the presence of black magic."

My lips repeated the words. "Black magic?"

Nicholas chuckled, easing his posture. "Black magic? Those superstitious bastards."

The look on the captain's face did not soften.

Nicholas noticed it too. His laughter faded. "You believe them? You truly believe that Miss Monroe had something to do with Wrack's death? That's impossible."

"Only the blackest of arts could take a man so swiftly from this life," he snarled. "The sailors will be committin' the body to the sea shortly. Miss Monroe, be prepared to stand on trial for the murder of Thomas Wrack at the first bell of first dog watch today."

With a whirl of his black duster, the captain was gone.

Stunned, Nicholas and I stared at each other. The meaning of the captain's accusation had yet to sink in.

"Stay here," Nicholas commanded and strode out of the cabin, closing the door behind him before I could protest.

Five minutes passed before I heard footsteps approaching down the hallway. A soft tap sounded on the door, then it opened wide to reveal two mangy pirates whom I did not recognize. They looked similar enough to be brothers. One held a ring of keys. My heart thudded heavily at the sight of them.

"Miss Monroe, please come with us," one demanded.

Still huddled on the small bed, I asked "Where to?"

"To the brig," the other replied.

My breathing grew shallow, "No, no, I can't! Why?"

"You've been charged with a crime, miss. You must wait there fer yer trial."

"Please, no," I begged. The very thought of the brig made my stomach lurch. Images from Wrack's assault flashed in my memory. I shut my eyes against them, but it was no use. I could see his sneering face. I could feel his wet tongue sliding up my cheek. I could smell the stench of his breath and the nauseating scent of fresh blood. "Anywhere else," I pleaded, my eyes still shut.

"Cap'n's orders, ma'am," the first pirate said. He stepped forcefully into the room.

I was out of options. I would rather go willingly than be manhandled by these loathsome men.

"I see. I'll do what is necessary," I bargained, "but I need to wait for Mr. Holladay to return first."

The man in the room took a step closer to me. "We have our orders, miss."

There was an apologetic note in his voice, and I sensed he'd rather not force me to follow his orders.

I slowly pushed my covers off, then cinched the tie around my robe a bit tighter. I placed one bare foot on the floor at a time, wanting to delay this as long as possible in hopes that Nicholas would return. I smoothed my hands over my mussed hair, taking my time to rake out the tangles with my fingers, though my hair was impossibly matted with dried blood. Finally, I stood.

The men escorted me down the hallway without touching me, for which I was thankful. We crossed the ship's waist in an odd procession. A few sailors were scattered about the deck and the rigging and stared at me unabashedly. I was surprised that more weren't out to see what was happening. Perhaps they were…caring for the body. I looked for Nicholas, wishing he would notice what was happening and put a stop to it, but I could not find him.

The men led me down the ladder, deep inside the ship.

The brig had not been touched since the night of Wrack's attack. As my eyes adjusted to the darkness, I saw the jagged bits of the broken jug, the spent candle, and even the book I had been reading, the pages brown with dried blood. I halted, faltering in my resolve to play nicely. The two men looked at me, ready to pursue if I fled.

"I can't go back in there," I begged.

"Just for a bit, miss," the man closest to me said. "It will only be a little while."

The other pirate—the one with the keys—went forward to the swinging gate that served as the door to the prison. He examined the lock. "Marks shot it to bits. It ain't gonna hold." He slammed the door to the frame several times, each time it failed to catch and swung back out. I hoped this meant I could not be held here.

"The cap'n'll have somethin'," the other pirate said. He reached to take my arm in his burly grasp. I couldn't help but recoil. "C'mon," he ordered sternly.

I forced mysel to walk forward into the cage, horrible images racing through my mind. The pirate with the keys ascended the ladder while the other man closed the door behind me, holding it in place. The sound of the metal door clanking shut reverberated in the expansive room. I shut my eyes fiercely, trying to imagine a prettier scene, but I could only see a jeering Wrack prowling around the perimeter of the brig, striking the key against the bars.

CHAPTER FOURTEEN

I INHALED DEEPLY, TRYING to calm the swelling panic in my breast. Lingering smells of rum and blood met my nose and I stifled a gag.

The man standing guard fidgeted uncomfortably. He must have believed me guilty. He was afraid that I would put some kind of fever curse on him, too. The absurdity of the situation angered me. I was tempted to chant some mumbo jumbo just to scare him away. I was sure it would work, but then what? I was on a ship with limited space. One-hundred pirates against me. Well, against Nicholas and me. Still, there would be nowhere to run and I couldn't afford to make things worse.

We waited in silence. The other man returned with a mass of chain and a padlock the size of my hand. Without a word passing between the two men, they wrapped the length of the chain around the gate and the door frame, sealing it with the padlock, and hurried out of the hold.

Afraid to move a single inch, I simply stood still like a lost child.

Maybe I truly was meant to die. I should have drowned

in the hurricane with my father or at least been scorched to death by the tropical sun as I drifted unconsciously in the jollyboat. I should have died at the hands of these pirates, whether during the attack on the other ship or when I was trapped in here with Wrack. It would happen now. I would be tried for a nonexistent crime and punished however the captain saw fit. I was terrified, but wished desperately for all this to be over. But more than that, I wished to see Nicholas. I needed him.

My wish was granted shortly. I recognized the sound of his steps as he came down the ladder. A sense of calm washed over me. He would let me out of here, straighten out this entire mess.

He was not alone, to my dismay. He was accompanied by the two pirates who had escorted me down not long before. They lingered near the staircase, talking in whispers.

As Nicholas walked closer to me, I rushed to the brig's door, reaching out through the bars. My embrace was unmet. He stayed several paces back, his demeanor formal and stiff. The calm I had felt just seconds before disintegrated.

"Are you all right?"

"I'm fine," I responded slowly pulling my arms back into the brig. "Can you let me out?"

"You'll have to stay down here."

"How long?"

Nicholas looked away. "About six hours."

It felt as though the wind had been knocked out of me. Tears leaked from the corners of my eyes. "Nicholas, what is happening?"

His stoic face relaxed briefly. "It's sheer madness. The men are afraid. I think they were surprised by the damage you did to Wrack. They think you're trouble."

"The damage *I* did to Wrack? What of the damage *he* did to me?"

"They're pirates. Do you think they care?"

I turned away, hiding my tears.

"I don't agree with them," he added hastily. "Wrack deserved every bruise you gave him. He deserved far more. I am honestly sorry that he died. Believe me when I say I had something far worse planned for him."

I looked back at Nicholas. "Will there really be a trial?"

He answered with a curt nod.

"But you're the quartermaster. Aren't you responsible for punishment? Don't you have a say in this?"

"I break up quarrels and oversee duels. Minor infractions. I wish I had more sway with a full-on trial, but I don't."

I swallowed hard, my last bit of hope fading. "What will happen at the trial?"

He shifted his weight slightly. "You'll answer their questions."

Why was Nicholas being so vague? I needed to know what I would face. "What if they find me…guilty?"

His jaw clenched and his nostrils flared The thought was just as worrisome to him. "They can't. There's not enough to go off."

"But what if they *do*?"

"It won't happen," he said and as I started to contest this answer he cut me off and continued angrily, "But *if* it did happen, the captain can order whatever punishment he sees fit."

My imagination flooded with visions of possible punishments. "What do you mean? What are you keeping from me?"

"I cannot say what he intends. But it is not good. I have rarely seen him in such a mood and it's like he's mad." He put one hand on his hip and the other hand pinched the bridge of his nose. I could see the muscles of his jaw ripple as he tensed. "And I don't know if it is best to play along, to give the captain his way. That may be all he wants. It may be that he is proving his authority since some of that was taken away with you. Although he claimed you, no one cared—including me. Maybe I made this worse, trying to protect you. No," he corrected himself immediately. "Things would have been worse if you were left to the devices of Black. I am convinced that this is a show of authority. The crew has been volatile, disobedient. He will make this into an example, but I doubt it will result in an extreme punishment for you. It has nothing to do with you."

"But if he's making an example, proving his authority, won't he need to follow through with a harsh punishment?"

Nicholas dropped his arms to his sides, looking at me intensely. "I swear to you now, Tessa, I won't let any harm come to you," The sternness in his voice made me shiver. I believed every word.

His posture relaxed and he stepped a bit closer towards me, but not nearly close enough. Lowering his voice, he said, "Look, I hate to leave you down here, but I need to take care of business upstairs."

I closed my eyes against the pressing tears and nodded.

"Things will turn out fine. Try not to worry."

Nicholas left and the two pirates followed him. They left the hatch above the ladder open, affording me a bit of light.

I noticed the crate was still within reach and went immediately over to it. I felt very vulnerable in the black dressing gown and I wanted to dress fully. My clean undergarments were still knotted around the brig's bars. I untied them and put them on. I pulled the blue silk gown into the brig and dressed hurriedly, worried that someone might come down any moment.

I brushed my hair, combing out the dried blood and rum. Once it was hanging in sleek ripples, I pulled it off my shoulders into a low ponytail at the nape of my neck, securing it with the black satin sash from the yellow ball gown. Several rebellious tendrils framed my face.

I was lacking a corset, a petticoat, stockings, and shoes, but I felt more complete than I had in a long while.

The hours crept by. I listened for the bells on deck proclaiming the time. Precisely when the first bell of the first dog watch rang, three men descended the broad ladder. I stood nervously, anxious to be out of the brig, yet terrified of what waited for me on deck.

Two pirates I had never seen before led the captain down the ladder towards the brig. With his flowing black robes and ghostly pallor, I was convinced that the captain was Death himself, coming for me at last. As one pirate opened the lock and removed the chains from the brig, the captain stated formally, "Miss Tessa Monroe, your trial for the killing of Thomas Wrack has now commenced."

Without being instructed to, I followed the procession up the ladder to the ship's waist to the trial that would decide my fate.

CHAPTER FIFTEEN

THE CAPTAIN, TWO GUARDS, and I walked to middle of the main deck where a crude courtroom of sorts had been organized. The captain took his seat behind a makeshift desk and I was instructed to sit in a solitary chair facing it. Dozens and dozens of pirates looked on, sitting and standing wherever there was room. Curious eyes even glared down at me from the rigging.

I squinted in the brightness—I hadn't seen sunlight for weeks—and scanned the crowd for Nicholas, but didn't find him.

In the full light of the afternoon, Captain Black looked more terrifying than ever. With his snow-white skin, wispy hair, and blood-red eyes he looked like a demon from beyond the grave. I could hardly stand to look at him, he was so terrifying, yet I found it impossible to look away.

The captain took a pistol from his waist and pounded its butt on the desk.

"The trial of Miss Tessa Monroe officially commences.

Miss Monroe is hereby accused of the murder of Thomas Wrack. Who be the accusers?"

The majority of pirates raised their hands above their heads, cheering and hollering.

The captain stared directly at me with his grotesque eyes. "Looks like majority rules. Any last words?"

My last words? Had I just been found guilty? This was insane. I hadn't even heard the full accusation nor had the chance to defend myself. This was my life! Not some silly pastime for bored pirates. My face flushed hot.

"That was it?" I cried, standing abruptly, not caring that I was challenging the captain. Nicholas was convinced that this trial was a show of authority to remind the crewmen of their station, but this...this *trial* did none of that. And now I was convinced that my punishment would be the captain's message to the crew.

The little composure I had was dismantled. There was no way that manners or proper display of behavior would hold any sway upon these madmen. Something inside me snapped. "That's what you call a *trial*? Wrack—" the name felt dirty in my mouth "—was not even murdered. Give me your reasons. Let me defend myself!" I looked into the crowd surrounding me, hoping to find a shred of sympathy.

The captain bellowed a laugh and struck the pistol butt against the desk again.

"She's a right funny lass, ain't she, boys?"

A wave of cackles rippled through the onlookers.

"Sit down, Miss Monroe. We are all gentleman here," he gestured to the audience of pirates who chuckled raucously. "We be more than happy to give you the trial you ask for."

I sat down nervously. Was this all just a mockery to them? Would my arguing prove to be a foolish move?

I looked across the sea of faces and finally saw Nicholas. He was on the forecastle deck leaning casually against the foremast, surrounded by a thicket of dirty men. Our eyes met, but his gaze was less than generous. There was no reassurance there. I remembered our last encounter on this deck, surrounded by the same pirates. Nicholas had betrayed me then. Would it be any different today?

"Of ye who have accused this pretty little thing, what reasons do ye hold to?"

"She had the motive!" a faceless voice called out.

"She broke Wrack's nose!"

I twirled around with each flying comment, trying to locate my accusers, but the allegations came from all sides.

"She killed Wrack in his hammock!"

"She's a witch!"

This was outrageous. Forcing myself to look into the captain's blood-red eyes I said, "You have no proof!"

"Just like all women, they always want more," the captain snickered, eliciting lewd chuckles from the crowd. "Tell me exactly what it is that ye be wanting from us lot o' pirates." He seemed entertained but I sensed a real threat under the carefree demeanor.

I thought as quickly as I could. Everything I said would be taken quite literally or twisted back on me. I needed to be clever in my requests, making sure to protect myself in every way. "First, I demand to know what charges are against me. Second, I demand the right to refute any charges or comment made. Third, I demand that honest testimony and real proof be presented to the court. No opinions, no assumptions."

"Is that all, miss?"

I hoped it was. "Yes."

Captain Black stood and leaned over his desk sneering at me, "Miss Monroe, you are hereby charged with the murder of Mr. Thomas Wrack. Do ye plead guilty or innocent?"

"Wrack was not murdered," I shot back.

"Can you prove that with honest testimony or real proof?" he asked sarcastically.

"Sir, you told me yourself this morning in the quartermaster's cabin that Mr. Wrack died of a sudden fever. Unless you claim that you lied, I use your word as honest testimony and proof that Mr. Wrack was not murdered by anyone."

He exhaled sharply through his nose.

I smiled smugly.

"'Tis black magic!" a voice hollered from my left.

The captain addressed me again, "Miss Monroe, you are hereby charged with witchcraft resulting in the death of Mr. Thomas Wrack. Do ye plead guilty or innocent?"

"What? You cannot change the charge!"

Captain Black sneered at me. "You are hereby charged of murder and of witchcraft. You are found innocent on the charge of murder. Happy?" He mirrored the smug look I gave him a moment before. "Now onto the charge of witchcraft. Do you plead guilty or innocent?"

I looked to the crowd for help. Surely anyone could see the injustice. No one seemed to care but me. Not even Nicholas.

"Guilty or innocent?" Black boomed.

"I am innocent."

"Let it be known that Miss Monroe denies the charge." The captain walked in front of his desk and looked at the group of pirates to either side of us as he continued his charade as prosecutor and judge. "Miss Monroe, how did you happen to be on this vessel?"

I stole a glance at Nicholas. If only I knew what he was thinking. Was he on my side now, hiding inconspicuously among the crowd to protect both of us, or was he proving allegiance to his crew? I debated whether or not I should tell the captain about our chats in the galley. Revealing Nicholas's involvement with me may prove dangerous for him—but it could be the alibi I needed.

I answered honestly, "I do not remember, sir."

"Can anyone else answer the question?" he asked the crew. No one answered.

"Gibbons!" he called.

A pirate shuffled forward ever so slightly and removed his knitted cap.

"I believe you can clear up this matter. Speak."

Fixing his stare on his feet, the man told of how he was the first to see the wreckage of the ship. He informed the quartermaster and was instructed to look for salvageable goods. While the crew was hauling up buckets of rum they spotted a floating jollyboat with me inside.

The captain asked for others to confirm this story. Several did.

"The lone survivor of a hurricane," Captain Black said to me. "How did ye manage that?"

"I do not recall, sir. I was unconscious."

"Just lucky, eh? Or perhaps ye had some help from an otherworldly source."

The implication was inconceivable.

The captain continued his questioning, "What happened next? What can ye remember?"

He circled my chair like a shark.

Deciding to leave Nicholas out of my story, I said, "I came onto the deck during your ruthless attack on that poor ship."

Captain Black wheeled on me, "This is a court of law, Miss Monroe," he said sarcastically. "We need to be objective. Best not let pesky opinions of yer benefactors taint yer testimony."

My jaw clamped shut. Black contorted everything I

said. I wanted to scream. Logic and justice were impossible.

"I apologize, sir," I said, hoping that the contempt I felt did not manifest in my voice. "I came on deck during the...battle—" I hoped that was a less offensive word "—and was confronted by two members of the crew."

"Which members?"

"One was Wrack. I do not know the other one."

"Who was with Wrack that day?" the captain asked the crowd.

His question was met with silence.

"Me thinks you lie," he said in a playful tone. It made me sick to my stomach.

"It's the truth," I insisted.

"Anyone? Anyone admit to confronting Miss Monroe on this very deck during our latest mission?"

No one moved.

The captain resumed his cocky pacing around me.

"It was Beck," a clear voice from the crowd said.

Nicholas.

"Tell me about it," the captain challenged.

Nicholas did not step forward, did not stand any taller, just continued to slouch against the foremast, picking disinterestedly at his fingernails.

"Beck and Wrack approached the girl. I knew she was meant for the captain only, and didn't want any overzealous appetites to force them to break command. I simply reminded them of that, and they let 'er be."

"Beck!" the captain called.

"Aye?" I recognized the burly pirate as he stepped forward.

"Would that be the truth?"

"Aye, for the most part," he confirmed.

Turning back to me the captain prompted me to continue.

"I was sent to the brig."

"And who sent ye to the brig?"

My eyes flickered to Nicholas. He lazily stood against the mast as if he were taking a break from the day's labors. I could not read his posture or his face. "Th-the quartermaster," I finally replied.

"How long were ye in the brig?"

The days and nights had all blurred together. "I do not know for certain."

Captain Black called for the ship's log and examined the records. "A fortnight and a day. A right long time to be in such miserable circumstance. What did ye do to cause such punishment?"

The image of Nicholas raising the cutlass at me flashed across my mind. I mimicked what he had said, "I insulted the quartermaster."

"How did you insult good ol' Marks?"

My heart faltered. I wrung my hands and tried to concoct a believable tale. What would it take to insult someone gravely enough to be locked in the brig for two weeks but wouldn't make me appear more treacherous to these men?

"She spat on me," Nicholas called to the captain. "And she called me a naughty name," his tone was jaunty and laughter pealed from the crowd. I was glad for his interjection but at the same time I felt rebuffed by his laughter. I glared at his lax figure.

"Spitting on an officer. What an insolent little strumpet."

Captain Black paused and scanned the crowd. He stopped when he found what he was looking for and the corners of his mouth lifted in a devilish grin.

"I understand you made a sort of friend, Miss Monroe," Black sneered.

I followed Black's gaze to Skidmore.

Sweet, quiet Skidmore. He seemed utterly incapable of telling a lie. Skidmore knew everything there was to know about me. About Nicholas. With the captain's gaze locked on him, he looked terrified. There was no way he could remain collected under the captain's scrutiny. He would break. He would tell of the mutiny. His testimony could put a noose around my neck.

My hope plummeted as I heard the captain call him.

"Mr. Skidmore. Please step forward."

CHAPTER SIXTEEN

CAPTAIN BLACK PACED BEFORE me with delight.

"Skidmore, tell the court about Miss Monroe's behavior when you saw her in the brig."

Skidmore was standing near Nicholas. He shifted uneasily, pulling at his beard of straw. I silently begged him to defend me, save me.

"Miss Monroe was mostly quiet."

"Mostly," echoed the captain. "Did she or did she not act out aggressively when first placed in the brig?"

I sighed dejectedly. Any hope of my friend defending me melted. The captain would get whatever he wanted out of Skidmore.

Skidmore avoided my pleading stare. "She was upset." His response was so quiet I wasn't sure if I heard him correctly.

"How did this *upset* girl act that day in the brig?"

"She threw her furniture against the bars."

"And she screamed like a banshee," the captain added triumphantly. "We all heard her."

Skidmore's head bobbed slightly.

"And we all saw Wrack after Miss Monroe finished with him. It takes a certain amount of…*nerve* to attack a man who was only bringing ye a bit o' rum."

I shot to my feet. "He attacked me! He was *not* bringing me rum!"

"Sit down, Miss Monroe," Captain Black growled.

I sat.

"Did he or did he not bring you a jug o' rum?"

I sensed a trap. "He had a jug, but—"

"And he let himself into the brig to deliver a generous amount of rum."

"He let himself in the brig to violate me!"

The captain ignored my outburst. "The two of ye must have exchanged words. He must have stated his purpose of being down in said brig."

"He was down there to hurt me," I seethed, my hands balling into fists at my sides.

The captain stopped his pacing and stared directly at me, his hands clasped behind his back. "Did he tell ye that?"

I did not know how to respond. Of course Wrack didn't proclaim his intentions—what criminal would? My lips moved eagerly but no sound came out.

"Answer the question, Miss Monroe. Did Wrack tell ye he came to the brig in the middle o' the night to *violate* you?" He strung out the syllables of the word "violate," as if it were a foul obscenity.

"N-n-no," I stammered.

The captain leaned in towards me. His face was only inches from mine. His breath reeked and his scarlet eyes danced. "Did he say why he were there?"

"He said he was there for refreshment," I replied, mimicking his suggestive tone.

The captain backed away and looked at the pirates.

"See, men? Just a bit o' rum in the wee hours of the night. Who of us has never enjoyed a bit o' late-night refreshment?"

The trial had turned in a direction that frightened me. I desperately needed to regain control. "He did not mean rum." Trying to twist the captain's words, I argued, "Who would come down to the brig in the middle of the night just to drink rum with a prisoner? A *female* prisoner? He said 'refreshment.' He meant me!"

"So in yer opinion, when he said 'refreshment' he meant you?"

"Yes," I nodded emphatically.

"What caused ye to form this opinion?"

How could I explain that cold feeling of dread in the pit of my stomach when Wrack entered the hold that night? "The fact that he was there in the middle of the night. The way he looked at me."

I could tell I wasn't convincing anyone. My head swam. I fumbled for any logical blow.

"He ran the keys along the bars." I mimed the movement.

The captain's cottony eyebrows shot up, surprise widening his eyes. "Solid evidence indeed!" His feigned look of surprise twisted into a look of ridicule. "Opinions and assumptions, miss. Opinions and assumptions."

I trembled from frustration. The captain already had his mind made up. This was all a game for him. He wouldn't even listen. Yet as I sat there, replaying my answers in my mind, I knew that the things I said were somehow lacking. Even if the captain or the other pirates were listening, my story seemed hollow. Though the captain was toying with me, he was playing this game by the rules I designated.

If I couldn't gain any footing, with all the rules I established, was it because I was wrong?

Was the captain right?

Wrack had never really *declared* his intentions. In truth, all he did was offer me rum, explaining that he needed to place it in the brig because it was too large to fit through the bars. And that was entirely legitimate. He must have done something—something that proved his intentions, something the others could agree with. I thought hard, remembering the series of events that night. Wrack came down the ladder. He was a bit sneaky, but that wasn't a crime. He offered me the rum. He had keys to the brig. He explained that he needed to put it in the brig. Then he opened the door and...and I attacked him before he ever touched me. *I attacked him.*

No.

There was a threat. I knew it. I knew it then and I knew it now. I had not overreacted. His actions after I slammed the door into him were not brought on by my behavior. He was a predator. The fact that I tried to thwart him did not justify how he treated me.

"He was drunk," I argued with new determination.

The captain waved dismissively. "Most of us are drunk right now," he spread his arms wide to his audience like a fabulous entertainer. Cheers and whistles sounded.

"Were ye angry with him for his midnight visit?" he continued, still putting on a show.

"Yes."

"Do you admit to assaulting Mr. Wrack?"

"I was defending—"

"Miss Monroe, do you admit that you assaulted Mr. Wrack?"

"He was threaten—"

"Miss Monroe, one more time. Did you or did you not assault Mr. Wrack?"

Captain Black towered over me, his crimson eyes boring into mine.

"Yes." My voice was feeble.

"How did the aforementioned scuffle end?" He spun away, his duster whirling dramatically.

"Mr. Skidmore and Mr. Nicholas pulled him from me," I said.

The captain spun on the heels of his boots. "Mr. *Nicholas*," he said mockingly, "tell us what happened."

Nicholas had not moved an inch. It was infuriating to look at him, lounging easily against the mast.

"My keys were missin'. Wrack was missin'. I heard screams from the hold and thought to investigate in case there be trouble," Nicholas replied absently. "We discovered that Wrack had locked himself in the brig with the young lass. He looked to be forcing himself upon her. I shot the lock on the door and we removed him from the temptation."

"Fair enough." The captain slyly looked at me. "And if I may ask, what was the temptation wearin' that night?"

The question blindsided me. I didn't answer.

"Skidmore! What was Miss Monroe wearing that night?"

"A dressing robe." His voice cracked.

"And nothin' else?"

Skidmore looked down and shook his head ever so slightly.

"Miss Monroe, tell us what happened after Mr. Wrack was removed from the hold."

I cleared my throat. "I was taken to the quartermaster's room where I recovered from my injuries."

"Were ye alone during that time?"

"I slept a lot."

"Certainly. But that's not what I asked. Who was with ye?"

"The quartermaster, mostly." This turn in questioning confused me. I couldn't decipher Captain Black's motives or anticipate his next question.

"Who else?"

"Mr. Skidmore."

"Now I know I have personally seen the quartermaster and Mr. Skidmore working their watches for the past three days. So I know they did not keep you company every moment. Marks, Skidmore, can you confirm that Miss Monroe had time by herself when she was recovering?"

Skidmore's eyes caught mine briefly, then he stared at his feet. Reluctantly, he affirmed. "Aye."

Nicholas stood taller against the mast and crossed his arms over his chest. He seemed defiant when he said, "For brief moments."

The sudden change in his demeanor meant two things to me. First, it meant that Nicholas was defending me. I had not been abandoned. Second, it meant that the direction the trial had taken was much worse than I anticipated. Nicholas was exposing himself now…for me.

"And now for me own bit o' testimony." The captain addressed the crowd. "This very mornin' when I informed Miss Monroe and our noble quartermaster that Thomas Wrack had given up the ghost, this lady's exact words were 'I'm sorry.'" He rocked on his toes then slammed his heels down victoriously. "She apologized!"

The crowd of pirates erupted with gasps and shouts.

"I did not!"

"Do ye deny what ye said?"

I thought very hard, remembering exactly what had

happened during that conversation. The captain told me that Wrack had died of a fever. He implied that I knew about it.

"The words were not an apology, they were for clarification," I disputed.

"Oh. To clarify what exactly?"

"You seemed to be accusing me. I was unsure of what you meant."

The red eyes grinned at me. "Seems awfully strange to apologize to me when I be the one accusin' ye of a crime."

"It was not an apology!"

He held a hand up to me, halting any further rebuttals.

"After that, Miss Monroe was taken to the brig to await trial. That brings us to the current time."

This was not going well at all.

He could not be serious. I stared at Captain Black in complete disbelief, my jaw slack. But I no longer saw the playfulness, the enjoyment in his demeanor that was there before. Somehow, this situation had turned very grave.

"What we have here," the captain pointed a bone-white finger at me, "is a girl who is the sole survivor of a hurricane. A girl insolent enough to insult a ship's officer and spit upon him. A girl who admittedly assaulted a member of the crew without good reason—"

"I had reason!"

"Quiet!" he bellowed. The captain seemed more dangerous than ever. A shiver cascaded down my spine.

"...without good reason," Captain Black reiterated. "A girl who wore nothin' more than a scant robe until this very day. A girl who admits to bein' very angry with Mr. Wrack for his visit. A girl who, as a *prisoner*, attacked a crewmember simply because she *assumed* his intentions were ill. A girl who had enough time alone to put a black spot upon a sailor who was in perfect health the prior day!

"Ye have heard the testimonies, men. And as requested,

this trial cannot take any assumptions or opinions into consideration, only honest testimony and proof."

He paused dramatically. He had an undeniable charisma, and I hated him all the more for the way he spun webs around my words.

"I may be judge and hangman upon this vessel," he said to me. "But I do not presume to be the jury too. Men, sound off if ye find Miss Monroe guilty."

A thunderous chorus of "Aye! Aye!" and the stomping of feet on the deck sealed my fate.

Captain Black turned to me gleefully, his red eyes burning. "Tessa Monroe," he said over the commotion of the cheering pirates, "ye be found guilty of witchcraft and the resulting death of Thomas Wrack."

This was utterly unfathomable. I was completely aghast. This entire charade had been a complete mockery. I could not believe that there was any seriousness in any of it. My indignation kept me from being as frightened as I should have been.

"Fetch some rope and tie a noose! That witch be dancing the hempen jig from the yardarm and we won't be missin' that!"

CHAPTER SEVENTEEN

ANARCHY BROKE OUT ON the main deck. Hollers and cheers sounded all around. I sat like stone in the center of the deck while raucous figures hurried past me in all directions. I was a world apart, stilled by denial and foreboding, while those around me were spurred on by the bloodlust of my pending execution.

Was it true? Was I just pronounced guilty of witchcraft and sentenced to be hanged?

In that moment I realized I must already be dead and stuck in Hell. How else could I explain all the impossible things that had happened? I had been waiting and hoping for death to save me from my fate on this ship, but that would never happen because I was already dead and in a never-ending purgatory.

Sounds were distant and my eyes unfocused. This was not real. No thought of fight or flight came to me. I was paralyzed.

The piercing sound of a gunshot tore me from my daze. I jerked towards the noise and saw a dozen pirates standing on the forecastle deck looking onto the chaos below. Nicholas stood at the head of the group, his pistol still pointing into the air.

"Avast!" he hollered. "Black Jack, come forward to hear your peers."

Captain Black looked menacingly at the pirates assembled on the deck a few steps above him. His indignation was obvious—but was I also sensing a hint of worry?

Nicholas placed his hands on the railing and leaned forward, looking down upon the captain. "Since we be votin' on things, some of the boys, along with myself, thought it might be time to vote upon your captaincy."

"What is this?" fumed the captain.

"We call it democracy. Though someone such as yourself might call it mutiny." Nicholas exuded a playful confidence.

A new feeling washed over me. It elevated my breathing and quickened my pulse.

It was hope.

Captain Black stared at the mutineers one by one, his eyes alive with malice. When they settled on Nicholas, they changed. I knew what he was feeling. I had felt it at Nicholas's hands before. Hurt...shock...disappointment. It was the look of absolute betrayal.

I felt a twinge of pity for the man.

The captain recovered from his shock. "I have been captain o' the *Banshee* nigh on four years—"

"Aye, and we think that be long enough."

Captain Black drew a long, slender sword from its sheath as if to attack someone. "And how do ye think you will go about effectin' this change?"

"By a simple vote," Nicholas responded as if the answer were stupidly obvious. "The crew voted to make you captain and, according to the articles of this ship, which we all signed and conduct ourselves by, the crew can vote you down."

Just a few nights ago in the sanctuary of his room, Nicholas had told me the crew was ready for a mutiny. The timing was perfect. This must have been what Nicholas had been arranging while I was locked in the brig. He knew there was a chance that I would be found guilty and that the punishment would be as severe as death. The only way to derail the outcome of the trial would be with an action as bold as mutiny. I shuddered to think of these extreme circumstances and the risks that this stranger took for me.

The pirate ways were unfamiliar to me, but I knew what a mutiny meant. I knew it could grow ugly. What if this coup d'état failed? What would Black do to Nicholas? I did not really need to ask that question. I knew.

Captain Black stared down the crowd, assessing the spread of this rebellion. Though there were far more pirates watching Nicholas than standing behind him, none of them came to the captain's defense.

Still pointing his sword at the general crowd, as if threatening every last man on the ship, he growled, "Let's do this."

A very tall, slender man with a greasy black ponytail that hung past his waist carried a leather folder filled with worn parchment. Opening the folder and referencing the papers, he said, "According to the articles signed by every member of the crew, when it comes to booty, the cap'n gets first claim on unique items, the quartermaster gets second claim, followed by the bos'n and gunner. The rest be divided among the crew. Money be split evenl amongst the crew, with the cap'n and quartermaster each gettin' an extra share. Other appointed mates receive half an extra share."

"Do any of ye dispute these articles?" Nicholas asked the crew.

No one argued.

"Go on."

The man with the black ponytail directly addressed the captain now. "Two months back when we raided the port at Eleuthera, ye took for yer own that rapier—" he gestured to the sword the captain held "—and the silver tea set."

"What of it?" growled the captain.

"Them're *two* unique items."

"Aye," Nicholas chimed in, "And I'd been eyeing that tea set," he said with a boyish grin.

"An' we all know that when it comes to countin' coins," the black-haired man continued, "ye have Squeamy Pete do all the dividin' in the privacy of yer own cabin with none else to look on. Dividing plunder is the responsibility of the quartermaster."

Another pirate—one who wasn't standing with Nicholas's small group—called out, "Aye! An' we all notice that Squeamy Pete seems to be havin' more money than the rest o' us."

"Yer payin' 'im off for cheatin'!" another voice from the crowd bellowed.

"Ye didn't even show yer scabrous face during our last chase just a fortnight ago," someone else pointed out.

The captain challenged this accusation, "Ye know I cannot be out in the sun fer lengths of time."

"A cap'n that can't fight with his men ought not to be cap'n!" an angry sailor hurled at him.

"The fearsome nature of my looks has won more battles than their delicacies have cost!" Captain Black shot back, his eyes glinting like bloody pools.

"And yer fearsome nature has beaten many o' us lowly dogs!" Another voice, another pirate.

The mutiny was swelling.

"And what about her?" Nicholas spat, pointing at me. He stalked across the forecastle deck and down the ladder to face the captain directly at the ship's waist. His insurgents followed him. "You claimed her as your unique prize, and now you move to hang her? 'Tis only because you're afraid she will do to you what she did to Wrack when you force your will. If it be anyone else, they'd meet with the cat's nine tails, not the gallows."

This was the heart of the matter—my safety—disguised in this rebellion. Not gold. Not plunder. I was the reason that Nicholas did this. This man hardly knew me, yet he risked his life to preserve mine. My heart thudded.

"What about the rum?" a grey and weathered man spoke out. "We be forced to drink rum watered down past the point of recognition while ye take all the good drink fer yerself!"

A mob was forming. Onlooking pirates had mingled with the mutinous few behind Nicholas so there was no longer a division between groups. They moved on the captain, surrounding him. More and more complaints echoed from the raging crowd until I could no longer distinguish individual voices or their grievances.

The beating of my heart escalated with the rowdiness of the mob. The crowd would overthrow the mutant captain and his authority, reversing his verdict and negating the sentence for my hanging. I still didn't know if they would try me again or if I could ever escape the clutches of this damned ship, but at least I would live to see the sunset. That was enough for now.

A sudden silence fell across the crowd. The sound of the sail flapping in the wind replaced the angry shouts. Confused, I craned my neck to see through the crowd, to understand the sudden quiet. The thicket of men surrounding the captain shrank back, leaving a wide circle where they had just been grouped so tightly. The captain stood just as he had before, sneering at his challengers.

Peering through the crowd, I finally noticed a small movement at the captain's feet. My hand flew to cover my mouth and my eyes widened in horror. Lying before the captain was the man with the long ponytail, writhing in agony, pink bubbles of blood frothing from his mouth. He clenched his gut tightly, twisting upon the deck, his hands glossy with blood. The captain stared down at him wearing an expression of satisfaction. His long rapier dripped with the sailor's blood.

In stillness, everyone watched the grisly scene. Strange gurgles and hiccups came from the dying pirate as he continued to gyrate and twitch. His frenzied eyes searched the crowd, looking for aid or at least a bit of comfort in his last moments. Not one person moved. Not one word was said. I could not look away from the nightmare before me. My eyes refused to blink. Then it was over. The gurgling ceased and the man lay still, his eyes wide open. A pulse of blood coming from his abdomen was the only movement now.

Quietly, gruffly, Nicholas said, "I move to strip Black from the office of captain of the *Banshee*."

"I second the motion." It was Skidmore.

With an eerie reverence, each pirate raised a hand. When all had voted against him, the former captain threw his sword down with a tinny *clank*.

Black walked up directly up to Nicholas and stared him down with flashing eyes. "You just marked yourself, lad. You and your witch."

With his last threat lingering in the air, the dethroned captain stalked away into the bowels of the ship.

CHAPTER EIGHTEEN

STILL MOTIONLESS, I WATCHED the crowds dissipate. Nicholas ordered several men to tend to the body. I watched in gross fascination as they straightened the corpse and placed gold coins atop its now closed eyelids. Two other sailors emerged from the forecastle and approached the body with a sheet of cloth—the dead man's hammock—and wrapped it around the body. A cannonball was included at his feet. Nicholas sewed the canvas shut, the final stitch going through the nose of the body. The congregation grew and most of the pirates were present to bow their heads and pray for the dead man's soul.

Nicholas opened a gate in the railing, and the pirate named Gibbons dragged the cocooned body across the deck and pushed it off the edge. I flinched at the imminent splash and closed my eyes against the finality of it all. Other men pulled up buckets of seawater and mopped the red trail smeared across the ship's waist.

One by one, the men disappeared. A silent ghost left behind.

A soft touch at my elbow pulled me from my trance. Nicholas.

He pulled me into his arms and I melted against his chest, not a word passing between us. His embrace was fierce. The emotion of the day caught up to me, and I quivered in Nicholas's arms, crying quietly. Warm hands stroked my hair, rubbed my back. I nuzzled as deeply as I could into the soft cotton shirt that smelled deliciously of ocean air. Then Nicholas grasped my shoulders and pulled me back. His grey eyes stared intently into mine. Finding what he had been searching for in my eyes, he pulled me close to his chest and wrapped his arms around me once more.

Moments passed. My shaking slowly subsided. Nicholas looked at me again and softly brushed away the tears on my cheeks with his thumb. Taking my hand, Nicholas led me up the steps of the forecastle deck to the bow of the ship where we leaned across the railing. I avoided his gaze, afraid of what he would see in my eyes. I had doubted him. And he had risked everything. His life. The lives of those who trusted him. The image of the dying sailor flashed across my mind. I kept my eyes fixed ahead. I was afraid of him seeing my shame, knowing how undeserving I was.

We stood side by side looking across the hazy horizon in silence. His relief was palpable. He had been as scared as I. But he'd pulled off a mutiny and kept me alive.

Together, we looked out at the never-ending waves of blue. The sun was sinking over the horizon, casting a golden hue across the world. Alabaster clouds with a magenta fringe spotted the pale sky. The evening was beautiful. Calm.

The events of the day swirled together in a jumble. It seemed like a dream. It would be less surprising for me to wake up down in the brig or even in my bed back in

London than to actually acknowledge the day's events.

An ocean breeze tossed my hair about my shoulders and stray strands tickled my face. Gooseflesh prickled my skin. I absently hugged myself, rubbing my hands along my arms. Nicholas put his arm around me and pulled me into his side, warming my arms with his hands. His contrasting warmth made me shiver more.

"Your hair is red in this light," he said softly, tucking a rebellious lock behind my ear.

I remained silent. Words would not come. I did not know how to talk about what had happened, or if I should even attempt to do so. Yet how could I converse about more trivial matters after such huge events?

My eyes lingered on the setting sun. Nicholas divided his attention between looking at me and at the ocean. There was no awkwardness in our silence. Just a restful stillness, a recess from the world.

The sun dipped behind the ocean and the magic of the moment disappeared with it.

"Are you hungry?" Nicholas asked me.

I nodded, still unable to speak.

He led me down to the galley where a dozen men were lounging about. It was quite crowded. A hush fell over the men as soon as we entered. An old pirate as weathered as a torn sail hovered over the metal stove.

"Bratman," Nicholas addressed him, "two dishes."

"Comin' up," Bratman said without turning away from his work. He spooned porridge made from boiled beans into two tin bowls and handed them to Nicholas. It was then that he saw me in the galley, standing timidly behind Nicholas. His expression instantly changed from boredom to suspicion.

"Bratman, meet Miss Monroe," Nicholas said to the man, measuring the cook's reaction.

I curtsied. "Pleased to meet you, Mr. Bratman."

The old man turned back to his work on the stove without a hint of acknowledgement.

Nicholas turned and scanned the room. The men met his eyes steadily, every one unwelcoming. I think Nicholas had intended to eat in the galley, to introduce me to the men and familiarize us with each other. There was a tangible tension in the air, and it was obvious that such an arrangement would be a mistake. After pouring two cups of watered-down rum, Nicholas nodded towards the staircase, and I happily escaped the galley.

We went back to the forecastle deck and made ourselves comfortable sitting side by side propped against the bulwarks.

"You were remarkable today," Nicholas started.

"Oh, no I wasn't. I was…I don't know…cornered."

Nicholas touched the fading bruise on my jaw. "You're quite a force when you're cornered."

"Maybe."

I liked the porridge. Its soft texture and mild taste was ambrosia after the hardtack I had been subsisting on in the brig. I finished my dinner much too quickly.

Shyly, I looked up at Nicholas. He had hardly touched his food. He was paying far more attention to me. I cleared my throat. "I don't even know what to say. How to thank you…"

Twilight's orange glow deepened into a purple canvas dotted with the evening's first stars. A perfectly-shaped crescent moon shimmered gently over the sea. Sitting just above the horizon, I felt I could reach out and touch it.

"There is no thanks needed, luv, believe me. That you are alive and safe is all I want."

I blushed. I liked his professions more than I should.

He ate his porridge and took a swallow of rum. Then he took my hand in his.

"How are you?" he asked fervently.

I sighed heavily. "I wish I knew. I still can't believe everything that happened today. I can't stop shaking."

He stared at the hand he held for a long moment, breathing unevenly.

I looked at him in the pale light of dusk. Still looking at our interlocked hands, an expression of pain pulled at the corners of Nicholas's mouth. I could sense his hesitation. It concerned me.

Finally, he met my eyes. "Are you frightened by me?"

Though his question caught me off guard, it was the vulnerability in his voice that surprised me.

"No," I answered honestly. "Why would I be?"

"You saw me today. You saw me for what I really am—a pirate."

"Remember, piracy is not who you are, it's just what you do," I countered teasingly.

"Tessa," he pleaded, "I need to know. Are you frightened by me?"

I took my time collecting my thoughts. I played through the events of the day, sorting through the feelings that overcame me. "You're right. I saw you today—for what you really are. You are so strong, so in control, and completely brilliant. Once you started the mutiny, there was no question in my mind that everything would work out."

"Well, that makes one of us."

"Nicholas..." I began, but trailed off, too timid to say what was on my mind. He waited for a moment, then gave me a prodding look. My heart pounded. I was embarrassed to ask, but his look comforted me. He had exposed himself entirely a moment before.

"Why are you so good to me?" I whispered.

He chuckled quietly and squeezed my hand. "The moment I saw you, I just...just wanted to take care of you. It was overwhelming. This beautiful creature, all alone with no one. I knew you would need someone…and I wanted it to be me. I *want* it to be me," he corrected himself. "I didn't even know you, but that didn't matter."

"Thank you," I said softly. It was all I knew to say, but I meant it wholeheartedly.

"I have never met anyone like you. And I don't mean a noble woman. I cannot explain it. After we fished you out of that jollyboat, I was so thrilled when we found your heartbeat. Really, we thought you were dead. I don't know why it mattered so much to me, but it did. And even then I found myself protecting you from the others. I was taken by your beauty. And you were so fragile. I figured I pitied you. That's how I explained my draw to you. But even then, I knew it was more than pity, even if I wouldn't admit it to myself." A tender smile creased his face, lighting up his eyes.

I sat in hopeful anxiety. "If it wasn't pity, what was it?"

Nicholas traced circles on the back of my hand with his fingers. Several times he looked as though he wanted to say something, but nothing ever came out. Finally, he said, "You look right pretty today. I like the dress."

"It's a lovely color," I flatly agreed. "Answer my question."

Nicholas shrugged "It doesn't matter."

"It matters to me."

"Tessa, I don't know what to do with you," he said somberly, a distant look on his face.

His tone surprised me. Worried me. "What do you mean?"

"You certainly have a way of finding trouble. It won't be long before something like this happens again." Nicholas sighed, his gaze unfocused in the distance. "As happy as I am that I have you here by my side now, I have to let you go. I have to get you off this ship."

CHAPTER NINETEEN

THE INTIMACY OF THE moment evaporated like sea mist in a hot sun. A heavy feeling found its way into the quiet night as Nicholas's comment sunk in.

He did not want me. Well, maybe he did. But he couldn't take care of me—or wouldn't. A small part of me had started to imagine a dream with only Nicholas, a world where he would always be with me.

I tried to hide my hurt as I said, "I have thought of it, too, and I think returning to London would be the best course of action."

"London?" he asked weakly. I couldn't read his face.

I shrugged. "It is the only place I know anyone at all. Perhaps an old family friend would take me in."

"London." His voice was practical. "Makes sense." After a long pause he continued, "You will need to get to Barbados or St. Kitts. You'll find regular sailings to London from one of those ports." He continued to trace delicate patterns my hand.

I felt hollow. My time with Nicholas had taken an unwanted turn. I wished to get lost in his solace. I wanted his sureness to comfort me and blot out the horrors of the day. I longed for his closeness, his warmth. But we were cold now, leagues apart though our fingers still mingled.

I hated thinking of what would come next. Returning to London was a dreadful notion, but it was the only choice I had. I did not want to think about it at all. I wanted to forget all that had happened today and what would happen tomorrow.

But Nicholas would not let me forget. He seemed all too eager to plan my departure. Hadn't he just said he wanted to be the one to take care of me? Obviously, he only intended to care for me until he could pass the responsibility to someone else.

What had I been thinking? We were from separate worlds. He had his life at sea and seemed so content. I had nothing, not anywhere. Not even here. A frustrated ball of anger pitted in my stomach.

I pulled my hand from Nicholas's grasp and stood. "If you will excuse me, I am rather tired." I kept my words formal. I was crestfallen that things between us were not as I had thought. "I will show myself to the cabin. Have a pleasant night."

As I turned to walk away, Nicholas called in surprise, "Tessa, wait."

He sprang up and was instantly beside me, gathering my hand in his.

"Yes?" I answered passively.

"What's wrong?"

"Nothing."

"I can't help but feel that something is wrong," he pressed, wide eyed.

That ball of anger in my stomach spread. I was a fool, falling for Nicholas and his erratic emotions. I was simply a pleasant distraction, but not worth keeping around. He could not alter his life just for me. It was foolish of me to expect that. And now he realized it too. I did not need to wait for his explanations. The rejection was already stinging. Why let it get any worse?

"Of course something is wrong," I exploded, yanking my hand from his grasp. "You are a pirate. A romantic night under the moonlight won't change a thing." I continued my exit.

"Wait!" he called again, rushing to catch up to me. He stood in front of the ladder, blocking my way. "What just happened?"

"Please let me pass."

"You're upset. Did I upset you?"

Not answering his question, I moved to pass him on the ladder. He did not let me.

"Just talk to me. I know what you have been through today, but I can't even imagine what you're feeling—"

"I'll tell you what I'm feeling. I am feeling…angry and sad and alone and…angry! You are so *infuriating*!"

"*I'm* infuriating? I'm not the one who just switched personalities."

"Will you let me finish?"

Nicholas rolled his eyes. "Please, finish."

I struggled to find the words. "I think I know you. And everything changes. You befriend me. You deceive me. You imprison me. You risk your life for me. And now this! After everything—after the things you've said and the way you made me feel…And now, now you're treating me like a bale of cotton that you'll keep in the hold until you can unload me at some convenient port! I can't tolerate it anymore. I am *not* a bale of cotton and I will not allow myself—"

His lips crushed into mine, a solid arm cinching around my waist, pulling me into his firm body, kissing me deeply. The angry ball in my stomach grew larger, furious at his shameless arrogance. But I was too startled to protest. His mouth was hungry and rough. And so suddenly that it surprised me, the angry ball in my stomach evaporated into butterflies. Nicholas kept his eyes open, catching my gaze when I dared to look at him, sending shivers of excitement to my toes. His intensity overwhelmed me, and I was swept up in the splendor of his kiss.

When I finally pulled away, I felt dizzy. Before I could catch my breath—and my racing thoughts—Nicholas pulled me back in. I thought briefly of resisting, but instantly succumbed to his insisting kiss. I shut my eyes and my lips melted into his, finding a rhythm that pulsed with my blood.

Nicholas stepped back abruptly, looked squarely in my eyes and said, "You are a complete lunatic. Sleep well."

He strode past me casually and leaned forward on the bow of the ship without so much as a backward glance.

I stared after him for a moment in complete disbelief, then dashed down the ladder, across the deck, and into the cabin.

CHAPTER TWENTY

MY MIND WAS REELING. I tore off my dress and flopped onto the bed. I shut my eyes tightly and willed myself to fall asleep, knowing it would be impossible. I deepened my breathing, hoping to settle my racing blood. A storm of emotions surged within me. I could still feel the pressure of Nicholas's lips on mine and see the determination of his stare.

As I sorted through my jumbled thoughts and the words leading up to the kiss, my fury returned.

How could he just dismiss me like that, after everything that had happened today? He gambled his life to save mine, then acted as though it meant nothing. He said things I had only dreamed of hearing, then swept them aside like clutter on a table.

And the kiss.

I had never been kissed. Not like that.

My lips felt as if they were on fire. I touched them to be sure they weren't.

Nothing Nicholas did made any sense. Was his kiss a declaration? From any other suitor, I would unequivocally think so. But with Nicholas…I couldn't be sure. He was a gallant swashbuckler and romance came naturally. Maybe he would be the same way with any girl on any given day.

I pressed my fists against my eyes. I hated feeling so helpless, so confused. Being near Nicholas altered my judgment the way a vein of ore upsets a compass. How could I sort my thoughts with him outside my door? I was at sea; I couldn't just walk away.

Even if I could—would I?

As angry as I was with Nicholas, I only wanted to be with him. Why couldn't I just go find him, talk to him, be with him?

Even if I could set aside my pride, would he want to talk to me? The way he turned his back on me after he kissed me…the memory made me burn. He took what he wanted when it was convenient for him, and I was left in that aftermath.

I pounded the lumpy pillow and rearranged myself on the wooden excuse of a bed. I fussed and fumed late into the night, trying to distract myself by reciting poetry from memory and conjugating Latin verbs. But when my mind was not preoccupied with some fully engaging activity, thoughts of Nicholas instantly appeared.

I replayed every conversation we'd had that day. And I replayed the kiss—frequently. Every time I remembered the heat from his mouth or his firm grip around my waist, my stomach flipped erratically.

Footsteps pounded down the hallway and Nicholas let himself into the cabin, slamming the door behind him.

Finally, he must have come to his senses and was here to offer an apology.

Mulling over whether or not I would accept it, I propped myself on an elbow.

Nicholas paced the tiny cabin, paying me no attention at all. He was absorbed in his own mind, breathing heavily. The scene of this tall man stooped over and pacing back and forth in this puny room would have been quite comical if I had not sensed his growing anger.

I waited another moment for him to let me in on this new game of his before asking, "What's wrong?"

Only after I spoke did Nicholas glance at me. He seemed almost surprised that I was there, lying in the bed.

"Everything," he responded darkly as he continued his truncated pacing.

I waited for further explanation but Nicholas did not offer one. "And *I'm* the infuriating one." I flopped onto my back and pulled the covers over my eyes.

He sighed heavily. "The crew is having a meeting. Discussing the mutiny, voting in a new captain. I assumed that they would choose me."

"And they didn't," I added when he failed to finish. "That must be very disappointing." Maybe he'd notice my sarcastic jab.

Nicholas growled, turning towards me. His hands were in fists. "It is not about disappointment, Tessa. I do not *want* to be captain. But I am afraid of what will happen if anyone else *is*."

"Oh." My voice softened as I realized this wasn't some kind of manipulative performance.

"I think they'll put in a bloke named Diggot."

"And he's a problem?" I asked, keeping my voice hushed.

"Aye. A right suspicious fellow. He's a bawdy old gossip, but he's popular for reasons I have never understood."

"Have you appealed to them? Explained about this Diggot fellow? Maybe they will listen to you. You're quite popular yourself."

"I've tried. It's beyond that."

"So you don't like the captain. Put up with him awhile

and as soon as the voyage is over, leave this crew and join another."

Nicholas stopped his pacing long enough to stare me down with a look of severe condescension. "You don't understand. This is a pirate ship. The crew doesn't take kindly to an accomplice jumping ship and making nice with a group of enemies."

"So go back to carpentry. You could have your own shop now."

"You don't understand!" He said again, his voice getting louder. "I am a *criminal*. I can't bloody well walk off this ship and become a respectable landowner with chickens and cows. *I don't have that luxury*."

I shrank back. "I understand," I snapped. "You dislike the captain and cannot do much about it. It's not ideal, but it's not the end of the world."

He wheeled on me, grabbing my shoulders. "Dammit, Tessa! He thinks you need to hang!"

His face froze in horror. He had not intended to say those words.

"Hang?" My voice cracked.

Nicholas stood and faced away. Quietly he added, "The crew agrees with him."

My pulse thudded behind my ears. I imagined I would hear the sound even louder with a noose strangling me.

"Maybe we can delay it," I thought out loud, my logic coming back slowly. "At least until we make port somewhere."

Nicholas nodded, pressing his palm to his forehead. He was still avoidant; there was more he was not telling me.

"Nicholas."

He glanced at me.

I sat up, tucking the blanket under my arms for modesty. "Please sit by me."

He sank next to me on the bed, tense and agitated. I

touched his hand and he was suddenly still.

"We can figure this out," I said, "but you need to tell me everything."

"I'm so sorry, Tessa. I did not mean to do this to you. I did not come here to shout at you and frighten you; I just needed somewhere to think. I am so *frustrated*! Things are out of control. Things I thought I could handle. And I don't know what to do. Everyone can see that I have an agenda that is different from theirs. And they do not like it. I don't know why. It doesn't hurt them. But the more I resist them, the more distrustful they get. And when I try to keep quiet and go along easily, they steer things in a direction that is simply unacceptable. Everything I do...Nothing helps. It just keeps getting worse."

We both sighed.

"So they still want to hang me. Can we delay a few days? Make it into port?"

"Maybe. Maybe there could be a retrial," Nicholas mumbled to himself, sounding logical for the first time. "A new captain would need to levy the accusations, hold the trial, decide the punishment." He met my gaze and said, "It might buy us a couple days. Maybe that might work."

I nodded eagerly, trying to give Nicholas hope I did not feel myself.

"You would go back to the brig."

I bit my lip. Maybe I would rather hang.

I nodded again.

"Maybe a raid. Yes, that would work." Nicholas stood, his eyes flashing. "I'll order an attack on the next ship we see. In the commotion, no one would notice if you escaped. Skidmore would help."

It was a miserable plan: attacking a random ship just to cause a diversion.

"No."

He looked at me, confused. "Huh?"

"I cannot have that on my head. I cannot let you stage a raid just for me."

"It will save your life!"

"But cost so many others! I could never live with myself."

"Dammit, Tessa. I will not see you hanged. I'll kill everyone in these blasted seas if it will keep you alive."

I looked at him with narrowed eyes. "Find another way."

"Fine. No raiding. But maybe we could lay chase as if we were going to. Give us a little more time."

"As long as you guarantee the raid will fail."

"They fail more often than you think. Especially with a new, pompous captain—bound for failure, really. I'd control the direction and take us near a port. It would be easy to convince Diggot to stop to sell our goods, make trade, and resupply. Yes. It will be perfect."

"Then I could sneak away. You could help me. Somehow I would make my way to St. Kitts, find someone who would have known my father—the governor ought to help me and send me back to London if necessary."

Nicholas stared at me incredulously.

"It might be a bit complicated, but it will work," I reassured him. "I can do it."

"Yes, you could," he conceded, but I could tell he was thinking of something else.

"What?" I prodded, suspicious of the far-off gaze in his eyes. "You don't think I can?"

Ignoring my question, he said, "I can give you funds to sail to St. Kitts." His voice was sullen. I sensed that something more was bothering him.

"There's something else. What is it?"

He shook his head sadly. "I thought I might escort you."

"Yes! That would be brilliant!"

"I can't."

"Of course you can. If you think that I will not let you, that it would be improper—"

"It is necessary for me to stay here. Prevent them from pursuing you."

"Oh." I felt as sullen as Nicholas sounded.

We sat quietly, mulling over the haphazard plan. Nicholas looked at me, his expression pained. He leaned in close and pressed his lips against mine.

"I have to keep reminding myself that you do not belong here," he murmured. "You are a lady. I can't keep trying to turn you in to something you are not."

"And what is it you are trying to turn me in to?"

"Mine."

CHAPTER TWENTY-ONE

"TESSA!"

I had barely drifted back to sleep when Nicholas's urgent whisper sounded at the door. He opened it and let himself in.

He grabbed the blue dress off the floor and held it out to me. "Put this on."

"What is it?" I asked.

"Shh!" he hissed. Nicholas turned his back to me in an attempt at privacy. "Dress quickly."

I nervously climbed out of bed and pulled my dress on.

"Change of plans. We're leaving now. They are planning to hang you in the morning. Maybe me too."

"What! Why?"

"I was trying to buy you time, as we discussed, but they would not hear of it. My defending you and all the time I have spent with you has not gone unnoticed. They think you have put some kind of witchcraft devil spell on me. That I am a danger to the crew because I rose up against Black. It was Black who forced that idea. It's vengeance for him. He wants me dead."

I finished the last of the buttons on my dress and touched Nicholas on the shoulder to alert him that I was ready.

"What now?" I whispered.

"Follow closely and keep quiet."

Outside the quiet sky was a deep grey. The sun had not risen yet, but would shortly.

We tiptoed hurriedly to the starboard railing and peered over the edge at the churning water below. A jollyboat was floating alongside the ship.

"It's time for us to get off this vessel." He pointed in the distance. I followed his finger but saw nothing but a blurry horizon. "We are not far from some cays, some islands too, hopefully. We got a good current here and there's a good shot at making it."

We were running away.

Despite all that could go wrong with being adrift at sea in a small jollyboat, the idea of escaping the pirates permanently and having Nicholas all to myself was thrilling.

Nicholas opened a gate in the gunwale and tossed a rope ladder overboard. It was fixed to the ship and dangled precariously along the hull down to the jollyboat. "Watch your step. I will be right behind you."

I nervously lowered myself down the flimsy jack ladder. The crashing waves seemed leagues away.

"Quickly, now," Nicholas prodded.

Descending the ladder was as slow as it was awkward. My feet fumbled to find each hold, and it was next to impossible to see what I was doing in the ashy light of early morning.

Nicholas anxiously watched my slow progress, throwing quick glances over his shoulder.

After one such glance, he vanished from my view

momentarily only to rush back and look over the caprail at me dangling on the jack ladder.

"Go! Tessa, go!" he barked. Judging by the volume of his voice, it was apparent our intentions were no longer secret.

I dropped as fast as I could, relying more on the strength of my arms than the surety of my footing. Nicholas disappeared from the railing again. I continued downward.

"Deserter!" an angry voice called from the ship.

I froze. We were caught. I craned my neck, hoping to see something of what was happening on the deck above, but I could only see the railing and the towering masts against the glowing grey sky.

"Tessa, leave! Now!" Nicholas's voice was panicked.

I forced myself down. I was better than halfway to the small boat below. I needed to hurry off the jack ladder so Nicholas could follow. It wouldn't take him half as long to shimmy down the rope.

Three faces peered over the deck at me. None of them belonged to Nicholas.

"It's the witch! She's escaping!"

They reeled in the ladder, intending to haul me back aboard the *Banshee*. I tried to keep up the pace of my descent, but they were stronger than I, and the distance to the jollyboat increased.

The jack ladder lurched; I slammed against the ship's hull and the rope slipped out of my sweaty hands. I plummeted, grasping at the rope as I rushed down. My fingers curled around the last bit of the ladder, the hot pain of friction tearing into my palm. I could not keep my hold and I plummeted through the air again. My attempt was enough, however, to slow my fall so that I dropped squarely into the jollyboat without hurting myself.

"Nicholas!" I yelled.

The ladder was gone. The pirates had finished reeling it up. Nicholas would have to jump.

His face appeared over the railing. Brandishing his cutlass, he severed the rope that anchored the jollyboat to the *Banshee*.

"Jump!" I screamed.

"Go! Get outta here!" he bellowed.

A group of men rushed at Nicholas and pulled him from my view.

"No! Nicholas! Nicholas?"

The boat rocked peacefully next to the *Banshee* just as before. Slowly, so slowly that I did not notice it at first, the distance between the jollyboat and the ship grew. I was adrift now. Each wave pushed me farther from the *Banshee*. Away from Nicholas. I waited for him to jump. The distance between the boat and the *Banshee* grew. The sounds of the scuffling onboard the ship faded and I could only hear the sloshing of the waves and my own frenzied breathing.

In desperation I called out for Nicholas again and again.

He could still make it. He was strong. He could swim the distance. He could still make it.

My eyes ached from staring so hard at the ship, a shrinking toy on the horizon. Its peaceful bobbing and graceful sails betraying whatever violence was occurring on deck.

"Nicholas!"

I clutched the sides of the boat in a death grip. Desperation crushed me and I nearly jumped from the boat to swim back for him.

It was too late. I had drifted too far. He was not coming.

CHAPTER TWENTY-TWO

ENDLESS BLUE STRETCHED IN all directions. The pale blue of the sky melted into the bottomless blue of the ocean as far as I could see. The glaring white sun was the only thing interrupting the blue monotony. The brownish-grey speck that was the *Banshee* faded hours ago.

I sat stiffly, clutching the edges of the jollyboat in disbelief, dried tear stains crusting on my cheeks. This had been the great escape plan? Now what?

The sun was climbing the eastern sky, casting its blinding light on the dancing waters. The air was already heavy at this hour. It was going to be a hot day.

Nicholas said there was land nearby. He knew better than to plant us both in the middle of the sea without the prospect of nearby civilization. To do otherwise be certain death—and an unpleasant one at that. Two oars lay in the bottom of the jollyboat, but without knowing what direction to paddle, I dismissed them as useless.

A grey canvas bag was next to the oars. It contained three sizeable flasks filled with fetid water; a stash of hardtack and dried, salted beef; a dirk; and a wide, tar-covered hat. I was glad for Nicholas's foresight in packing these things before he fetched me; glad that the canvas bag had made it into the boat even though he did not.

The presence of the bag kept me calm. It was not much, but it would keep me alive for a day or two. Hopefully by then…by then, what? Perhaps the ship would return for me so they could execute me properly instead of letting the blistering sun finish me?

I clutched the bag to my breast. It represented more than my survival. It was a tangible symbol of Nicholas. He was supposed to be with me. This escape was meant for the two of us. Maybe it was childish, but I drew comfort in the bag, a symbol of his intentions.

The sun climbed higher and higher in the sky. I was desperately hot and reluctant to drink the water. I worried that I'd guzzle it all in a minute. I allowed myself a sip. After tasting the water, that fear immediately vanished. I would have to be dying of thirst before I would swallow that stuff again.

I removed the hat from the bag and dipped it in the ocean. Water beaded up and rolled off the top, which had been smeared with tar for such purpose, but the underside absorbed the moisture. I placed it on my head and felt much cooler. At least I would not die with a sunburned face.

The day passed slowly. I wanted to lie down across the benches and rest, but I was afraid that if I were not constantly shifting my weight, the boat would capsize.

A shrill cry broke the silence.

Startled, I looked around for the source of the piercing noise. High in the sky a wisp of cloud slowly moved with the breeze. As my eyes focused on the small white spot, I realized it was not a cloud at all, but a gull loping in the atmosphere. My heart soared. If a bird were nearby, land was too.

I squinted into the sun and contorted my neck to watch the gull, afraid of blinking and losing sight of it for even a second.

The bird careened through the sky, and the boat seemed to follow it. Nicholas said there were good currents here. Maybe the ocean was taking me where I needed to be.

The sun drifted lazily into the horizon, taking its light with it. Fear swelled in me when the bird faded in the day's dying light. I scrambled to see the full breadth of the sky. I'd lost the gull.

Dejected, I plunked myself down upon the floor of the boat and leaned against a wooden bench and slept a shallow sleep.

With the peach glow of the sunrise, I looked for signs of life or land. I was disappointed—but not surprised—when I saw neither.

Rifling through the canvas sack for food, my first impulse was to eat the hardtack and save the more nourishing beef for later. But when I remembered that I could very easily die in this jollyboat today, whether from hungry sharks or severe heatstroke, I decided to eat what I wanted. I nibbled on a small piece of tough beef and watched the sunrise turn the entire sky in to a gleaming, golden treasure. The ocean reflected every nuance of the sky, the sparkle of the waves adding magic to the sight. It was the most magnificent sunrise I had ever seen. I should have been watching it with Nicholas.

Despite my dire circumstances, I felt a sort of self-possession I had never known before. I no longer lived in fear of what another person might do to me. I feared pain. I feared the absence of my agency—something that had been all but stripped from me aboard the *Banshee*. Adrift in this small boat, I was threatened by the heat of the sun and the depth of the ocean, but it was a threat I was somehow better equipped to face.

I thought of my father and what his last moments of life had been like. Had he survived the hurricane only to die while drifting on a calm sea? Perhaps he had been crushed by the ship's implosion, or just simply drowned. Had he, like Nicholas, placed me adrift in a jollyboat in a final attempt to save my life?

I shuddered to think of what might be happening to Nicholas. My imagination spun with the brutal pirate punishments I'd heard of. Lashings. Dunking in the ocean. Marooning on an island. Keelhauling.

The image of Nicholas dangling in a noose flashed before my eyes.

He said they wanted to hang him. He could already be dead. Maybe they had not even bothered to execute him formally; maybe they impaled him with their swords when they pulled him away from the railing.

No. I refused to believe it.

Nicholas was an officer. Until two weeks ago, he had been respected by his crew—as respected as a pirate can be. His skills were valuable. They would not want to lose him. But they would punish him. No doubt about that.

The day passed much like the day before. I shifted my weight constantly to counteract the lunging of the boat. It was exhausting. I forced myself to take occasional swallows of the stale water to stave off dehydration. I searched the sky for more gulls but found none. In the late afternoon I spotted a grey mass on the horizon and laughed joyously, thinking that I saw land. My heart plummeted when the shadow shifted and rolled across the sky—a distant storm.

The ocean grew agitated during the night, and the

wind sprayed across the pitching waves. Black clouds sheathed the sky, muffling any light from the heavens. Claustrophobia enveloped me. It was strange to feel confined when I knew I was surrounded endlessly by sky and sea, but in the darkness of this heavy night, I could not see past the edge of my small boat. Unfounded fears of shadowy sea monsters haunted me. I was too terrified to sleep. The night felt everlasting.

Even the rising sun battled with the darkness of the thick clouds. Finally, though, there was enough light to see the unchanging scenery around me. Instead of endless blue, I was encompassed by eternal grey.

I looked behind me and cried in surprise when I saw a fat gull sitting on the boat's edge. The startled bird took flight. I watched in eager delight as the bird sailed through the sky towards a faint shadow on the horizon. I sprung to my feet for a better look, dancing wildly to keep my balance.

There was a definite shadow on the horizon. Its shape was indistinct, but it was an unchanging, solid mass. Land.

I grabbed an oar and paddled towards the shadow. With no landmarks to gauge my progress, I couldn't be sure I was propelling the boat along or just wasting my energy. No matter. I was too anxious to simply sit still and wait on the tide.

The grey mass grew, becoming darker and more distinct in shape. Though it seemed small, lush vegetation and palm trees flourished on the isle. Shelter. Land. Fresh food. Fresh *water*. I almost cried.

The sun was setting. I had to get to that island before it was too dark to see. If I didn't, the ocean's current might pull me away and it would be impossible to recover from that. I would take no chances. I fought my burning muscles and paddled harder. When I finally felt the oar brush against sand, I grabbed the rope still attached to the jollyboat and plunged into the ocean.

Water rushed over my head and I bobbed to the surface, laughing with glee. I swam forward and the boat floated easily beside me. My feet finally found the shifting sands of the ocean floor. I walked backwards, leaning against the pull of the boat with all my might. It offered greater resistance with each step I took. Every inch of me ached. I was tempted to let the boat drift away, but I knew it could provide essential shelter during the night. It could be the difference between life and death.

With shaking legs and burning arms, I heaved the boat onto the beach.

I had made it!

I collapsed and dug my fingers into the golden sand.

"You were right, Nicholas," I cried. "We found land. You were right."

CHAPTER TWENTY-THREE

I DECIPHERED MY SURROUNDINGS the best I could in the deepening twilight. A broad white beach stretched down the length of the island as far as I could see. Towards the interior of the island, the sand bled into a forest of palms and ferns obscured with ominous shadows.

Not wanting to sleep on the sand, I climbed into the jollyboat and curled up in the bottom, giving myself up to exhaustion.

Soft raindrops woke me in the night. Annoyed, I crammed the tar-covered hat on my head. Its brim was full of water that splashed down the back of my neck. I shivered, grumbling under my breath. Inspiration struck and I placed the empty canteen on a bench to catch the fresh rain.

Exhausted though I was, it was too much to ask to sleep through the strengthening storm. Brilliant flashes of lightning danced around me, the accompanying thunder rattled my chest. The wind lashed at the surrounding trees, and waves pounded the beach, battering the jollyboat. I worried that the tide would carry me away. Begrudgingly, I uncurled myself and hopped out onto the sand. I pulled the boat a bit farther onto the rain-soaked beach, then dragged the rope towards the forest. I fought my nerves as I stared into the black abyss of a jungle.

Quickly, I knotted the long rope around the slender trunk of a palm, hoping it would hold. I dashed back to my boat and huddled inside.

My stomach rumbled with hunger.

The canvas bag was lying in a shallow puddle at the boat's bottom, soaking wet. I groaned. The hardtack was ruined, a soggy mess. I pulled out one of the strips of dried beef. Though the seasonings had been rinsed off, it was edible

I tried not to think of what would happen after the beef was gone. I imagined myself marching placidly through the jungle and finding bunches of wild fruit and nuts growing on low-hanging branches that would sustain me like royalty.

It was a naïve notion. I was a stranger in the Caribbean. Even if food were that easy to find, would I even recognize it? I hoped so. My life depended on it.

I pushed away my thoughts of food and replaced them with thoughts of Nicholas. I replayed our last kiss again and again. Losing myself in romantic reverie, I imagined how our courtship would blossom under more traditional circumstances.

I imagined myself back in England, preparing for a night at the theatre. I would wear my favorite ball gown— a dress of dusty lilac silk that made my alabaster skin glow. My cinnamon hair could be styled fashionably on top of my head with intricate braids and cascading ringlets, elegant yet soft. A string of pearls, white gloves, and kid-leather shoes. The butler would announce Nicholas's arrival. I would glide effortlessly down the stairs, masking my enthusiasm with a wistful smile. Nicholas would be waiting for me in the grand foyer, a dashing smile softening the angles of his face. Barefoot and wearing his canvas breeches and flowing cotton shirt, he would…he would….

Wait.

That was not right.

I changed the image in my mind. Nicholas would be waiting for me in the foyer, wearing…a silken suit and a white wig? A long coat and leggings?

I could not picture it at all, try as I might. He simply looked absurd in any civilized clothing I could imagine.

Annoyed at this disruption in my fantasy, I let him remain in his sailor's garb and continued with my dream. Nicholas would be waiting for me in the grand foyer, a dashing smile making my blood rush. Barefoot and wearing his canvas breeches and flowing cotton shirt, he would rush to meet me halfway up the stairs, entwining an arm around my waist and kissing me longingly without a word passing between us. I smiled, heart fluttering at the thought.

No, that was wrong too.

Nicholas would wait for me to descend the stairs, all the while admiring my beautiful gown. As I approached him, he would casually reach for my hand, pull me within inches of his face and stare directly into my eyes.

No…Nicholas was not behaving himself. I thought back upon other outings I'd had where an impeccably dressed gentleman met me in the foyer with a hat under his arm, bowed graciously, complimented my gown, and exchanged pleasantries while offering me his arm. It was a familiar script. I knew it well. So why couldn't I put Nicholas into that role?

* * * * *

The storm subsided, though a lazy rain still dribbled down. The sun broke through the clouds in another magical sunrise, splashing the fractured sky with crimson and gold.

With the dawn breaking, I had enough light to explore my surroundings better. I stumbled out of the jollyboat stiffly. My legs trembled underneath me. More than likely they were tired and overworked, but I wondered if I had spent so much time on the sea that I had lost my *land* legs. I smirked at the thought.

I checked the canteen I had left on the bench. An inch of water sloshed in the bottom. Not much, but it was something. I set it back on the bench, hoping to catch a few more droplets.

I scanned the beach deciding which direction to explore first. To my right, the beach faded steeply into a short hill that jutted into the ocean, limiting my view of the coast. To my left, untouched sand extended as far as I could see. I picked up my skirts and walked in that direction.

The coastline curved smoothly and I followed along the driest sand I could find. Tiny crabs scuttled across my path in jerky movements. They matched the color of the sand exactly and it took me a moment to realize that the sand itself was not moving. I faintly wondered if the creatures were edible.

I walked until I could no longer see the jollyboat. That was far enough.

I walked back to the boat.

The air was thick with moisture. The heat of the sun did nothing to dry my limp, clammy dress. My head ached and my sore body still shivered from the dampness that encompassed me.

Once back at the boat, my energy was expended. I settled my reluctant muscles between two benches and drifted off to sleep.

CHAPTER TWENTY-FOUR

I WEAVED MY WAY through the large crates, barrels, and bins at the dockyard in England. Some were being loaded onto ships while others were being distributed to vendors. Peddlers called to me, trying to entice me with colorful birds, bolts of luxurious fabrics, baskets of exotic spices, and piles of tropical fruits. I ignored them all. I was searching among these crates, searching for something I had not yet found. Beyond the docks, dozens of moored ships gently swayed in the breeze, their countless masts looked like an army of javelins piercing the sky.

As I meandered through the shipping goods, I finally found what I was looking for. Arranged on the dock in neat rows was a traveling zoo. A barker csalled for patrons to visit, "Only three shillings!" he shouted.

I dropped three coins in his hand and crossed into the zoo. A cage of monkeys. Oversized rodents. Two zebras. These distractions held no interest for me. I kept my meandering pace without stopping to take in the sights. I briefly paused at a caged tiger. Its eyes were glazed, and its fur was matted. It panted as if in boredom. I had expected to be awed. I was disappointed. I continued towards the last cage. I knew it would hold the best animal. The closer I got, the more whispers from the crowd I could hear.

"The fiercest of the fierce!" a small boy exclaimed.

"I've never seen anything like it!"

"So majestic."

"How frightening!" a woman shrieked with excitement.

All crowds vanished as I finally stood before the rusty, tarnished cage and looked at the wild creature within.

It was Nicholas.

He stood in the center of the cage, his eyes fixed on nothing. Forlorn. I wondered what was so majestic and fierce about him. I could not get him to look my way, could not make him behave as he would have in the wild. I was angry. Disappointed.

Then his eyes locked on mine. They were the color of the morning sky. They were wide with shock, shimmering with pain.

A small wet, spot of blood appeared in the center of his abdomen and spread. He clutched at his stomach, his hands turning glossy and red. He looked at me, horrified.

I held a long, thin rapier dripping with his blood.

I startled awake.

My breathing was shallow and my head spun.

I shook the image out of my head.

It was just my mind reliving the horrors on board the ship. It did not mean anything.

It was not prophetic.

It was just a dream.

Just a dream.

I rubbed my eyes and shifted uncomfortably in the jollyboat.

By the look of the sun's position, I guessed it to be late afternoon. The air was as sticky as ever.

My head pounded. My throat was raw. My hand shook

noticeably as I reached for a canteen. I took a sip of water, hoping to soothe my throat, but swallowing only exacerbated its pain.

I tried to pull myself out of the boat, but failed. My limbs were weak. I sank down, trembling.

I needed something to eat. I cautiously counted the strips of dried beef. Four. Could I survive on one a day? Would the water last that long? I was down to the last canteen. Plus the small amount of rain I caught, which was hardly worth counting. That would give me four days. Then what?

I ate my ration of meat slowly as if the more time I took to eat it, the longer it would sustain me.

It was time to explore the forest, to see if I could find water and food. I turned to look at the tangle of green. Though the sun shone high in the sky, the forest looked dark and foreboding.

I maneuvered myself out of the boat, my skin feeling as if it were on fire. I steadied myself against the boat's bow while a wave of dizziness clouded my sight.

Slowly, I made my way into the dank jungle.

Though uneasy with the constant whispering of the leaves and the suffocating shadows, I was in awe at its unequaled beauty. I had thought I had seen green before. As a child, I had run freely across rolling hills so green they put emeralds to shame. But this…this was something else entirely.

The soil beneath me was the color of coffee. I placed my bare feet carefully, taking care not to injure them. Each step stirred up the heady scent of damp, decaying leaves. Such a different fragrance than the salted air of the ocean. I inhaled deeply.

Every few moments, I stopped to examine the world unfolding around me. Brilliant pink flowers spilled from vines overhead. My fingers grazed mottled tree trunks as smooth as marble. The canopy overhead was so densely woven that I could scarcely see the sky.

I picked my way through the tangle of trees slowly, certain that a fresh stream or bunch of bananas was just beyond my vision. I could no longer hear the rhythm of the ocean nor could I see the beach. Anxiety bubbled in my chest. I pressed on. There was a water source somewhere. I needed to find it.

After what felt like hours of meandering, a patch of yellow caught my eye. A half-dozen birds were clustered on a gnarled mass that hung from a tree. They flitted about the clump, chirping and hopping, pecking at it and at each other. I looked closer at the clump. It wasn't a gnarled branch like I thought, but a bouquet of long, brown pods. And the birds were eating them.

As I stood watching the birds feast, I realized the shadows were deepening. It wouldn't be long before the sun set. I didn't have much time.

Sizing up the tree, I estimated that it was at least twenty-five feet high. I couldn't climb it. Not only had I never done such a thing in my entire life, and even if my skirts wouldn't hinder me, there were no branches within reach.

I looked around the forest floor to see if I could find anything to throw at the clump of food. At the base of the tree, I noticed several pods that had been knocked loose. I picked one up.

With a little effort, I pried the hard pod open with my fingernails. Nestled inside was soft, reddish flesh surrounding six seeds. I sniffed it. I licked it. The flavor was mild but sweet. Pleasant.

I removed the pits and devoured it.

I ate the insides of three more pods I found on the forest floor. I looked up again at the birds above, feasting away. I salivated.

I found a moss-covered stone and launched it at the clump of fruit. The stone sailed through the air and missed the target widely, hitting the branches of an adjacent tree on its descent. The birds startled and flew away.

I glanced again at the dark forest behind me, knowing I would not see the beach but still searching for it. Darkness was quickly encroaching.

I would have to return tomorrow.

But how would I ever find this tree again? This tree that would be my salvation?

I needed to leave a marker.

My hands flew to the black ribbon tied in my hair. I removed it and fastened it around the trunk. I stepped back to view my work. The shiny black satin easily blended in with the dark shadows of the jungle. It would be impossible to see. I retrieved the sash and tied my hair with it again.

I scanned myself for any other ideas. There was only one other thing I had—the Wedgwood blue dress. I would be able to recognize that from yards away. The color was bright enough, unusual enough….I searched for a piece of the dress I could easily tear off for a marker.

I futilely tugged at the hem. The silk was too tightly woven. I transferred my efforts to a sleeve. The stitching stretched but nothing gave way. Though I had initially admired the fine workmanship of this dress, I was now cursing it. Any cheaper seaming would have popped by now.

My angst grew along with the shadows of the jungle. I needed to make my way back to the beach while I could still see. Yet, I just as desperately needed to find this tree tomorrow.

My eyes searched the ground, looking for a tool to help me. If only I had brought the damn dirk! I crouched down and fingered several rocks, tossing aside the smooth pebbles. I picked up a thin, flat rock and grazed my thumb over its edge. It was sharp enough to double as a blade. Once I severed just one stitch, I knew the seam would easily unravel.

Taking the sharp-edged stone in my right hand, I awkwardly hacked at my left shoulder. I was too timid, too light-handed. I tried again.

A rustling in the brush not ten feet away from me caught my attention. Apparently it caught the attention of some birds too, for a brightly colored flock took to the sky. I didn't know what had startled the birds, but if they were leaving, so should I. With one last effort, I pulled my sleeve taut with my left hand, crunched my eyes closed, and slashed violently at the dress with my right hand.

Sharp pain splintered down my shoulder. I opened my eyes to see what I had done. I had effectively ripped half the sleeve off the dress, so that mission was accomplished. I had also managed to score my skin from the top of my shoulder down to the hollow under my arm. Thick blood was already oozing at the cut. I hissed against the pain, angry at myself for this stupid wound. I threw the makeshift knife to the jungle floor. It landed with a wet thud. Working quickly, I yanked off the severed sleeve and mopped up the blood on my shoulder.

My eyes continued to stray to the place the rustling noise came from. Though I saw nothing nor heard nothing more, I knew something was there.

In the little light I had left, I struggled to find a way to attach the sleeve.

A jagged branch stub poked from the tree's trunk near my waist. Quickly, I speared the sleeve onto the barb and managed to wedge a splinter into my pinky. Sucking on my finger, I hurried towards the beach, glancing over my shoulder one last time at the suspicious spot in the bushes.

I emerged from the jungle just as the golden sun began to cast the world in an amber glow.

At the water's edge, I gingerly examined my shoulder. The cut was deep and blood throbbed out of it. I sparingly dripped my precious drinking water on my shoulder to rinse away the dirt and blood. I clenched my teeth and grimaced. Not from the pain, but at my own carelessness. I was wasting my drinking water cleaning up after my own stupidity. If I were to die of thirst, I would deserve it.

CHAPTER TWENTY-FIVE

IT WAS MIDMORNING WHEN I awoke. I was glad to have had a solid night's sleep. A dreamless sleep.

I stretched slowly, noting the same raw headache and raspy throat that plagued me yesterday, only today they were more intense. As I stretched, my wounded shoulder resisted stiffly, throbbing with pain.

I winced as I fingered the gash on my left shoulder. The cut was an angry red and oozed a diluted sort of blood. Yellow puss crusted around the edges. My entire shoulder was puffy and pink. The skin was hot to the touch.

From the headache and sore throat that had persisted for two days, I knew I was falling ill. Now that my shoulder was obviously infected, my situation was grave. Stranded on a primitive island without medical aid, an infection like this could kill me.

I rinsed my shoulder again with as much water as I dared to use.

My only chance of survival was finding help. I hadn't seen any signs of civilization on the island so far. But I couldn't afford to make any assumptions. The Caribbean was full of fledgling colonies, savage nations, and buccaneer hideouts. Unless this was an oversized sandbar, something that could save my life could be on the other side of the jungle.

I forced myself to eat my daily ration of meat before setting off on a one-way exploration. Either I would find the help I desperately needed or die.

I left the sanctuary of the boat and headed northeast along the rocky coast throwing a parting glance at the jungle. I had finally found fresh food but at the expense of my health. And now I had to walk away from it or die from infection. The irony stung as much as my shoulder.

I pressed onward, following the shoreline so as not to get lost. If something was to be found, I would find it, even if I had to circle the entire island. My faltering steps took me around the bend of land where the terrain grew tougher. The golden sand turned in to jagged pebbles that ripped the soft skin of my feet and the beach disappeared into a rocky hill.

The storm clouds overhead unleashed their fury and raindrops the size of cherries poured down. Every crash of thunder rattled my nerves. The rain in London had never been like this.

The wind raked across me and I shivered uncontrollably. Every time I shook, the pain in my shoulder shot straight to the tips of my fingers. Before long, the dull ache evolved into an insufferable fire.

I crawled up the hill—slick in the rain—grasping at plants as I made my way to the stony crest. Resting on my hands and knees, I looked around. The clouds tumbled ominously above, lit by flashes of lightning. The ocean churned dramatically below, white froth topping the black peaks. The jungle bent under the force of the blowing gale. Strands of my hair lashed against my face like a dozen wet whips.

Shivering so intensely that I could hardly coordinate my movements, I half skidded, half fell down the rocky hill and plopped into a patch of ferns. I did not get up. As the sound of the ocean grew distant, I humorously thought how this nest of ferns was the softest thing I had lain on in a while. My head spun. I closed my eyes.

The sky was still light when I regained my faculties. I did not know whether I had slept one hour or twelve. The rain had ceased but the wind continued its violent course.

I looked at my cut. The infection was worse. My entire shoulder was stiff and swollen, the open wound filled with milky fluid.

My dress and hair were still damp, but I was no longer shivering. In fact, I was hot. Too hot. I pressed my hands against my cheeks. They felt cold and clammy against the burning skin of my face. I had a fever.

Pinning my left arm to my side, I trudged to the water's edge. I splashed my face with the frothy water, instantly cooling my burning cheeks. A few drops of seawater dripped on my infected shoulder and I screamed in pain.

Light-headed, I sat down for a minute to catch my breath. I fought the urge to sleep again and forced myself to continue my journey.

I staggered on, oblivious to the rampant storm, the harsh terrain, and the bloody footprints that trailed behind me. In a stupor, all I could do was take one more step. Just one more step.

The hours blurred together, and my thoughts were lost in the fog of fever. When I happened upon a fresh stream, I had enough instinct to drink as much as my raw throat would allow.

I trudged on through twilight, one foot in front of the other. When it was too dark to make any more progress, I collapsed where I was, not caring to find a cozy spot for sleep. I scanned the landscape, hoping to see the flickering light of a distant flame in the darkness. Hoping to see a sign of life. Hoping my journey wasn't in vain. Hoping I wasn't looking into my death.

My sleep was shallow and I shivered constantly. My head felt hot to the touch and my feet were like ice. When the purple haze of dawn spread across the sky, I trekked on. I stopped frequently, my energy draining too easily.

The coastline shifted into rocky cliffs and became more dramatic, more dangerous. I kept the ocean in my line of sight, but deviated from the shore. I decided it would be safer and easier to follow the road. My feet fumbled in the wheel ruts but the path was clear and easy.

Wagon ruts?

I squeezed my eyes tightly and shook my head, trying to jar some coherent thoughts.

I bent over and touched the ground. Yes, a road. Well worn. With wagon ruts.

I did not know how long I had been following it, how long it had shadowed my course. I felt stupid and elated at the same time.

The fear that had been pushing me onward vanished. I sank in to the mud, completely spent. I curled up against the violent shivering, my arm screaming with agony. I had gone as far as I could. I sent up a prayer that someone would find me here in the middle of the road. Then I gave myself away to a feverish swoon.

CHAPTER TWENTY-SIX

MY EYES WERE CLOSED but I was awakening. Though my head still ached with fever, I was more comfortable and warm than I had been in quite a while. Strange, soft whispers surrounded me. Whispers of the ocean? Of birds?

I shifted slightly and opened my eyes, expecting to see the sky. To my astonishment, a roof was over my head. I quickly rolled onto my right elbow and saw two women staring at me.

I squinted my eyes closed and shook my head. When I looked again, the women were still there, whispering to one another.

Trying to calm my racing heart, I forced my mind to work slowly. I was in a building. I was lying in a bed—a real bed. Sunlight streamed through a nearby window. And I was alive.

My aching joints and clammy palms told me I was still ill, but I felt much better. My cut was covered in a sticky mud-colored poultice, but I could move my shoulder.

I turned my attention to the women watching me. Their

eyelids were lined and brightly painted, their lips were an unnatural shade of red, and their hair was cropped short. Their ragged dresses revealed far too much of their bosoms. Prostitutes.

"Where am I?" I said, but no sound came out. I cleared my throat and tried again.

One woman—a Negro—turned to her blonde friend and said, "Let Mother Ivy know she's awake." The blonde woman left.

"Hello," the Negro said, kneeling on the floor. She held a cup towards me. "It's cider. Might help with your throat."

I gingerly sat up and accepted the cider. It smelled delicious and I took a sip.

"I'm Hannah, by the way," she said. There was a certain reassurance in her deep, throaty voice. It was comforting and rich. Like velvet.

"Thank you for the cider." I looked down at my healing shoulder. "And for this."

Hannah shrugged. "I didn't do that. It was Mother Ivy. She fixed you up proper."

"So she's the one who found me then? On the road?"

Hannah looked out the doorway of the room. I followed her gaze. "Liam!" she shouted, "I know you're there. I can see you. Come on in. The girl's awake."

A boy hesitantly entered. When his eyes met mine, his face split into a gigantic grin.

"It was Liam here who found you. He's Mother Ivy's son. He has a habit of wandering where he's not supposed to. Guess it was good he did."

Liam stood sheepishly before me, smiling widely with his hands shoved in his pockets. He was about twelve and couldn't take his enormous brown eyes off me.

"Thank you, Liam," I croaked with my raspy voice. "You are my hero."

He beamed.

"What's your name?" Liam asked. "I wanted to name you Agatha but Mama said you already had a name. No one knew it, though."

The precocious boy made me smile. "My name is Tessa. Though Agatha is a fine name too."

"Are you a mermaid?"

I wiggled my feet for him to see. "No. Human. Just like you."

The blonde woman entered the room followed by a sour-looking woman with a severe grey bun. Mother Ivy, I thought.

Mother Ivy scowled at her son. "Go to the kitchen, Liam, and stop flitting about."

"Yes'm," he said, his eyes dropping to the floor. He quickly disappeared.

"You decided to live after all," Mother Ivy said brusquely. She was not a warm woman.

Unsure of what to say, I took another sip of cider.

Hannah stood next to Mother Ivy. "Her name is Tessa."

I cleared my throat and tried to look at the stern woman. "Thank you for…everything. My arm feels much better."

Mother Ivy nodded curtly. "Glad to hear it."

The three women stood in a row, the two prostitutes sandwiching their Mother Ivy. They stared down at me and the tension grew thicker. I was waiting for an explanation from them and they were waiting for an explanation from me.

"Might I ask where I am?" I stammered nervously.

"Maybe she has no memory," the blonde whispered loud enough for me to hear.

Hannah scoffed. "Of course she has a memory. She knew her name."

"I'm sorry," I said as I pressed the heel of my hand

against my aching head. "Let me explain. My name is Tessa Monroe. I was adrift at sea on a jollyboat and landed on a beach. Then I cut myself and got sick. And now I'm here. Except I don't know where exactly *here* is."

"Port Winslow," Mother Ivy answered.

"Port Winslow," I repeated. "How did I get here?"

"My disobedient son happened to find you dying on a road."

I nodded and paused a moment to digest this new information. "Port Winslow," I said again, "I've never heard of it."

"Small port, really," the blonde sassed. "Not somewhere the likes of you would ever visit on purpose."

I wasn't sure what she meant and it made my head hurt trying to figure it out. And then something clicked. I was in a port. "But even a small port harbors ships, right? I need passage to St. Kitts."

Mother Ivy snorted softly. "If you were on your way to St. Kitts, then you're definitely lost. Besides, this is a different kind of port. You'll not be finding passenger ships in the harbor at all."

"There must be something. I mean, I can't stay here forever." I said it more to myself than the stoic ladies before me. I thought about what Mother Ivy said. No passenger ships. "So this port…trade port, right? Not really a colony, is it?"

Hannah and the blonde nodded. Mother Ivy remained still.

"Do pirates ever come here?" I felt silly asking such a loaded question, but I could see the answer on the women's faces even though no one spoke. "There's someone who could help me. A Mr. Holladay. Nicholas Holladay. Does he frequent this port ever?"

"Never heard of him," Mother Ivy said flatly. "Sounds a little rich for our lot."

"No," I shook my head grasping for the right thing to say. "No, he's a pirate. Quartermaster. Marks. They call him Marks. He sails on the *Banshee*. I don't suppose you've seen the *Banshee* recently?"

"Marks?" the blonde balked. "You know Marks?"

Realizing that the blonde prostitute knew my Nicholas twisted my stomach. Still, it offered some hope for escape. "He's a friend. He might have asked about me?"

"Haven't seen Marks in ages," the blonde prattled on. "Not that he's worth much when he visits."

"Hush, Charlotte," Mother Ivy commanded. "Now Miss Tessa, you're obviously improving, but not entirely well yet. Rest up and we'll figure out what to do with you when you're worth something. Ladies, let's leave our guest in peace. There's work to be done."

Hannah and Charlotte left the room with Mother Ivy slowly following. She paused in the doorway. "I'll send Liam with some food. You must be hungry."

"Thank you," I responded politely, but it wasn't genuine. Something about this place made me feel just as trapped as the brig on the *Banshee*.

CHAPTER TWENTY-SEVEN

As SOON AS I smelled the food, my stomach roared for it. Liam laughed as he handed it to me.

"Hash," was all he said.

"Ah, it smells wonderful. Why don't you keep me company while I eat?"

He didn't need to be asked twice. Liam eagerly plopped down on the floor beside my bed.

I ate the hash voraciously. It was the best food I'd had in months. I wanted to swim in it.

I was only vaguely aware of the boy staring at me but I couldn't care until my plate of hash was almost gone and my stomach finally stopped rumbling.

"You really are hungry," Liam laughed again. "Must be feeling better for sure."

I nodded. "I thought I was going to die. And I probably would have if you hadn't found me on that road."

Liam beamed.

We sat quietly for a moment. Liam seemed completely content doing nothing but staring at me. But I was quite uncomfortable with it.

"So, Liam, where is your father?"

"Don't have one."

"Oh," I mumbled, feeling foolish for asking.

Liam did not seem offended though. "Where is your father?"

I shrugged. "I am not sure I have one either."

Liam's interest was piqued. "What do you mean?"

"I was sailing from England and our ship sank. I haven't seen my father since then. I was rescued by pirates, but I don't know what happened to him. I think he probably drowned."

I was amazed at how simply I stated these facts to Liam. There were no tears or dark, brooding emotions. It was easy to share it with such an honest little face.

"Do you have a mother? Who takes care of you?"

That question hurt my heart, just a little. I forced a smile. "Well, you do, now don't you?"

Liam's chest puffed.

"I need to make my way to St. Kitts, though. Or Barbados. When I am better. How do you think I can get there?"

He shrugged like the answer was so simple. "Just get on a boat that's going there."

I smiled. "Yes, that makes perfect sense. But I am worried that not all the boats are safe. Some of the boats might have pirates on them that will be mean to me."

"It's a legitimate fear, Miss Tessa," Mother Ivy was behind me, standing in the doorway of the room. Liam hadn't noticed her either. He jumped up at the sound of her voice, his eyes on his feet.

Mother Ivy floated into the room, her long skirts kicking up little storms of filth as they glided along the dusty floor. Her presence was imposing. I wanted to mirror Liam and stand at attention with my eyes on the floor.

166 | L A R A   H A Y S

"Take the dishes, Liam."

The boy did as he was told and hurried off.

"I hope you'll make yourself at home here, Miss Tessa. You'll need to stay for a while. First, you're not well enough for anything yet. Second, it may take some time until we find you passage to St. Kitts. Port Winslow is something of a…" she trailed off, searching for the right words.

"A pirate haven?" I offered, showing her that I wasn't as naïve as she may think.

"Well, if you want to put it that way. Port Winslow is a pirate haven. It has its own rules but it's not the safest place, especially for a girl like you. We'll need to be very selective of what crew we trust you with."

Memories of Wrack's attack flashed in my mind. I swallowed hard.

Mother Ivy continued. "We'll have patience and wait for a good crew that's headed to where you need to go. Don't worry; there really are some honorable buccaneers left." I saw her smile for the first time. It was chilling.

"Yes, I understand. But I don't want to be a burden. If there is any way—"

"Fair is fair, Miss Tessa, and I'm glad you recognize that. Wait until you're well, and then you can contribute a bit around here. That way you'll earn your place to stay."

"Contribute?

"You'd be a wonderful asset to my bordello, what with that pretty face of yours—though you are skinny. You could pocket the profits, save money for yourself."

It sounded more like an offer than a demand. "Is there something else?"

Mother Ivy seemed unsurprised at my response. "It was worth asking," she said, her thin lips smiling knowingly. "You can clean rooms and serve in the tavern.

It will only buy you a bed to sleep on and food to eat."

"I'll make that trade gladly."

*****

After several days of resting, I regained my strength and Liam showed me around Port Winslow. I hoped to find some alternative to working at the bordello. The port was small, however, a haven for illegal trade and salacious activity. I returned from my tour dejected, admitting that I would rather work in Mother Ivy's tavern than the other local businesses, which all seemed to be run by perverted drunkards.

I returned to Mother Ivy ready to earn my keep.

My bed was moved into a dormitory where the six other girls slept. In addition to lodging and food, I was given two new dresses, stockings, and shoes. The gowns were low cut and showy, but at least they were clean.

As I went about my duties at the bordello, I learned to silence my imagination. I did not want to wonder about what transpired in the rooms I tidied. Working in the tavern was better…and worse. Better because Liam was in the kitchen, ready with a smile and easy conversation. Worse because the patrons at the tavern were disgusting heathens who treated me like one of the prostitutes. Still, I looked forward to my work in the tavern because it allowed me to search the faces of the men and eavesdrop on conversations. I was bound to hear some bit of information about Nicholas, about the *Banshee*, or even Captain Black.

My new sisters wanted very little to do with me. Except Hannah. She constantly sought me out and treated me like a friend. And soon enough, I considered her a friend as well.

I cried myself to sleep every night. I was humiliated. I was a lady from London! How had I ever become a kitchen wench in a bordello?

I found a place on the island I liked to go to be alone. It was a large, grassy promontory jutting out over the ocean. The view was breathtaking and I could imagine my life at the bordello was nothing more than a distant nightmare. As one of the highest points on the island, it offered me the best vantage point to scan the horizon for ships, hoping to see something I could sail away on.

Watching the sunrise alone on the promontory became a tradition. I think Liam, Hannah, and the others understood my loneliness, for no one ever intruded on my sad ritual. Every morning I watched the delicate colors of the sky eat away at night's blackness. The ocean reflected the transformation, an inky abyss coming alive in the light. One by one, stars disappeared. I remembered times when I found their beauty captivating and warm, but now they seemed like harsh pinpricks of searing light in the velvet sky and I was glad when they were all gone.

Cruel and severe, the early-morning stars mocked me. A billion stars in the sky, staring down at me, telling me how alone I was. Speaking a celestial language of their own that I could not understand. I was always surrounded, but forever alone.

Looking across the sea of stars, I concluded that time did not exist. Oh, the sun rose and set, the tides came in and out, but time didn't really move. The world continued her repetitive rituals, but they had lost all meaning.

I looked to the lush jungle for any clue that would tell me I was wrong. The jade foliage was deceiving. It could be December or June—there was no difference. I was in an eternal summer, a garish recycling of the same day. Identical days without season, a perfect paradise on the side of every sunrise. It wasn't natural.

A breeze ruffled my hair and the clouds shifted above, revealing a luminous sliver of a moon in the fading night. Its brilliant light glittered on the ocean and illuminated the beach below like a strip of quicksilver. A delicate moon— so daintily formed. It was a wonder that the small crescent emitted so much light. I remembered the last time I had seen this moon—this perfectly-shaped crescent in a twilit sky.

It was on the deck of the *Banshee* the night after the trial. Nicholas was next to me, holding my hand in his, his arm around me to keep me warm. Nicholas kissed me that night. That night was the last time I saw him.

My throat grew thick and I breathed unevenly. Silent tears rained down my cheeks, tears that came all too easily these days. I hugged my knees to my chest and rocked silently, feeling like the light of the moon uncovered everything I was hiding from myself.

I had lived in this hellish whorehouse for a month. This was more than a holiday, more than a vacation. Soon, another month would pass and then another. I was not going anywhere. This was permanent. The opportune ship with kind pirates that would take me to St. Kitts was not going to come. It didn't exist. Mother Ivy was deceiving me, feeding me hope while she got her free labor. This island was now my life; the bordello was now my home. There was nothing for me but this.

The constant waves of the sea and the evergreen glow of the jungle could fool me into thinking that time was frozen, but the phases of the moon told the truth. Time *was* passing. And I was passing with it.

I felt more helpless now than I had in the brig of the *Banshee*.

I tried to ignore the moon from then on. How futile! Rather, I grew obsessed with the moon—searching for it every night, even watching for its filmy presence during the day, calculating its shape as it waned into darkness then grew full again, marking the passage of time in a way that I could not deny.

CHAPTER TWENTY-EIGHT

I DROPPED A PLATE of cabbage and ham in front of a man, set down a mug of ale, and walked towards the kitchen for my next order.

"Wait up, moppet," he called, "This order's not quite right."

I hurried back to the table, afraid of a scolding from Mother Ivy if a customer I waited on was unhappy.

"I'm sorry sir, isn't this what you ordered?"

"Oh, the food itself is fine, but I find something lackin' in the service. Shouldn't you give me a smile, wish me a pleasant day, and set aside a room for me?" His hand snaked around my waist.

I pulled away discreetly. "You certainly deserve a smile and to have a pleasant day," I forced myself to say as pleasantly as I could. "Now eat up." I tried leaving again.

"Hold up!" He caught my skirt and pulled me back. "How 'bout that room? Yer new around here, ain't ya? I can tell yer a classy thing. And what I wouldn't give to show you—"

I covered my ears. "Please, sir. I'm only a scullery maid.

Only a scullery maid. If you would like a room for later, I'll have Mother Ivy arrange something." I tried to leave again but he still had my skirt.

"You *are* new around here. Gotta say, yer innocence is even more attractive than yer purty face. Here in this port, I get what I want."

I pulled back, trying to free my skirt from his grip. He grabbed my wrist. The memory of Wrack in the brig bubbled up from where I buried it.

"Don't touch me!" I flung a pewter mug at him, hitting him square on the nose and drenching him with ale.

The man stood up and struck me across my 1face. "Dammit, whore! Why did you do that?"

Mother Ivy appeared out of nowhere, her calm, ominous presence presiding over our dispute. "Miss Tessa, it appears you've been clumsy with Mayor Winslow's order. Please get him a new one and make sure we do not charge him for any of his services today. And please prepare the suite for him and have Hannah waiting. I'm sure he'll appreciate some relaxation after such a stressful supper. Will that satisfy you, Mayor?"

I nodded submissively and slipped away.

"No, Madam, that won't satisfy me at all. You see, I like the looks of that one. Plus, she's got spunk. Have her meet me in the suite, and I'll pay for my supper."

I paused on my way to the kitchen. This was Mayor Winslow, the man who owned this island. The man who ran this port. Keeping him happy was crucial for keeping a business hopping. Mother Ivy would cave. Mother Ivy would send me to him. I would have to run.

"Oh, mayor, I am glad to hear that you admire my taste in who I hire. I certainly pride myself in being a good judge of character. You've been away, so you don't know the entire situation here. Miss Tessa is a pretty little thing and she's a good waitress. Keeps the tavern running smoothly, even if she is not all too generous with her kindness. She's lovely to look at and that's why she's here. Whet everyone's appetite a bit. But the thing is, she's doesn't exactly satisfy customers outside of the kitchen. And I won't have my customers unsatisfied. It would ruin my reputation. She stays in the kitchen. She'll bring you your food and Hannah will be waiting."

I hadn't expected her protection. I exhaled and scampered off to the kitchen for a new plate of ham and cabbage, vowing to do my best from now on.

* * * * *

After I was finished working, I lay awake in bed. My eyes drifted to the empty bed next to me—Hannah's bed. She was with the mayor now. I felt responsible. I felt sick. I tried to tell myself that the mayor—and other clients— weren't like Wrack. Hannah had chosen this life—though I am sure poverty forced her decision. Still, she never complained.

I rolled over and tried not to think about Hannah and the mayor. I tried not to think about anything.

A loud crack sounded from down in the tavern. I heard a woman scream then raised male voices, then sounds of a scuffle. Another crack sounded. Then another.

"Was that a gunshot? That was a gunshot," a girl two beds away said.

"Where's Mother Ivy?"

"Hide under your bed!"

"Everyone calm down," I shouted over the commotion. "We need to figure out what's happening."

"There was a gunshot. I heard a gunshot!"

"Ladies, sit down." Mother Ivy appeared in the

doorway holding a candle. She, too, was in her nightdress. "It would seem that something violent is happening down in one of our rooms. Now who are we missing?"

"Hannah!" I told her. "Hannah is with the mayor."

"Anyone else?"

The girls still clung to each other, screaming and crying.

Mother Ivy raised her voice. "Sit down on your own bed so we know who is downstairs. You have sisters in trouble. Sit down now!"

Everyone sat.

She noticed two empty mattresses.

"That one's Hannah's." I pointed to the empty mattress next to mine.

Mother Ivy turned her attention to the other empty bed. "Is this bed Penelope's?"

Penelope was a curvy girl, no more than fifteen.

Thundering footsteps pounded up the stairs and Penelope entered the dormitory a second later.

Mother Ivy hustled the girl into the room. "What's happening?"

Penelope took a deep breath, "A man broke in. I think he's going to kill the mayor."

"Liam!" Mother Ivy yelled. "Liam!"

The boy appeared.

"Liam, get the muskets. One for me, one for you." Liam ran down the hall and Mother Ivy followed him.

Penelope fell to the floor in hysterics, babbling about a man with a gun. The other girls huddled around her, trying to comfort her.

"Where's Hannah? Did you see Hannah?" I asked.

Penelope pressed her eyes closed, black tears smearing down her face. "Oh, Hannah. Hannah was in there when the shots went off."

I rushed off, ready to rescue my friend. I had no idea

how I would do such a thing, but my legs were in action before my brain was.

Hearing voices, I halted halfway down the stairs where I could listen while staying hidden from view.

"It's not my fault!" It was the mayor. He was pleading.

An angry voice roared back, "The way I see it, this is your island. You're responsible for everything that happens on it. Everything."

I heard glass break and the sounds of fists landing. There was tumbling and moaning.

"You have one chance before I pull the trigger and blow a hole in your neck so big you won't be able to scream as you die. Tell me what this is!"

The mayor was stammering, crying, really. Finally he said, "It's a piece of silk. I've never seen it before."

"What became of the owner?"

"The owner? I have no idea what you're talking about."

"Wrong answer," the voice seethed.

Something flitted across the floor and came to rest at the bottom of the staircase. It was my sleeve. My blue silk sleeve. The one I had attached to the fruit tree in the jungle.

I flew down the stairs and picked it up to make sure. Yes, it was my sleeve. Only one person would recognize it for what it was.

It took me a moment to make sure. With knee-high boots, a velvet red coat, and a tricorn hat, he looked strikingly different from the stripped-down sailor I dreamt of every night. But it was still him. The tawny skin. The wild, sun-streaked curls. The strong jaw and chiseled cheeks. They were clenched with malice now—a look I had never seen on my Nicholas before.

The barrel of his pistol was nestled into the flesh of the mayor's neck and Nicholas's eyes were burring with fire. I rushed towards the men.

"No!" I screamed.

"Don't move or I'll shoot," Nicholas said to me without taking his eyes off his target.

I froze. "Don't shoot. It's me, Nicholas. It's Tessa."

At the sound of my name, his focus hitched and he looked at me. "Tessa?"

A sob burbled from me as I ran to him and buried myself in his chest. I heard his pistol clatter to the floor and his arms wrapped tightly around me.

"Tessa?" he said again. He sounded so confused.

"Yes. It's me, Nicholas, it's me."

He lifted my chin and gazed intensely in my eyes, his eyes still full of fire. Then he crushed me in his chest. "I found you," he murmured into my hair. "I found you. I found you."

My heart thudded loudly, his heart echoing next to mine. I noticed an audience forming around the edges of the tavern.

"Are you all right? Did they hurt you?" he asked frantically, pulling back to look me over.

"I'm fine, I'm fine," I reassured. "I can't believe you're here," I whispered, looking up into his face. His expression was a stoic mask, but his eyes glistened.

He nodded brusquely.

"I thought you were dead," I murmured.

Nicholas pulled me away, grabbing both of my shoulders and looking into my eyes fiercely, "I thought *you* were dead," he said gruffly. He pulled the piece of blue silk I clutched in my fist. I remembered that it was covered in blood. "I was going to tear this place apart until I found you—or whatever was left of you."

I looked at him with wide eyes, astounded at his fervor. "You came for me." Tears soaked my lashes and overflowed onto my cheeks. Nicholas gently wiped them away.

"I'll always come for you," he said with a crooked smile.

It seemed so impossible. I knew I would wake up any moment. I knew this had to be a dream. We stood in the dimly-lit tavern ignoring the frightened onlookers, just staring at each other, then hugging, then standing back and staring again. Nicholas worked just as hard as I did to convince himself that this was really happening.

Mother Ivy broke the spell. "Back to bed, ladies," she said as she unloaded her weapon. "Looks like Miss Tessa has the situation under control."

CHAPTER TWENTY-NINE

WHEN EVERYONE WAS SURE that Nicholas was sane and that I was glad to be with him—and it took quite a bit of convincing for the mayor to forgive Nicholas—our audience dispersed and the tavern grew quiet once again. I showed Nicholas to the kitchen where we could graze on baguettes and fruit by the fire. Like I had been a month ago, he was enthusiastic about the ample amounts of fresh food. We sat at a small table, nestling our chairs closely together.

In the hot glow of the fire, Nicholas stared at me unabashedly, a faint smile pulling up the corner of his mouth. Suddenly shy, I looked at my lap and smoothed my skirt, lamenting the shabby nightdress I was in. When I glanced up again, his stare was still unbroken. I tried to hold it, but couldn't. I fed another log to the stove and when I looked back at Nicholas, he still stared. Blushing, I challenged his gaze and felt its intensity. When I wanted to break the stare, I resisted, feeling the pull of his eyes, craving the intimacy it created. Nicholas entwined one arm around my waist, cupped the back of my neck with his other hand and pulled me to his mouth for a slow kiss that heated me from within.

He pulled back and smiled, "I suppose I should apologize for that. I just had to be sure it was really you."

I felt my cheeks flush and looked away.

Wanting to ask a million questions—not knowing where to start—I fiddled with a dry bread crust. "So," I finally said cracking a smile, "you're not dead then?"

"No." He was positively glowing. If I looked the way I felt, I knew that my glow exceeded his. My smile had not faded since his arms engulfed me.

"How did you manage that? How did you manage all of this?" I gestured towards the bordello, still shyly shading my eyes with my lashes.

He followed my gaze across the darkness and sighed softly. "Aye. They were fixin' to kill me, maroon me, or something else unpleasant, not exactly sure what, but I'm glad I did not find out. Did some talking, some negotiating—which included using my entire stock of gold to pay off every last man on the ship. Anyway, convinced 'em to leave me be. They dropped me off at a port where I, uh, *procured* a modified fishing ketch and some supplies. As soon as I could, I set sail to find you."

"Impressive." What a grave understatement.

"Not really," he smiled at me in fake modesty. My heart danced every time I dared to look in his eyes.

"I am certain it is a much more involved story than you are telling."

He shrugged.

"And they just let you go?"

"Gold goes a long way with pirates. And I told them you would curse the ship if they did not give me my way."

I laughed aloud. "Having a reputation as a witch has its advantages. So then what happened? You *procured* your own boat. How exactly did you get it?"

"Now that is a story I will *not* be telling you."

I frowned and pushed out my bottom lip. I figured he employed less than legal means, but he did not need to hide that from me. I understood.

"Oh, don't be like that, pet." He brushed my cheek gently. "That's not fair."

I continued to frown, reveling that I held some kind of control over him.

"I got off in Cumaná. Did some bargaining with a dissolute group of fellows, and got the ketch. I won't tell you more than that. Pirate stuff."

"It can't be that bad."

"And that's what I'll let you think. But Tessa, you know I am a pirate. There are things I have done that I will regret until the day I die. Things I never want you to know about."

"Are you afraid I will think less of you? I won't. I've been surrounded by pirates lately. I know what they're about," I gestured to the tavern.

He nodded quietly. "You know far more than you ought to. And you know I am a pirate—no surprises there. But there are details you don't need to know. Stories I will never tell."

The subject was closed for discussion.

I was more curious than I had ever been. I remembered the grisly scene on the deck of the *Banshee* when I had come out in the middle of a raid.

That was Nicholas's life.

He had done things like that. He would have killed the mayor if I had not stopped him. I knew his past was full of horrors. But I also knew that he was not like Wrack, or

Mayor Winslow, or the patrons I served in the tavern every day. Nicholas was different.

I thought about his boat moored in the harbor. He had given up so much for that boat—all of his money and a lifetime worth of work. What else had it taken? What price had he paid to come to my rescue yet again?

"But how did you know I was here?"

He stared into the fire. "I know these seas. Judging by the currents, I figured you'd be in this general area—if you survived your go in the jollyboat."

"Mmm," I nodded nonchalantly, trying to hide my awe at his persistence. "But how did you know that I was exactly here?"

He laughed loudly. It was a beautiful sound. "I didn't! I checked every bleeding island, every cay, every last sandbar in the area, looking for some sign of you. Looking for a bashed up jollyboat, a tar-covered hat floating on the water, bleached-out bones—anything that would tell me what happened to you."

"Did you really think you'd find," I swallowed, "bleached-out bones?"

"Nah," he said with a wink, "it takes months to bleach bones."

My eyebrows shot up.

"Honestly, though, I thought the worst."

"And you still looked? Even though you thought I was dead?"

He nodded stoically. "I had to know what happened and do whatever I could. Give you a burial or something. I mean, whatever did happen was my fault. I had to know. It consumed me."

"And you found me here."

"This is probably the eighth place I looked. I saw the boat right away," he gestured loosely towards the ocean.

"Anchored my ketch and came ashore for a better look. There was still food in the jollyboat. Bad sign. If there was a chance you were alive, I knew the food would be long gone by now."

"Hey!" I nudged him with my shoulder. "I found fresh food in the forest, thank you very much."

"I constantly underestimate you." He stared into my face. After a moment, he continued. "I searched the area and I found that bit of your dress on a tamarind tree. I was sure that was all I was going to find. Didn't know whether you'd been eaten by cannibals or what. But I knew I was on Winslow's island and I wondered if maybe you'd made it here to port. But with that bloodied fabric, I thought some dogs must've had their fun in the jungle with you. I was going to peel Winslow's skin off one strip at a time until he told me who'd done it." He chuckled softly but I knew he was not joking. "And you," he stroked my cheek, "how did you do it?"

I stared into the embers, thinking back to those dark days. "You were right about the currents. They carried me right here. I was in the boat for three days. I can't say how glad I am that you packed the sack of food and water."

He nodded in agreement.

"I saw the island on the third day, rowed towards it the best I could. Then, when I was close enough, I swam and pulled the boat along behind me."

Nicholas raised an eyebrow.

"I did! Don't you believe me?" I nudged him again.

"I didn't say a word."

"I'm stronger than you think." I said it proudly, stubbornly, knowing it was true.

Nicholas said nothing, just eyed me steadily. It seemed he completely agreed. He prompted me to continue.

"I thought I was marooned. I was scared to leave the beach—the boat—but I finally ventured into the jungle hoping to find food. Which I did. But I could not reach it. I cut the sleeve off my dress to mark the tree so I—"

"And you cut yourself," Nicholas added.

I nodded, absentmindedly touching the fresh scar on my left shoulder. "Well, I needed a way to find that tree again. So I cut the sleeve—and my arm, which explains the blood on the fabric—and hung it as a marker. The next day I fell ill. My cut was gravely infected. I had no idea whether I was alone on the island, but I was hoping I wasn't. I followed the coastline until I found a road. I was too exhausted to go any farther and just collapsed. Mother Ivy's young son found me. I was brought here and Mother Ivy has taken care of me ever since. I work for her to earn my keep."

Nicholas pulled back, his eyes growing stormy. "You work here?"

"What choice did I have? I have to earn my keep."

"There is always a choice, Tessa," Nicholas growled. "If I ever imagined you turning to prostitution for survival, I would have never sent you away."

"Oh! I work in the tavern. I serve food. I never have...I would not ever do...that..."

Nicholas exhaled slowly, his eyebrows relaxing. We both chuckled. I nuzzled close to him again.

He casually played with a strand of my hair. I analyzed his features. His face was stoic again, but something more was brooding underneath. He looked perfectly sculpted in the dying light of the fire. The golden flickering emphasized his high cheekbones and full, sculpted lips while deep shadows intensified the chiseled angles of his face. I was reminded of the first night I saw him in the lantern light. He was more breathtaking now than he had been then.

Abruptly, he stood, "Walk with me on the beach?" I slipped my arm through his.

Leaving the bordello, I tiptoed carefully on the cobblestone walks.

"No shoes?" Nicholas noted.

"Upstairs," I replied, turning to fetch them.

"Don't trouble yourself."

He scooped me into his arms and carried me to the sound of crashing waves.

CHAPTER THIRTY

NICHOLAS CARRIED ME OVER the dusty streets of
town and set me down once we reached the beach. It was
a clear night and a brilliant moon hung in the sky,
illuminating our way. The beach was peaceful, calm. The
lazy waves shimmered in the moonlight. A soft breeze
tousled my hair.

We walked hand in hand for several steps before
Nicholas stopped and faced me. His jaw was set and his
eyes were piercing.

"What is it?" I asked nervously.

"I've not had my fill of you yet, Tessa. Please, just stand
still and let me look at you."

His fingertips touched my face, traced the bow of my
lips, leaving a trail of fire in their wake. He tucked my hair
behind my ear, his fingers wandering from the hollow
behind my ear down the length of my neck. My breathing
grew shallow. I was dizzy with delight. His fingers trailed
down the length of my arm, sending a waterfall of chills
down my spine. Burning and chills. Fire and ice.

Leaning to whisper in my ear, Nicholas said softly,

"Don't move." His lips grazed my earlobe, then traced the line of my jaw, his hands circling my waist. Though I tried not to move, to be perfectly still as he requested, I couldn't help but tilt my head back, welcoming his kiss. I drew an unsteady breath that I hoped was masked by the sound of the waves.

He pulled my hand to his mouth where he tenderly kissed each of my fingertips, my palm, the inside of my wrist. He gently placed my arm back by my side and stood back, crossed his arms and looked at me from head to toe.

"Are you quite done?" I joked, though I was so breathless that I feared it sounded like a reprimand.

"Yes," he answered cockily. I longed for a different answer.

Not knowing how to react, I resumed our leisurely walk, keeping my eyes down. Nicholas matched my pace.

"What are you thinking?" I asked.

"I was just thinking that I came here to save you, but you didn't really need any rescuing."

"Are you mad? I've been dying to get off this island!"

"I can't believe how well you've managed. You found land. *Inhabited* land. You found food. You weathered storms. You got a job and have a place to stay and food to eat. Really, what do you need me for?"

"Well, maybe I do not need to be *rescued* because I am already safe and cared for, but I still need to get off this damn island!"

Nicholas gave a deep belly laugh. "This *damn* island? Never heard you talk like that before. I think these working ladies have influenced you!"

"Then take me away!" I threw my arms up and twirled. "Though I don't really know where to go."

Taking my hand and looking at me shyly, Nicholas said, "I have never seen London."

There was vulnerability in his reply. Knowing how assured and brazen he always had been, seeing his heart unguarded touched me. He was asking me to rescue him.

"London? Really?" I cried, amazed at his implication. He was declaring himself, willing to make a life with me.

He grinned wildly, obviously pleased by my reaction.

The dreamlike image of a caged Nicholas flashed through my mind. "Oh no," I muttered under my breath.

"What?"

I tried to get my thoughts straight. "The thought of you coming to London with me is exhilarating, but in all honesty, I don't think it would suit you."

His smile faded into an unreadable expression, though he matched my steady pace down the beach.

He thought I was rejecting him. Babbling, I tried to explain myself better, "It's not that I wouldn't like you to come to London. It's just that, I can't really imagine you *enjoying* London."

His tension eased. "Aye, I know it will be different. But it will be an adventure."

I said nothing. Things might be not be as bad as I imagined. I was not *that* girl anymore, that admiral's daughter, so it might be different.

"Isn't London what you wanted?" Nicholas asked after a moment.

The waves washed farther onto the sand. I gracefully sidestepped the encroaching tide to avoid getting wet.

"It makes the most sense for me to go back to London."

Nicholas looked at me carefully, trying to see what I would not say.

"Familiar places, familiar people. An easier place to start over. It makes the most sense," I repeated weakly.

He searched my face. "Is it what you want?"

I wasn't entirely sure. "I don't know. Is there somewhere else, here in the Caribbean we could go?"

The smile was back.

"No, probably not," he said still grinning.

I stared at him blankly. Was this a joke?

He laughed loudly at the confused look on my face. "See, Tessa, I'm a pirate. Or at least I *was* a pirate. And while you might be ever so forgiving in seeing past my rowdy youth, most local lawmen aren't so magnanimous. There's not a respectable island in the Spanish Main that doesn't have a price on my head."

I pursed my lips slightly, staring at the way the sand squished between my bare toes with each step. Dozens of crabs darted this way and that, giving the illusion of shifting sands.

He tilted his head down, trying to look at my face. "Tessa?" he asked.

"Hm?"

"Tell me what you are thinking."

"Just thinking about you. And me." I blushed at my boldness, glad for the camouflage of night.

"And what are those thoughts?"

"Just that in a way, we are both very much alone in this world. Nowhere to go. No one to belong to."

"I saved your life, so I think you belong to me," he teased. He lifted my chin and pressed his lips to mine.

"Fair enough," I countered back with a smile, "but if I belong to a homeless renegade, where does that leave me?"

He skipped in front of me excitedly, and walked backwards so he could face me as he spoke, "Does it really matter, Tessa? I have that ketch. That is all we need. We'll go to London. Just the two of us. It will be a fresh start. Whatever you're afraid of, don't be. Everything will be fine."

He stopped walking and took both of my hands in his. His words tumbled out breathlessly. "Look, I don't know everything. I haven't got it all figured out yet. I don't know what you came from, or what you expect. But I think we fit. You and me. Two homeless renegades. Belonging to no one but each other. And, so, we will make our fate as we go. That is all I can promise. But it's all that I want."

"Nicholas," I started, unsure of the pounding heart in my chest, "back in London, I knew everything. I knew my place. I knew the type of person I would marry, what kind of vocation he would have, where I was likely to live. I knew every step I would ever take."

Nicholas stared at me intently, eager for my response.

I paused for a deep breath then continued. "That all changed when my father died. It's been so unsettling not knowing what the future holds. I have nothing. No one. I gave my life up as a lost cause, thinking I would die any moment. Now, it is as though you have given it back to me. And it's like...it's like an unopened gift. I don't know the next move anymore. It is still unsettling, I can't deny that. But..." Nicholas dropped his head slightly, peering more earnestly into my eyes, "...making our own fate. I like that." I smiled broadly and confidently repeated my new conviction. "We will make our fate as we go."

He planted a swift kiss on my lips, then began running down the beach, pulling my hand. "Come see my boat!"

CHAPTER THIRTY-ONE

LAUGHING, WE RAN HAND in hand down the moonlit beach, the gentle waves splashing in our wake.

"Why didn't you anchor in the harbor?" IS asked.

"The jollyboat's there," he pointed. "That's where I started my search. Besides, she's small enough that she moors just fine in shallow waters. Look at her. Isn't she great?" Nicholas was beaming.

We splashed through the tide and climbed the jack ladder up the side of the ship to the deck. Nicholas bounded across the ship's waist, throwing his arms wide in presentation.

Still catching my breath I managed to gasp, "It's wonderful."

A single deck stretched the entire length and width of the ketch. Though it was easy to see that the vessel was old and worn, it was well taken care of. The boards of the deck were scoured clean with tar tightly sealing every seam. It looked as though it had once been painted black, but it was faded to a charcoal grey. Two masts stretched from the deck. The canvas sails had been patched in several places. I fingered the massive spokes of the ship's wheel, located towards the aft of the vessel. I imagined the days ahead, Nicholas—or possibly even myself—at the helm, the endless turquoise seas, gulls crying overhead with a hearty ocean wind filling the sails.

Nicholas opened a hatch in the deck and climbed down a ladder. I followed without bidding. I squinted into the darkness, trying to make out my surroundings. The ladder led into an opening that extended the width of the ketch— a foyer of sorts. I could barely stand erect without grazing my head on the low ceiling. Nicholas had to hunch to navigate the room.

A glassed-in porthole on either side let the bright moonlight in. A large, square, wooden table was bolted to the floor. Nicholas opened the two doors on the forward side of the foyer. The starboard door revealed a roomy galley with a small, iron stove, mismatched cupboards, and crates that served as chairs. The portside door concealed a small cabin full of crates and barrels.

Two doors similarly graced the aft side of the wide foyer, opening into two spacious cabins. Aside from the furniture secured to the walls and floor—a chest of drawers, and a desk—one cabin was entirely bare, though three portholes made it very welcoming. The other cabin was obviously Nicholas's quarters. Though identical to the room next door, it was fully furnished. I was surprised to see a four-poster bed piled with blankets and pillows. A plush, though tattered, armchair sat in the corner. Wrought-iron sconces dotted the walls.

"This is beautiful," I breathed.

Nicholas beamed as he grabbed an armful of pillows and blankets off the bed, then hurried up the ladder to the deck. His energy was contagious and I found myself following his every move with laughter and excitement.

"Here," he said, picking a spot on the deck and tossing

the bedding down. "Perfect for stargazing." He plopped onto the pillows and gestured for me to join him.

I nestled into the comfortable pile and Nicholas wrapped an arm around me, tucking a soft blanket under my chin. I laid my head on his chest.

"What a clear night," I murmured staring at the gilded sky.

He absentmindedly stroked my hair. "Mmm," he agreed.

"So many stars."

It felt so natural lying in his arms. My heart beat placidly, my breathing easy. It felt like home.

"Sometimes when I look at the stars, I think of my mother."

"How old were you when she passed?"

"It happened when I was born. I never knew her."

"I'm sorry."

"Some people say that it was better that way—that I wasn't old enough to remember her or miss her. But in some ways it is harder. Maybe I do not know exactly what I miss about her, but I still do. And there aren't any memories to help fill that void of what she would have been to me."

"You know, many cultures believe that the stars represent those who have passed on," said Nicholas. "A sky full of angels. It seems to me you've done the same. What a beautiful way to memorialize her."

"I like that."

I was captivated by the beauty of the million twinkling lights above. It seemed so wrong that just a few nights ago I found the stars cold and harsh. I felt sorry for that thought and somehow wanted to apologize to the stars above for thinking such a thing. "There is nothing more beautiful than the stars at sea."

"I can think of one," Nicholas whispered, pulling me closer.

I snuggled even deeper into his side, sighing with happiness.

"I have always heard that sailors use the stars."

"Most definitely."

"How?"

He pointed out a constellation—a bowed line of stars. "Do you see those stars?"

I shifted until my face was right next to his so I could see where he pointed. Our closeness made my heart flutter. Trying to concentrate, I followed the line his finger made. "Yes."

"And then here," he traced a square at the end of the line of stars.

I nodded.

"That is the starry plow, though others call it by different names—the Butcher's Cleaver, Churl's Wagon, the Great Cart. The Dutch call it the *steelpannetje*—the saucepan. It is part of the Ursa Major constellation."

"I see it!" I said happily, seeing the shape of the seven bright stars. "But I have to say it looks more like a saucepan than a plow."

"Look here, where the two stars form the edge of the plow—or the edge of the pan, if you will."

I nodded.

"Follow the line those stars make," he drew an imaginary line along edge of the pan to a brilliant star blazing in the sky, "and then you find Polaris."

"The North Star."

"Aye. The most important star in the sky to any sailor." He adjusted slightly so he could look at me. I continued to stare at the sky. I worried that if I took my eyes off the constellation, I wouldn't find it again. More than that, I was afraid that if I looked at Nicholas, every coherent thought would fall out of my brain, and I was enjoying this moment far too much for that.

"Why?"

"It never moves; it is always directly north. Helps any navigator determine their latitude—how far north or south they are. Explorers have used it for centuries. Anyone can set a course by that star—it never fails. I've always thought of her as my angel in the night. Keeping me on my course, never letting me down."

I nestled closer, laying my head back on his chest. Nicholas cradled me there against his heart, tucked securely under his chin. I could feel the soft rumble of his speech and the steady thrum of his heart. It was a comforting feeling. Staring at the North Star, in the warmth of his arms, I thought of the moment I met Nicholas and all that transpired since. I remembered the many times Nicholas had been there for me, never letting me down, even when I doubted him. *My* angel in the night. And though I couldn't know what would happen tomorrow—if I would be dining extravagantly or choking down hardtack—I did know that I could set my course by him. He would be my North Star.

With the countless stars glittering around us, I felt as if we were the only two people in the universe. We talked late into the night, sharing secrets, telling jokes, watching as the swollen moon glided across the sky. I didn't want the moment to end. But I realized that when we set sail, my dream would come true—every night would be like this. We really would be the only two people in the universe. This moment would last forever.

CHAPTER THIRTY-TWO

WE REMAINED ON THE island for three more days. Nicholas had tentatively mapped out our voyage. We were much farther south than I had imagined—about a dozen leagues off the coast of New Granada. Because I was British and Nicholas was a wanted pirate, we would be unwelcome in most of the ports along the Spanish Main. Our only choice was to make port at pirate havens. This still held some danger since Nicholas had been branded a mutineer and a deserter and I would be—as he put it—a desired commodity among such immoral company. But we would only port as often and as long as absolutely necessary.

Our first stop would be Curaçao where we would stock up on supplies. Though Nicholas had used most of his gold to buy his freedom and had little to barter with, he was sure we could figure something out. I was afraid he meant stealing, but I didn't dare ask. He knew I didn't approve of such things, but because our survival depended on it, I did not pry. I convinced myself that ignorance was indeed bliss. If I was unaware of illegal activity, I couldn't be upset about it. We would continue north, stopping in New Providence for supplies, then aim for Bermuda. From there, we would sail to London.

We had two options for establishing a life in London. The first was for Nicholas to sign on with a merchant ship. No one in London knew he was a pirate, so it should be easy enough for him to gain employment, especially as a seasoned seaman and a trained carpenter. Or—and this was the option that I rather preferred—I could solicit help from my father's associates in helping Nicholas establish a carpentry shop. If we were unhappy there, we'd set sail and try again somewhere else.

Mother Ivy was quite generous and gave us plenty of food stocks for our journey. She told me I had earned it. With the help of Liam, Nicholas and I scoured the island and found things we could use for bartering in ports. We loaded the ketch with beautiful shells, natural fibers, and piles of coconuts.

When the day of our departure arrived, I hugged all the girls from the bordello and even Mother Ivy. I saved my goodbye for Liam until the last.

"Goodbye," I whispered, my voice cracking. "You were a true friend to me."

"I don't want you to go," he said, trying to be brave.

"Don't forget me. I will never forget the handsome, brave man who saved my life."

Liam smiled tensely and I could see moisture welling in his dark eyes. He pulled something out of his pocket—a necklace he'd made from beautiful shells and carved wooden beads.

"It's lovely. Here, help me put it on."

Liam slipped the necklace over my head and quickly kissed me on the cheek.

"Thank you." I kissed his cheek and made him blush.

With my farewells said, we climbed aboard the ketch,

and Nicholas unfurled the sails and hoisted the anchor. We drifted out with the tide. I waved and waved to Liam, who was perched on the promontory watching us sail away.

Nicholas was able to man the small ketch himself. I found myself admiring him as he climbed into the rigging and set the sails to catch the wind. He had such strength yet moved as easily as a bird on the wing. The wind tossed his hair and whipped his shirt, and I blushed when I caught myself staring at his well-muscled chest.

Once the sails were set, Nicholas led me to the helm. Standing behind me and guiding my hands, he helped me steer the ketch into the bright sea before us.

"Now, as a matter of ceremony, we have to sing," Nicholas announced as he turned the wheel.

"Sing?"

"Aye, pet. Bad luck if we don't sing a sailing song as we set out from the harbor."

"Like an invocation hymn?" I asked naively.

Nicholas laughed loudly. "I'm sorry. Did not mean to laugh at you. You are just so...you're quite endearing. No, we need to sing a chantey. A sailing song."

Slightly embarrassed, I muttered, "I'm not familiar with any chanteys."

"I will teach you. Most chanteys are designed to allow sailors to coordinate their strength to the rhythm of the song to get tough jobs done."

I nodded, familiar with the nearly constant, boisterous singing heard upon any ship.

"But there are a few other special chanteys," Nicholas continued. "Those sung only when sailing home and those sung only during departure. This one is a fine sailing song. It celebrates the adventure waiting for us. And it's suitable enough for a lady's ears," he added with a wink.

With no hesitation he belted out his song:

Set us out to sea, my boys
Western winds are blowin'
Fill the sails and ride the waves
Ain't no need for rowin'

Blow Ye Winds
And Take Me Away
Across the Seven Seas
Hey! Hey!
Blow Ye Winds
Not a Finer Day
Across the Seven Seas
Hey! Hey!

Set upon the blue, my boys
Can you say what's yonder?
Ain't no need to stop just yet
There's a big world to wander

Blow Ye Winds
And Take Me Away
Across the Seven Seas
Hey! Hey!
Blow Ye Winds
Not a Finer Day
Across the Seven Seas
Hey! Hey!

"You know," I said looking at him over my shoulder, "your sailor's accent grows much thicker when you sing chanteys."

He quickly kissed the top of my head, "Aye, me beauty," he said in a brogue so heavy I could hardly understand him, "not but once in a g'while that a swabby be unfetterin' th' canvas an' catchin' a hearty wind by the lee to seek 'is fortune upon th' briny deep with such a pert lass on his arm."

I laughed into the wind.

"Nay, me ducky, you'll not be distractin' me so easily. It be your turn to sing."

I groaned good-naturedly and let Nicholas lead me in song. There was something freeing about standing at the helm, belting into the wind, singing a song that hundreds of seamen had sang before me, a song meant to herald grand adventures and welcome the unknown.

After finishing a second round of the chantey, I left the helm and leaned back against the bulwarks. Nicholas stayed at the wheel. His hair blew freely about him. His eyes shifted from the vast horizon to the sails above, his practiced hands turning the heavy spokes of the helm as necessary. He sang quietly to himself, and grinned like a child when he caught me staring.

"I have never seen you like this before," I said to Nicholas.

He smiled as if he did not know what I was talking about. "Like what?"

"Look at you. You could not stop smiling if I promised you Rome."

As if to prove my point, his smile grew wider. "No need to promise me Rome. I already have everything."

"What do you mean?"

He looked knowingly at the never-ending sea. He closed his eyes and turned his head up. His face held the look of pure serenity—like a patron saint worshipping the sun.

Then he looked calmly at me. "This is it, luv. This is the greatest day of my life."

"Setting sail is just that exciting, isn't it?" I agreed, a grin playing on my lips, as I looked across the azure waters.

"That it is," he affirmed. "There's nothing quite like a strong wind in the sails and the sun shining on your face. But that is not what I said. I said that this is the greatest day of my life."

"Today? The greatest day of your *entire* life?" I looked again at the sea and the sky, trying to determine what made this voyage so particular.

"So far."

He grinned wildly. His grey eyes shone in the sun. I looked at him curiously, waiting for an explanation.

"Like you said, setting sail is always exciting. But today is different. For the first time in my life, I'm a free man. It's just me. And my ketch. I have my own ketch!" he practically shouted. He bounded to my side gleefully, turning me to look across the water. He swept an arm across the scenery. "I can go where I want, do what I please. It's a freedom I've never known." Nicholas stared into my eyes. "And there's you. Standing there like you don't even know you are the greatest gift the sea ever gave me."

He nodded once, a confident, satisfied gesture. "No, I can't say I have ever seen a finer day."

CHAPTER THIRTY-THREE

ALONE WITH NICHOLAS—REALLY, really alone—for the first time, I found myself nervous. It seemed rather impious to be sharing such close quarters without a chaperone. Nicholas found this particularly hilarious when I explained my sudden shyness.

It was nothing Nicholas did or said. He was a perfect gentleman, even before I admitted my apprehension. Nicholas had insisted I sleep in the furnished cabin while he took the cabin next door. And though we indulged in many passionate kisses, he was always the first to pull away, more easily satisfied than I.

I tried to help with the chores as much as I could, but I hardly knew what to do with myself. Despite what I had learned in the tavern, I was a horrid cook. It was easy enough to pour rum and boil water, but anything beyond that took Nicholas's expertise. He seemed more than happy to fill the role of caretaker. From cracking coconuts, to constantly tending the lines and the sails, he seemed to radiate joy in all the tasks that his newfound freedom required.

I admit that I followed Nicholas around like a puppy, but by watching him I learned to make myself useful. After seeing him scour the deck with salt water and a holystone two days in a row, I decided to start on the chore while he was aloft in the lines, reefing the sails. I hauled up a bucket of water from the ocean, retrieved a holystone, plopped onto my hands and knees, and began scrubbing.

When Nicholas came down to the deck, he glared in disapproval. "What are you doing?"

"I thought I would help," I said timidly, surprised by the reprimand in his voice.

"I don't need help." His stern look softened when he saw the hurt in my face. "I mean, thank you, but really, leave it alone and go rest."

I sat back on my heels, and pushed a stray lock of hair away from my face with the back of my hand. "I don't need to rest. I want to help."

"I have it under control." I could tell he was trying to spare my feelings.

"I know you do, but I really want to do my share."

"You do plenty," he argued feebly, then noting my furrowed brows he beamed, "You keep me company."

"I refuse to be completely helpless," I insisted with a sigh.

"I don't want you feeling helpless, it's just..." he trailed off.

"Am I getting in your way?" I asked, suddenly realizing that the answer might be yes. I dreaded being unhelpful, but more than that, I would hate making things worse just by being here.

"No, you are fine."

"Am I doing it wrong?" I eyed the wet boards surrounding me and the holystone in my hand. It had not looked complicated when Nicholas scoured the deck, but it was my first attempt at anything like this. I could be ruining the ship for all I knew.

"No, Tessa, it isn't that. Just...don't. Just get up and stop scouring the deck."

He pulled me up by the arm and took the holystone from my hand, tossing it aft. His arms snaked around my waist, pulling me close.

"I'm a sailor. This is what I do. Let me do it."

"What am I supposed to do?"

He raised his eyebrows as he looked at me and said, "I don't know. Whatever it is that ladies do."

I pushed away from his chest, taking a small step back. "What is it you think ladies do? Laze about and stare at the ocean all day? I am not useless." A hint of sarcasm touched my voice.

"Tessa, believe me, I *know* you are strong. It's nothing to do with that. I just don't want you working like that."

"Why not?" I grumbled.

Nicholas pulled me close to him again. I put on a show of resisting him, but let him wrap his arms around me. "You are fixed on defying me, aren't you? I know you can do it. But I just really want to take care of you—" I opened my mouth to protest, but he pressed his finger against my lips and continued, "I know you don't need me to take care of you, but *I* need it. Please. Just let me."

His grey eyes glistened with nothing but affection. I couldn't resist. I surrendered with a hug. "Fine. I won't scour the deck. But I can't do *nothing*. I get so bored when you are working."

"I don't want you to be unhappy. But you won't scrub floors like a scullery maid. Maybe you could mend the sails. Something less physically taxing? We will sail into Curaçao in four days and I promise we will purchase some things that will make life at sea more pleasant. Books and sewing and anything you want. Sound reasonable?"

"I suppose," I said, still moping a bit. "It's just that scouring the deck seemed easier than cooking."

Nicholas laughed and hugged me tighter. "There's no winning, is there?" He planted a swift kiss on the top of my head then dashed aloft to tighten a luffing sail.

That night when I presented Nicholas with a dinner of bland boiled fish, I couldn't help adding, "Bet you wished I'd finished the deck while *you* cooked."

He ate the fish heartily and never complained.

* * * * *

Though I complained of boredom—Nicholas allowed me to help with very little—the weeklong trip to Curaçao was a happy one. Compared with the confinement in Nicholas's cabin aboard the *Banshee*, my imprisonment in the brig, being aimlessly adrift in a jollyboat, stranded on an island, and working among prostitutes, I was now in paradise.

The daily workings of the ketch intrigued me and I peppered Nicholas with hundreds of questions. I admired his agility as he climbed the ratlines, secured the sails, shimmied down the masts, tied knots, and performed a dozen other chores daily. He was strong, too. It was difficult not to stare at the way his arms hardened and rippled as he tacked the lines and managed the boom. He tried to teach me how to read the ocean—an art form as mysterious to me as a forgotten religion. All of nature is speaking, he would say. We just had to learn to listen. Despite his lessons, I could never see the invisible eddies Nicholas found so obvious or remember the significance of cloud height and shape. I surmised that sunshine and wind made Nicholas happy, therefore, they were good things.

I made peace with my idleness. I knew I was capable of helping more. And Nicholas knew it too. It wasn't that he *had* to take care of me. He *wanted* to. And I let him.

We decided to name the ketch the *Freedom*. Though Nicholas initially wanted to name it after me, I strongly objected, and we settled on a name that celebrated our liberation.

He kept to the sailor's schedule of never sleeping more than four hours at a time. I felt bad for the constant amount of work that he always needed to do, but he insisted that he loved it. Sailing was his calling and he said that he'd never had more fun at it. He claimed that sailing the ketch by himself was less work than he had ever done on the *Banshee*. I always felt guilty retiring to a full eight to ten hours of sleep each night in a comfortable four-poster bed knowing that Nicholas would keep working through the better part of the night.

I experimented in the galley constantly, trying to invent a delicious new delicacy. I made a type of scone with flour, water, coconut milk, and dried papayas. Dipped in molasses, my recipe masqueraded quite well as dessert.

When I wasn't wasting our supplies in the galley, I did my best to entertain Nicholas—I would fill his ears with idle prattle that he seemed to enjoy, and he taught me long-haul and short-haul chanteys. With no books to read, I recited verses from the Bible and recounted my favorite tales. Nicholas was quite taken with the story of Odysseus traveling home after the Trojan War. He requested that story often.

The days blurred together in a golden haze. The laughter, the work, the late-night revelations…each day was better than the last. On a boat so small with no one else to talk to, it was impossible to keep secrets. We saw each other at our worst and made each other better. An intimacy bloomed between us that could not have been born in any other way. Nicholas became my truest friend, my closest confidant, my partner, and my happiness.

I was in love with him.

CHAPTER THIRTY-FOUR

SEVERAL DAYS BEFORE WE were scheduled to reach Curaçao, a knock on my door woke me in the middle of the night.

"Nicholas?"

"Would you please come out?" he asked.

"Is something wrong?"

I squinted in the direction of the portholes. It was still dark.

"No. I just need to talk to you."

"Let me dress. I will be just a moment."

Concerned that something was amiss, I hastily threw on my tattered silk dress and hurried to the deck where Nicholas was standing at the helm with his back to me, staring into the distance.

I rushed to the other side of the wheel where I could look at him.

"Is everything all right?" I searched his face for the hovering doom that caused him to wake me in the middle of the night.

He looked surprised at my agitation and took my hand.

"Of course."

Still unconvinced, I scanned the horizon, looking for anything that might signal trouble. Nothing was out of place.

I turned back to Nicholas, confused. "You needed to talk to me?"

"Mm-hmm," he nodded casually and gestured to two wooden chairs he had arranged near the helm.

The setup briefly reminded me of the last time I had seen chairs arranged on the deck—at my trial. My foreboding deepened. I sat down nervously, unsure of what to expect.

I scrutinized his every move, hoping to glean some insight into why he summoned me. He was as casual as ever, gracefully sitting in his chair, then scooting it closer to me. I looked into his eyes, but he was looking somewhere else. I could not catch his attention. Did he even know what this was doing to me? My palms grew damp. Though the ketch wasn't in imminent danger, something was not right.

Nicholas held my face in his hands and kissed me slowly. I tried to discern any difference in this kiss, wondering if this was a kiss goodbye. Maybe I was just a bale of cotton after all, doomed to be left at port.

"Where are you, Tessa?" he whispered between kisses.

"Right here?" I answered uncertainly.

"No," Nicholas breathed into my ear, "you are not here with me. You are a hundred leagues away."

His lips found mine once more and though I kissed him back, I failed to mask my anxiety at this bizarre behavior.

"Tessa." Nicholas sat back in his chair and clasped his hands together.

I stared wide-eyed, bracing myself for the words that would come next. He must have realized that I had been right all along—that he did not belong in London. That he needed to stay here at sea. Our lives were too different. He would tell me that when we landed in Curaçao, it would be time to go our separate ways.

"I have been on my own a long time. A rat on the streets. A sailor on the sea. And a pirate officer after that. It has been a long time since I have answered to the laws of society or even thought about what anyone wanted but me. I do what I please and I take what I want."

I sat rigid in my chair, my hands tightly clenched in my lap. I reminded myself to breathe. My uneasy heart grew heavy, ready for the break that was coming next.

Nicholas finally seemed to see me and sense my worry. "Relax," he chuckled as he touched my knee. "You make me nervous."

Trying to be brave, I nodded vigorously. A little too vigorously, eliciting more laughter. How could he laugh at a time like this? I could understand his reasons for leaving, but did he have to be cruel? That was too much. I bit my lip to keep it from quivering.

Leaning towards me and taking my hand, he continued. "It occurred to me that I can't always be like that. It's not always about what *I* want."

I closed my eyes, ready for his final words.

"I need to do what is right by you. So I need you to tell me what you want."

My eyes flew open. "Wh-what *I* want?" I stammered.

He nodded, suddenly serious.

I replayed the words he said. I was not sure exactly what they meant, but I was fairly certain they did not mean goodbye. "I-I'm not quite sure I follow you." Maybe I was in too much shock to understand that he was letting me down softly.

His eyes locked securely with mine. "I want to be with you. I knew you were special from the moment I saw you and since then, every moment we have shared confirms that you're my north star. You are what I want to guide my journey by.

"Because of the life I've lived, I tend to act on my assumptions like they're gospel—like it's all that matters to everyone involved. But things are different now. So I need to know what you want. How do you feel about me...about us?"

He leaned back in his chair and waited, more serious than before.

Blowing out a sigh, I pushed my windblown hair from my face. "Nicholas! Do you know how much you worried me just now? I thought this was going to be something horrible."

A look of confusion flashed across his face. Then he realized what I had been thinking. He smiled apologetically. "I am sorry, I just..." he sighed, "I just did it again, didn't I? I figure out something I want—like talking to you about all this—and I discard everything else. As if this couldn't have waited until morning! I shouldn't have wakened you and I am so sorry for scaring you."

"It's all right," I smiled, still finding my emotional footing. "I'm glad you did. I admire your directness. It is refreshing in a world of ostentation and charades. I only hope that I can be as honest."

Nicholas visibly stiffened.

Now he was anxious. He had no reason to be. How could he not know that? It was so ridiculous, but as I was still recovering from my near heart attack, I found a small bit of satisfaction in his discomfort.

"Relax. Please. Now you are making *me* nervous. I just mean that I have spent so much time in that world of pretension that I find it very difficult to speak so candidly of my feelings."

I carefully weighed my words before I spoke, still

unnerved by my uncontrollable desire for the man that sat across from me. I desperately wanted to tell him how I felt. How I didn't want to spend another moment without him. How my entire future shone in his eyes. I wanted to tell him how special he made me feel and how afraid I was that I would be unable to make him feel the same way, and that he would tire of me eventually. My heart tattooed in my chest, and I grew too nervous to say a tenth of what I wanted.

"I agree with your sentiment and feel no differently." I regretted the words as soon as they were out. Though I wanted to check my longing somewhat, I sounded like I was finalizing a business venture.

Flashing a warm smile, Nicholas leaned in close to me and took my hand again. "Good. I want to do this right for you, but I don't quite know how. So I need you to tell me what to do."

He was nervous. I could tell from the softness in his voice, the hunger in his eyes. It was entirely endearing. My nerves returned and, again, I was apprehensive about what he would say next, although now it was a much different feeling.

"Do we...Should I...I mean...Do we need to marry?" he finally blurted. "You are just seventeen. I do not know if that is...if that is the right age...if you have other intentions. I just...I just...I just...I don't know. But I want to know. I *need* to know."

He seemed as if he was going to keep bumbling along and, as amusing as it was to see him as lost in love as I felt, I stopped him with a kiss.

CHAPTER THIRTY-FIVE

"Nicholas Holladay, did you just ask me to marry you?" I asked coyly.

Nicholas smiled crookedly, the gauzy moonlight illuminating his strong cheekbones. He flittered nervously. "No. I just asked you if I needed to ask you to marry me."

I thought that over, raising my eyebrows at his logic. "Oh. I see. Well, in that case, I suppose I do not need to answer."

A frustrated pain filled his eyes.

I teasingly slapped his arm. "If you want to ask me, then why don't you just ask me? Or maybe you don't really want to ask me. Maybe you think that you have to, and that's the only reason why." I scowled at him playfully, yet partially believing what I said.

"No, Tessa. It isn't that I feel *obligated*. I just wanna do everything right. And *if* I were to ask you, it would not be here on some old putrid fishing ketch in the middle of nowhere. Maybe in Paris. There would be dancing and jewels and romance. It would be perfect."

Reluctantly, I took my eyes away from his and took in my surroundings. A balmy zephyr breeze warmed the night. An endless sea of stars glittered across the sky. I sat next to the man I loved and we were the only two people in the universe.

"I cannot imagine a night more perfect than this," I whispered. "A sky full of diamonds. The ocean waves dancing against the ship. And you. It's really all I could ever ask for."

"But I am not asking," Nicholas insisted, a small smile on his full lips.

"I would say yes. But since you are not asking…"

Nicholas pursed his lips and scowled in mock annoyance.

"At least now there is no need for you to be so nervous next time," I offered in truce.

His face lit up. "That does help."

After a moment of comfortable silence, Nicholas said, "You still haven't told me what you want. I mean, before, you were a little apprehensive about being completely alone with me—"

"I'm fine now."

"I know. But still…You would be alone with me quite a lot. It's not the way things are usually done. And we are both a bit unusual ourselves, so I have no qualms. But I know it is not the life you always dreamt of. Just tell me what you want."

"Nothing sounds more wonderful than a hundred thousand days exactly like this."

"Good. Still…this is not what you dreamt about growing up. What I want to know is what you expected your future to be like. Back in London, before you met me. What were your expectations then?"

I rolled my eyes. I did not want to say. It didn't matter what I wanted then. This was bigger, this was more.

"Tell me," he insisted.

I stood and turned away.

"You really want to know? Fine, I'll tell you. Leisure. Vanity. Riches. That's what my life was going to be. Formal courtships. Dozens of suitors. I'd settle on the one who could offer me the most—an impressive income, a respectable profession...someone who could increase my status." I rattled off the words, knowing their sting. "He'd work endlessly, establishing an immaculate reputation for our family. I would busy myself with tea parties and concerts, forever entertaining the aristocrats of Europe. Eventually, there would be children. And life wouldn't be complete without a summer home on the banks. I would die an old woman, surrounded by wealth and reputation, but without a shred of passion in my life. Fairly standard dreams."

"Fairly standard," Nicholas repeated quietly to himself.

We waited in silence. I was afraid of what he was thinking.

"I want to know more," he said. "Tell me about your suitors. You've been courted before?"

"Nicholas, please," I begged. "This is nonsense. None of it matters anymore."

"I know," he said quickly, "Your expectations have changed. I understand. Mine are a lot different, too, compared to six months ago. I just want to know."

"Why?" I demanded. "You are comparing yourself to a life I do not even want."

He was taken aback. I must have unmasked his true intentions.

"I am not comparing," he defended, though I was unconvinced. "Knowing who you were then helps me understand you better now."

"Does it really? I don't compare myself to your past

conquests, and it hasn't seemed to hinder our connection."

"What?"

I should not have said that. I turned away, not wanting to answer, but knowing he would demand it.

"What past conquests?"

Nicholas stalked over to me, grabbing my arm and spinning me to face him. "What are you talking about?"

I pulled my arm from his grip. "I never pressed for details. But it was no secret that you frequented the bordello. All the girls knew your name."

"The bordello?"

"Charlotte," I said, watching for his reaction.

Nicholas groaned in vexation. "That trollop. She's just bitter because I never gave her any business. C'mon, Tess. I became quartermaster at eighteen. You really think I had time for conquests?"

"Frankly, I don't care to think about your past. I only brought it up because you refuse to let go of mine."

Nicholas gestured to the sails overhead. "Someday you will tire of this, Tessa. Maybe you'll tire of me."

"Are you insinuating that a fancy courtship and marriage proposal is all it will take to keep me by your side? To yoke me to you? You must think me so shallow."

I looked at him quizzically, eager for an explanation.

Nicholas pulled me to him and lightly kissed my forehead. "Goodnight, luv. It's time for me to go to bed. Again, I am sorry I woke you." He flipped over the sandglass kept near the helm to mark the passing of the hours.

Before I could argue, he bounded down the ladder and into his cabin.

"What? Wait!" I stormed after him. "You wake me up in the middle of the night, making me think something is terribly wrong. You propose marriage, then take it away.

You make me talk about things I would rather not think about. You question my loyalty. And then wish me a goodnight? We are not done talking."

Nicholas pivoted in his cabin. "It was very rude. I admit it and I apologize. But my watch is over and I have to sleep, or I will be worthless at sunrise."

"You cannot end our conversation like this."

"I'm exhausted, Tessa. We'll talk tomorrow."

"Remember when you said it was time for you to consider what others want? Well, I want to talk to you. Now."

Nicholas shrugged. He began unbuttoning his shirt, the soft cotton falling open over his chest. I covered my eyes and turned my back in shock.

"I really must go to bed," he said. "If you care to join me…"

I pounded to my room, slamming my door. "You're impossible!" I yelled. He never answered.

Nicholas was right—once he set his mind to something, there was little else anyone could do to stop him.

CHAPTER THIRTY-SIX

I SLEPT IN LATE the next day, avoiding Nicholas. I half expected him to bang on my door asking why I hadn't made breakfast. But he left me alone. I lingered in bed four bells into the forenoon watch—halfway through Nicholas's morning shift.

After dressing myself and plaiting my hair, I went to the galley and rummaged for something to eat. Finally, it was time for me to face Nicholas. I couldn't avoid him forever. And I didn't really want to—I was only hoping he would come to me first. I felt I deserved that.

Nicholas was nowhere to be found on deck. I wandered back to the lower deck, finding it strange that he would be asleep during his shift. The door to his room was ajar. I peeked inside, but didn't see him.

In turn, I looked through all the rooms on the second deck. Nowhere. I returned to the main deck and looked for him again, squinting up at the sales to see if he was aloft in the rigging.

Still no sign of him.

It took me a few moments to realize there was one place I hadn't looked—the bilge.

I had never even been in this ship's bilge, but it had to have one. I found a hatch to it in the storage cabin.

I lowered myself down the ladder and cringed slightly as the putrid bilge water immersed my bare feet. Nicholas was pumping the water out, making enough noise that he didn't hear me. I approached him slowly, not wanting to startle him.

It didn't help.

As soon as he saw me he visibly jumped. "Bloody hell, Tessa. What are you doing here? Go upstairs."

I grabbed the pump handle and pulled it down.

"I want to help."

"Not down here."

I continued to pump. Nicholas wiped beads of sweat off his forehead with the back of his sleeve then stood with his hands on his hips, glaring at me.

"Stop," he commanded.

He was not used to his orders being ignored. I relished in his frustration. I continued pumping, my arms already shaking with exertion.

Nicholas rolled his eyes. "I don't want your help. Go upstairs. Go…scour the deck."

I matched his glare. "Oh, so I am allowed to do that now?"

"Do whatever you want. Just…you can't be here."

Using all my energy to man the pump, I spoke in short bursts. "You promised…we would talk…so let's….talk."

He stood by idly, hoping I would give up. I refused.

"We'll talk later."

"We'll…talk…now."

He snorted. "All right. Go ahead."

"You're a…conceited…dolt."

"What? I'm a *dolt*?"

"Don't…interrupt…me….Not finished."

Nicholas stepped forward and halted the pump handle. "Stop. We'll talk."

Breathing heavily, I let go of the pump. "You're a dolt."

"You said that already."

I crossed my arms. "I told you to stop interrupting me. If you want to know the truth about suitors and courting, I'll tell you. There's a gentleman in London, the son of a banker, actually, who was quite fond of me. It broke his heart when I moved away. He actually asked me to stay behind, promising to make me his wife."

Nicholas looked away, his mouth pressed into an angry line.

"I refused him. Obviously. I'm here. And he's not the only one. Perhaps the most serious…the most recent…but there have been others."

I paused, waiting for a response. Nicholas held his tongue.

"I'm telling you this so you know that I have options. I'm telling you this so you know that I am choosing you. Because I want to be with you."

Nicholas shook his head and sighed, finally meeting my gaze. The line of his mouth had pulled into a frown. "I acted foolishly last night. I'm acting foolishly now. You really deserve much more than this." His gaze strayed to the bilge water lapping my ankles.

"It's nice that you think so," I replied. "But it would be nice if you would believe in my feelings for you."

A smile tugged at Nicholas's lips and his cheeks flushed pink. "I'm a dolt, Tessa. A right fool. I'm so crazy for you that I can't think straight. I can't even trust my own damn judgment anymore. Everything I've done for you has turned in to a mess."

"This isn't a mess," I reassured him, looking around. I shifted my weight and water splashed at my ankles.

"Well, the bilge is, but that's all. I've never been happier. *You've* never been happier. See beyond your paranoia and just enjoy it."

Nicholas laughed then, a healing kind of laugh that let me know everything was all right.

"I've been down here all morning to punish myself for how I treated you last night. I guess all I really had to do was realize I am a conceited dolt."

I grasped the pump handle again. "May I have a little help?"

"You need to go upstairs."

I began pumping. "You need to...learn to...honor my...decisions."

He chuckled again, and then joined me at the pump.

CHAPTER THIRTY-SEVEN

CURAÇAO WAS BREATHTAKING. SHOCKING pink, yellow, and azure buildings topped with terracotta roofs decorated the streets of Willemstad, the island's capital. Wide streets branched into quaint alleys and small manicured parks. Tented markets dotted the cobblestone courtyards, their goods proudly on display. Freshly mined salt. Textiles in every color of the rainbow. African slaves. Corn and peanuts. People of various sizes and colors, speaking different languages—Nicholas identified Dutch, Portuguese, Spanish, and indigenous—crowded the streets, creating an alchemy of exotic excitement and instant belonging.

Although it was easy to melt into Curaçao's bustling diversity, Nicholas was on guard. He wrapped his arm firmly around my waist, and kept me as close as possible. He explained that this affluent Dutch island had little to offer in natural resources but with its natural harbors, it made an excellent trade port. It was a haven for traders of all nationalities—as well as smugglers and pirates. Although Willemstad did not offer the best prices in the

Caribbean, it had absolutely everything. And that included its share of criminals.

After unloading our excess cargo onto the docks and exchanging our goods to the highest paying merchant, Nicholas led me into the trade district of Willemstad. As promised, our first stop was at a bookstore of sorts.

I browsed the inventory of books, most of them used and tattered. I caressed the leather-bound volumes of familiar favorites and thumbed through the stiff pages of foreign texts. I instinctively selected a sturdy copy of *The Holy Bible*, something both Nicholas and I viewed as a necessity on a ship. Though I had been raised with strict religion—church every Sunday, daily prayers, and Bible study—Nicholas revered the divine in a way that only a sailor could. Maybe it had to do with the constant reminder of mortality on an unpredictable sea, but God and religion were something that no sailor looked upon lightly.

I smiled to myself when I spied a copy of *The Odyssey* and quickly snatched it up. I found a volume of Chaucer's *The Canterbury Tales* in fair condition and added it to my pile. I selected a volume of blank pages to use as a diary and sketchpad, several quills and ink wells, and a small hymnal. Nicholas arranged the trade, shrewdly bargaining a decent price.

Next, we visited the grocer and bought a month's worth of cooking supplies including flour, sugar, raisins, honey, molasses, dried fruit and beans, smoked beef, tea, and rum. I thought it impossible that thirty days worth of meals would come from that handful of ingredients. Nicholas assured me that we would supplement with fresh fish we caught along the way and I felt a little better.

Clothing was next. A black woman with a French accent greeted us as we entered the dress shop. She piled bolts of various fabrics before me. I breathlessly admired the China silks and French brocades, envisioning the lovely gowns they could be transformed into. I was accustomed to the finest of things in England—all my gowns were specially made—yet I had never seen so many beautiful fabrics in one place. Nicholas instructed me to select anything I wanted, and while I was naturally drawn to the finest of fabrics and laces, I attempted to be frugal. I was no longer the admiral's daughter. I was now a renegade like Nicholas, which meant I could not afford silk.

The shopkeeper helped me select two ready-made cotton blouses and two practical linen skirts. Stockings, shoes, bonnets, gloves, undergarments, petticoats, a corset, and nightclothes completed my new wardrobe.

The shopkeeper quickly measured my proportions, then set about finishing the hems of my new garments. While we waited, Nicholas selected several items for himself and we were on our way.

We finished our shopping trip with necessary incidentals for the ketch such as a supply of holystone, canvas fabric and heavy thread for repairing the sails, ammunition for Nicholas's pistol, and tar for sealing the deck.

"There is an inn a few blocks away where we can eat and rest up," Nicholas said.

We had been in Curaçao for the better part of the day and I was growing weary from walking under the blaring sun. I was ecstatic to learn we would dine at an inn instead of choking down more hardtack on the ketch.

We reached the inn as the day's shadows were lengthening. The Spanish-style building was at least three stories tall, easily the largest on the street. I admired the soaring arches and intricate details of the unique architecture. Burning torches in black metal sconces encircled the entire exterior in a ring of fire. It was glorious. The building held an air of majesty and foreign culture. Despite all of England's cathedrals and quaint cottages, there was something more grand and beautiful in the lines of this Spanish inn. I could not peel my eyes away from the rustic wood accents and Spanish tapestries that hung on the walls as Nicholas made arrangements with the innkeeper.

"Tessa," Nicholas called, beckoning me to come to him. He was speaking with an aging Spaniard.

"He'll show us to our room," Nicholas interpreted.

"Our room?"

"Aye."

"We are not returning to the ship?"

"We deserve a night away from the ketch. Hot baths, warm food, soft bed. Hope that's all right with you."

"Mmm," I moaned happily, anticipating those delights.

"If you'd rather return to the ketch…" he teased.

"Not after you just promised me a hot bath."

We followed the innkeeper up a flight of stairs to a corner room. He opened the door widely and welcomed us. *"Bienvenido."*

Nicholas conversed with him in Spanish, then handed the man a silver coin.

"He'll send maids to fill the tub," Nicholas translated as he closed the door.

"I did not know you spoke Spanish."

He unloaded the armful of packages onto a table near the door. "Aye. I'm basically fluent in Spanish and French. Dutch and Portuguese? I can get by if I need."

"Whoa," I murmured under my breath, although I did not know whether I was responding to Nicholas's lingual abilities or to the beautiful room around me.

The spacious room was bathed in the warm candlelight of several ornate candelabra. I slowly caressed a beautiful side table carved from dark wood. Polished teak floors gleamed beneath my dirty bare feet. A raised, arched ceiling rose gracefully overhead. My fingers danced over the pitted texture of the stucco walls. Two oversized beds with thickly quilted linens flanked an arched doorway leading to a small balcony. I peeked behind a wicker partition to see the bathing and vanity area I had never been more excited to see a tin bathing tub, a washing bowl, and a portrait-sized mirror.

My mouth fell open as I stared at all the luxuries around me.

Nicholas chuckled softly as he took my hand and pulled me to sit with him on the bed.

"You are an admiral's daughter—I *know* you have seen this kind of comfort before."

I threw myself on the bed, swimming in the soft covers. "I think I'd forgotten. Besides, look at the architecture. It is amazing. I have never seen anything like it."

I sat up at the sound of a soft tap at the door. Nicholas let in two maids, each with steaming buckets of water. We wandered to the balcony while the ladies filled the bath.

The lights of Willemstad twinkled in the early gloaming. Vendors were closing their shops, locking away their goods, and preparing for the night. The laughter of drunken men spilled through the streets and ladies of the night called to them. In the distance, I could see the masts of the ships moored in the harbor and the churning blackness that was the ocean beyond.

"What was it like, coming into port?" I asked Nicholas, thinking of all the revelry below.

"Always exciting. We'd celebrate for days. The boys would get drunk beyond belief. Not I. I learned early on to stay sober and stop by at the gaming houses with the lushes—bettered my odds," he winked at me.

My thoughts drifted again to the women selling themselves in the streets below. "Did you ever...have anyone special?"

"Of my many conquests, you mean?" He nudged me playfully.

"I'm sorry. I shouldn't have asked. You need not answer."

"See? Sometimes you just need to know."

I nodded, expecting Nicholas to chastise me for my question. To my surprise, he answered me.

"Plenty of sailors are like that. Doesn't sit right with me, though. I never felt that gettin' sloshed and mingling with ladies of the night was the right thing to do. That's what happened to my mother. Never felt right about things like that."

"What do you mean that's what happened to your mother?"

Nicholas continued to stare at the activities below. He smiled faintly, but his eyes were sad.

"She was the daughter of a Negro slave and a white landowner. Her father's position saved her from slavery, but not from prostitution. Every night, the same thing. Even when it made her sick, she didn't stop. I imagine she thought it was the only way to survive. She could've managed another way, gone back to her father, something. I was an orphan before she was dead." He sighed and added quietly, "She had it all wrong."

"Your father?" It was far too rude of me to ask such things, but he was so open, so willing to tell me. I'd never been so honest in conversation before.

He shrugged. "A customer she knew for one night."

"I am sorry," I whispered, not sure how to react to these revelations.

"Don't be. She made a choice. She had options. But she

wanted to set out on her own. And that meant making certain…sacrifices. She was a strong woman, a good woman, but stupid. She does not deserve pity." His vitriol surprised me. I couldn't help but pity this woman. How could he be so unforgiving towards his own mother?

"So what do you know about your father?"

Nicholas shrugged. "Not much. Mum said he was an Irish sailor. Fair-haired, blue-eyed, tall, and handsome. Said he was kind. And that is all I know. Not even a name."

"So Holladay is your mother's name."

"Yes. Her name was Sophronia. Sophronia Holladay."

"It's a lovely name."

He grunted softly in response.

I was astonished by his confidence. In my world, no one would reveal such a story for fear of recrimination. If ever a scandal like this became public, the most one could hope for was to be pitied. He took no shame in his past and accepted no pity.

I was proud for him.

CHAPTER THIRTY-EIGHT

THE MAIDS INFORMED US that the bath was ready.

"You first," Nicholas said to me. "I will wait here."

I placed my new clothes in the bathing area and spread the wicker divider as far as it would go. I was certain Nicholas would stay on the balcony, but I was cautious nonetheless.

I undressed and, without thinking twice about the waste, I threw the Wedgewood blue dress and my undergarments into the rubbish bin.

A variety of soaps, oils, and lotions were arranged on the narrow vanity. I examined each delicate cut glass bottle, pulling out the stoppers and inhaling their scents. I poured several drops of an Oriental-scented oil into the bathwater, then sunk in indulgently, my chestnut hair floating in curls on top of the water.

The hot water made my skin feel tight and itchy, but I immediately relaxed. The heat was intoxicating. I sank lower into the water, submerging every bit of me. I'd not had a proper bath since I departed London—at least four months ago. It was a privilege I had taken for granted. I wanted to soak for hours, but I wanted Nicholas to enjoy the water while it was hot. After a few minutes of relaxing I scrubbed my hair and every inch of my skin with sweet smelling soap.

I dried myself with a plush towel and smoothed fragrant oil onto my legs and arms. After running a comb through my wet hair, I slipped into my new dressing gown and rearranged the wicker room divider to separate the bath from the vanity so Nicholas could bathe while I readied myself.

Though we couldn't see one another, Nicholas and I were only a few feet apart, him in the bathtub and me dressing in front of the mirror. It was strangely intimate, strangely comfortable.

"I've always enjoyed staying at a nice inn while in port," Nicholas said as I pulled on my new drawers and chemise. "Enjoy a little luxury and surround myself with some different company, if only for a few days."

"Not really one to fraternize with your fellow pirates, hmm?"

"Right," Nicholas laughed. "Like I said, it's not the lifestyle I wanted. Don't get me wrong. I love sailing, and I love the freedom. But if I could do it without the smelly shipmates, I would. And now, I guess I am."

"I was a fairly smelly shipmate before that bath."

He laughed loudly. It was a beautiful sound.

"So you have lodged at this inn before?" I asked, stepping into my skirt.

"Yes. It is much nicer than the taverns by the docks."

"I admit that I am delighted you shared your tradition with me. That bath was amazing. And I cannot wait to sleep on a real bed."

"Thought you'd like it. How are your new things?"

I had just finished dressing. I stepped back to view myself more fully in the mirror. I wore a white cotton blouse with puffed sleeves that gathered at the elbow into long, fitted cuffs lined with a row of dainty buttons. My plum-colored skirt that hung in soft folds to the floor, a double ruffle decorating the hem. Though I had never worn linen before, I loved the way it hung, its movement airy and light. A matching sash accented my narrow waist. I felt loose and free in the flowing top, without the restrictions of a tight bodice. I hardly recognized myself, but I felt a little more like I belonged at Nicholas's side.

"I love them," I answered.

I combed all the tangles from my hair, admiring its softness and shine now that the dirt and salt had been washed away. I twisted wet tendrils around my fingers, coaxing them into soft ringlets that hung to my waist.

Looking in the mirror, I saw a different person. My brown eyes sparkled warmly. My cheeks were rosy from the kiss of the sun and my complexion glowed. I smiled involuntarily, wondering whether my glow came from bathing and the thrill of new clothing or from the way I felt about the pirate on the other side of the thin divider.

I strolled to the balcony, admiring the bustling sights of the lively port. Though night had fallen, it seemed the town's activities were just starting. Voices carried on the wind, lively music floated up from the streets, and more and more lights blinked in the darkness.

I smelled Nicholas approaching before I felt his arms slip around my waist and his face nuzzle into my hair. He smelled like the ocean on a balmy day, refreshing and mysterious, yet unmistakably masculine. I inhaled deeply. Nicholas turned me around and pulled me into the room, stepping back to admire me in the light.

"Beautiful. The clothing suits you."

"And look at you," I replied coyly.

With a cocky grin, Nicholas puffed out his chest and posed for me. He was wearing his new attire. His weathered canvas breeches had been replaced with a fitted pair of chocolate brown trousers. He wore an ivory linen shirt with a burgundy waistcoat and a long, tailored jacket that matched his trousers. His wet hair was worn loose, sun-kissed tendrils falling into his eyes and framing his face. The look was finished with a polished set of knee-high boots. I stared unabashedly. He looked much more stylish than the sailor I had met onboard the *Banshee*, yet he was as roguish as ever. The dashing attire added to his rebellious charm. He was not the overstuffed, over-mannered gentleman that I feared excessive civilization would make of him. He was debonair, but he was still Nicholas.

My heart thumped wildly just looking at him.

I walked to him, running my hands along the lapels of his jacket. "You look simply delicious," I whispered, standing on my toes to kiss him.

Our lips met, melting into one another. Nicholas's hands tangled into my wet hair and I tugged at his jacket, wanting to be closer.

Breathless, Nicholas pulled away and said with a crooked smile, "I think you are hungry."

I reached to kiss him again, but he only pecked me swiftly on the nose. I pouted.

"Time for dinner, Tessa."

"One moment. Let me pin up my hair."

I moved towards the mirror but Nicholas stopped me. "Leave it the way it is." He pulled a tendril through his fingers.

"It wouldn't be proper."

"There's no bother for propriety in a town such as this. Leave it. For me."

I shook my head ever so slightly. "You always get what you want."

"Always."

Offering me his arm, Nicholas led me downstairs to the dining hall.

CHAPTER THIRTY-NINE

THE PLATE OF SIZZLING mutton, rice, and beans was pure bliss. I hardly remembered my manners as I inhaled the very last bite.

Waiting for dessert, we chatted idly. Nicholas dazzled me with his vast knowledge of all the islands and local culture.

My eyes constantly strayed to Nicholas. I had always found him pleasing to the eyes, but tonight he was especially so. With his hair loose and his dress slightly more refined, he was irresistibly dashing. I couldn't help but admire this new look.

As we finished our meal with freshly squeezed orange juice and rice pudding, a loutish man staggered into the dining hall, sat at a nearby table, and ordered ale. I hardly took notice of him until he took notice of us. He seemed to stare, squinting in our direction, leaning towards us slightly.

Instantly, I tensed.

It was important for Nicholas to be inconspicuous, and here was a gruff fellow, eyeing him coolly. Knowingly.

The man was dirty and shifty. His rags were tattered and he wore a frayed stocking cap on his grizzled head. His face was deeply lined, like crumpled paper—a sign that he had spent his days in the harsh sun. Maybe he was a pirate from the *Banshee,* and was here to satisfy a grudge he held against his former quartermaster and the witch.

"Something amiss?"

Nicholas's voice brought me back to our conversation.

"Oh. Sorry. It's just…there is a man staring at us. Over there." I inclined my head in the direction of our observer.

Nicholas turned slowly, not wanting to draw any attention. When he caught sight of the man, he laughed and stood up. The man did the same and approached Nicholas.

"Avis!" Nicholas said, clapping the gruff looking man on the back. "You old sea dog!"

"I was wonderin' if that be ol' Marks sittin' there!"

They were laughing and smiling, presumably old friends. I turned my attention back to my pudding, hardly paying attention to their exchange of pleasantries and sailor stories. My stomach felt as if it were bursting from all the supper I had feasted on, yet I could not resist the large bowl of sweet pudding. I was suddenly glad for the freedom of my new clothing. I would have never been able to eat so much in a suffocating corset.

My ears perked up when the man—Avis—mentioned the *Banshee.*

"Still quartermaster of that sucker blastin' excuse of a ship?"

"Keepin' out of trouble mostly, best we can. Just coming from southerly waters," Nicholas said, nimbly keeping his reply vague.

"Best stay that way. Bit o' trouble up northways."

"Can't say I ever shied away from trouble," Nicholas said with a cocky smile. "What's happening?"

The man coughed and continued, "If'n I didn't know better, I'd call it the Pirate Inquisition. Some flappin' jawed fruity tooty English navy man is huntin' all outlaws he can find. Some vendetta about pirates killin' his daughter or somethin'. Any excuse he can find."

Nicholas shrugged. "Doesn't sound too serious."

"He's got his whole fleet cruisin' the waters, killing any suspect man on sight. Heard that Carnegie went down."

"Really? Carnegie?" Nicholas sounded surprised. "Where's all this happening?"

"New admiral is stationed in St. Kitts. Gone haywire, I tell ya. Simply haywire."

My spoon clattered onto the floor.

The drunken sailor continued to cuss, "Cockleheaded bleedin' fussy. Come straight from England thinkin' the royal crown gives him the right to do what he pleases. Gets into a little pirate trouble along the way, an' instead of takin' it as a valuable lesson learned swift, he's gotta declare war—"

Without thinking, I shot to my feet and pushed my way in front of Nicholas.

"Do you know his name?" I demanded.

Nicholas grabbed my wrist and yanked me back a step.

Avis eyed me shrewdly, a sloppy smile on his drunken mouth. "Looky, looky, you got a cookie. Marks has been keepin' some treasures for hisself. Pleased to meet—"

"His name," I interrupted, my voice faltering. "Do you know the admiral's name?"

Avis stepped back slightly, seemingly offended at my rudeness.

He directed his answer to Nicholas with a sly wink. "We be callin' 'im Monstroe, like a monster. But his name is Monroe."

Nicholas's hand clutched mine.

I stared forcefully into Avis's hazy eyes. "Are you lying

to me?" I said, afraid to hang any hope on what a drunken pirate in Curaçao said.

His eyes darted from mine to Nicholas's. He let out a drunken guffaw. "Got yourself a live one, dontcha, Marks!"

Nicholas pulled me behind him, "Don't I know it," he replied good-naturedly. "So, it's Admiral Monroe, is it? Causin' all this trouble from St. Kitts?"

"Don't say I didn't warn ya."

"Thanks, Avis. Glad ya did." Nicholas clapped him on the shoulder again, "It was good to see you, a dirty surprise if ever there was one. Now, if you'd be obliged, I don't have much time in port and—as you can see—I've got better things to look at than your simian mug."

Avis winked at Nicholas and tipped an imaginary hat to me, then slowly shuffled back to his table.

CHAPTER FORTY

"MY FATHER!" I WHISPERED fiercely as Nicholas turned to me, our faces only inches apart. His expression of shock certainly mirrored mine.

Avis's story of pirates killing the admiral's daughter registered fully. Was that what had really happened? If both my father and I had survived the storm, we would certainly be together now—unless predatory pirates had taken advantage of such a vulnerable ship. It seemed just the opportunity pirates would exploit.

"But the hurricane, Nicholas, how is this possible?" I asked, not caring that suspicion colored my voice.

"I don't know," he said. His brow was furrowed and he softly chewed at his bottom lip. "I can't imagine how it happened. That ship was decimated. There was nothing but you."

"Avis's story...Why would my father think that pirates killed his daughter?" I pressed.

"He must have seen us take you in."

I pressed the pads of my fingers against my temples, closing my eyes against the storm of emotions that threatened to incapacitate me. With my eyes still closed, I said as evenly as possible, "I need to know something and I need you to tell me the truth."

My demand was met with silence. With my eyes still closed, I braced myself and continued. "How is it that both my father and I survived the storm, yet he made it to port and I only made it as far as your ship?"

"What!" Nicholas exclaimed, fully comprehending the unsaid accusation. "How am I supposed to know that?" He yanked my hands away from my face. I opened my eyes instinctively and met his gaze. He was angry. "You know everything I know."

Nicholas clenched his teeth, the muscles at his jaw flexing tightly. His eyes were sharp.

I glowered back at him.

Admittedly, I was falling for Nicholas. But I had seen too much. I knew what he was capable of. Not only had he manipulated me, but he had turned on his captain and bribed his crew. My affections for him changed none of that. I would never allow myself to forget what he really was.

"I know you're a pirate," I retorted.

He stared at me tensely. Though his jaw was still clenched—and his fists matched—his grey eyes were raw with hurt.

"I am not exactly proud of what I've become," Nicholas defended, "but I'm not ashamed of it either. I have never lied to you about anything."

"Is that so, *First Mate* Holladay? You *never* lied to me? Was my ship even lost? Or was it simply an easy target for a raid?"

Nicholas stared at me in disbelief.

"Was I your *unique item*?"

"I'm not going to listen to your bloody accusations." Nicholas backed away from me and turned to go.

"You're just going to leave me here?" I jabbed, still angry, still lashing, yet suddenly terrified of abandonment.

Nicholas turned back to me, his face a dark cloud. "Despite what you think, that's not who I am."

"Where are you going?" I demanded, the fear of being left behind growing stronger than my anger.

"I need a drink," Nicholas grumbled as he stalked away.

I sat down but kept my eye trained on Nicholas. He had better not leave me.

He retrieved a pint of ale and sat with Avis. I stirred my rice pudding moodily.

How dare he get so offended? My accusation wasn't against him—it was against Captain Black and all the pirates on board the *Banshee*. I would be an imbecile not to ask what happened.

Finally, Nicholas ambled back and sat across from me.

I avoided looking at him, but he seemed to have no qualms about boring into me with his fiery eyes.

We sat awkwardly. I toyed with conversation starters but nothing sounded right. I was still too upset to apologize but anything I said besides an apology seemed trite.

Crushed by the angry silence, I finally eked out an explanation. "Please understand, I do not remember a thing. What that man said…it just made me wonder."

Nicholas raised his eyebrows at me, seemingly enjoying my discomfort.

I continued. "I just needed to ask."

Nicholas took another swig of ale.

I knew I should stop talking, stop explaining, and let the burden of the conversation rest with him. But I could not get myself to shut up.

"I have a right to ask," I said haughtily.

Nicholas's eyes narrowed a little. He was waiting, knowing I would say more.

"And you have a right to be offended," I added.

He smirked a little. I couldn't tell if he was still angry. "I can't blame you for questioning. I just wish you didn't feel like you had to."

Finishing the last of his ale, he stood and dropped a handful of coins on the table.

"Finish your pudding and we'll get going," he said.

I pushed my dish away. I wasn't hungry.

"Where are we going?"

Nicholas deftly wove through the crowds in the tavern. I struggled to keep up.

"I am going to work the town a bit. See if I can uncover any more information. Maybe confirm this rumor. *You* are going to go to bed."

"I am coming with you," I said.

"No, luv. You're not."

"Nicholas, I need to do this. It's my father."

Nicholas turned and faced me, our faces just inches apart. "You cannot follow along. First, it's too dangerous. I'll be constantly worried about you getting your pretty little neck in trouble. Second, you should not be exposed to the places I am going. Believe me, you won't want to see the dark side of the city."

I started to protest, trying to find a solid argument for accompanying him. Nicholas talked over me.

"Finally, I cannot get the information with you next to me. No one will talk. We will get nowhere. So if you really want to help, please understand that the best way to do so is to stay in the room."

I agreed reluctantly. We entered the room and Nicholas strapped on his baldric and mashed a hat onto his curls.

"Is it even possible that my father is alive?"

Nicholas peered into my face, a look of tenderness in

his eyes. "We will go to St. Kitts. We will set out tomorrow. If your father is there, we will find him."

Loading his pistol, Nicholas said, "Lock the door. Don't venture on the balcony. I'll most likely be late. Rest if you can."

I stood still as he gently touched my cheek and breezed away, the heavy door thudding behind him. After his footsteps faded, I rushed to the balcony hoping to catch a glimpse of him. Perhaps I could overhear any conversations he might have on the street below. I waited for the better part of an hour but never saw him pass by.

Knowing I would not sleep, I prepared for bed slowly, hoping that my every action would help the time pass. I tried to read. I tried to write. The turmoil within me would not let me rest. I paced around the room listlessly, my vacant eyes refusing to focus on anything. I tried lying down, or at least sitting still, but could not. I analyzed the oils by the washbasin, repeatedly smelling each scent, rearranging the bottles from tallest to shortest, from roundest to thinnest, from darkest to lightest. I brushed my hair excessively, barely noticing when the head of the brush broke away from the bone handle. I paced the balcony, staring into the night, trying to make sense of the activity below. Every time I heard a noise from outside my room, I unlocked the door and peered down the hallway, even stealing a few steps towards the staircase, hoping to find Nicholas returning.

I stared at the candles in the room, judging the passage of time by the amount of wax pooling around them. The hypnotizing flames captured my attention longer than anything else had, small fires twisting and lurching in a scorching dance. There was too much time.

CHAPTER FORTY-ONE

THE CANDLES WERE HALFWAY melted when the sound of footsteps jolted me from my reverie. I dashed to the door, unlocked it, and tiptoed into the hall. Nicholas grimaced when he saw me outside the room.

He quickened his pace and herded me back into our room. "Get in there."

"What did you learn?" I pressed, ignoring his disapproval of my behavior.

"Same rumors, everywhere." He shrugged off his jacket and tossed it upon a chair.

"But what did they say?" I trailed him closely as he walked across the room.

"Same thing, Tessa. Angry admiral named Monroe is in St. Kitts. Has it out for pirates because his daughter was killed by them." He sounded indifferent.

"That's it? They all said the *exact* same words?"

Nicholas walked to one of the beds. I was right on his heels as he turned around and practically knocked me over.

"Tessa," he said sternly as he steadied me, "settle

down." He sat me down on the left-side bed. He towered over me with his hands on his hips, like an exasperated parent.

"There wasn't much difference to the stories. Some said the daughter was kidnapped while some said murdered. Some told me the name of the pirates or the ship that took you, but they were all wrong. No one mentioned the *Banshee* or Black Jack. But everyone knew the admiral's name. Definitely Monroe."

I quivered on the edge of the bed, my blood racing. I closed my eyes and let myself begin to hope.

Nicholas crouched before me, taking my hands in his. They were steady and warm. His voice was suddenly soft. "This is good news, Tessa. Be happy."

"I-I can't…but what if…what if they are wrong? What if it isn't true?" I questioned, avoiding Nicholas's eyes.

"You're scared to believe."

"If I let myself believe, and it's not true…it will be like losing him again." A single tear rolled down my face. Nicholas smoothed it away.

"I know." His voice was like velvet. "Tessa, I talked to more than twenty men tonight—merchant sailors, smugglers, traders, local business owners. They all said the same thing. It's not just a pirate legend. This is real. I can't make you any promises, but I think there really is a chance that your father made it to St. Kitts. Everyone knew his name. And the story about losing a daughter? Can't be coincidence."

I let Nicholas's words sink in. I searched his face. His features were calm and sure. I let out a broken sigh and nodded, letting his words comfort me.

"How long to St. Kitts?" I asked.

"About three weeks."

I nodded again, realizing all the questions forming in my thoughts would go unanswered until then. There was no use in driving myself—or Nicholas—crazy with my wild anxiety.

"And we leave tomorrow?"

"Yes," Nicholas promised, "at first light."

A hesitant smile pulled at my lips. "I can't believe it. I just can't believe it!"

Nicholas moved next to me on the bed and wrapped me in his arms. His lips found my forehead, leaving a small kiss. "Things will work out, you'll see," he whispered.

Sitting back, he asked, "Which bed would you prefer?"

I looked at the identical beds critically. "This one," I announced decidedly, patting the mattress I sat on.

"Are you quite certain?" Nicholas teased.

"Absolutely. I always sleep on my right side, and if I sleep in this bed I will be able to face the wall, which I prefer. If I were in that bed, I would be facing you, and I am worried that I make funny faces in my sleep."

Nicholas contemplated that seriously. "Not really— only when you're sick. Mostly you just mumble."

"It is inappropriate how much you know," I said, swatting him gently on the arm.

He abruptly stood, scooping me into his arms, then pulled back the covers of my bed. With me cradled against his chest, Nicholas leaned in and kissed me deeply, then finally laid me down upon the sheets and tucked the covers around me.

Having tucked me into bed, Nicholas retrieved the wooden room divider and repositioned it between our beds. "Now that's in case I make funny faces in *my* sleep."

He blew out the candles, then I heard him undress and settle into his bed.

CHAPTER FORTY-TWO

I AWOKE NOT KNOWING where I was. I strained my eyes to make out my surroundings. It took me a minute to remember the day in Willemstad. Then everything flooded back to me—the shopping, the inn, the bath, the dinner, and the possibility that my father was alive. I also had a groggy memory of Nicholas leaving. I couldn't remember if he had roused me or if I had awakened on my own, but I remembered him kissing me and telling me to go back to sleep, that he needed to go out for a short while.

I was still extremely drowsy. I wondered what had interrupted my slumber.

"Nicholas?" Perhaps his return had awakened me.

He did not answer.

Maybe he was already asleep. I listened intently for the rhythmic sound of his breathing but did not hear it.

I slowly stood up, feeling my way around the wicker divider between the beds. The faint light of the nighttime sky traced the shapes before me. I found his bed and carefully ran my hands over it, expecting to feel the solid lumps of Nicholas's legs under the covers.

The bed was empty.

I wished I knew where he had gone. At least I remembered him telling me he was leaving, but that was not enough right now. What could he possibly be doing that couldn't wait until morning? Probably gambling or drinking or some other loathsome activity he didn't want me to know about. I chided myself for that thought. He deserved more credit than that.

I lay back in my bed, snuggling deep into the soft mattress. Under different circumstances, I would have dreaded going back to the sagging bed aboard the ketch. But seeing my father would be worth all of that. I would happily spend a year in the brig of the *Banshee* if it meant seeing my father again.

As my breathing grew heavier, a tiny noise across the room pulled me back to consciousness. Fully alert, I listened hard. The noise did not repeat itself—if there even had been a noise in the first place.

I closed my eyes and tried to relax back into slumber, but I was too paranoid now. I kept listening for noises, imagining things in the dark. I fretted about Nicholas. Where was he? I was slightly annoyed—maybe more than slightly—that he would leave like this.

I tossed and turned in bed, hoping that my tired body would overcome my busy mind. It was probably a quarter of an hour before I heard a small noise again.

I sat up. It had come from the door. I looked into the darkness, hoping to discern what it was. I told myself that it could be anything, that I was thinking irrationally. This was a strange inn with new noises. Normal noises.

Still, I could not quite convince myself to go back to sleep. Surrendering to the paranoia, I decided take a light a candle. A quick survey of the room would put me at ease. I fumbled with the flint and steel on the bedside table, but I was eventually able to light a candle.

Sitting in bed, I slowly moved the candle in an arc so I could glimpse every inch of the room. As the candlelight fell on the room's entrance, a large shape illuminated. I startled and nearly dropped the candlestick.

My eyes focused on the unfamiliar shadow in the room. My heart hammered loudly as the shape took the form of a man wearing a low, wide hat. The figure didn't move. I think he hoped I would not see him, or that I'd assume my eyes were playing tricks on me.

And maybe they were.

I leaned towards the shadow, kneeling on the bed, and stretched the candle out as far as I could reach.

It was definitely a man.

I recoiled so quickly that wax splattered my hand.

"Who are you?" I did not recognize my own voice. It was so childish.

The man raised his chin slightly. Beneath his hat the light reflected off a pale face. His cold eyes glittered.

They were red.

A gloved hand rose from the folds of the jacket, pointing the sleek barrel of a pistol at me.

"Where is Marks?"

My stomach rolled with nausea at the sound of that voice.

Dumb with terror, I could only shake my head.

Captain Black strode towards me, sweeping his eyes across the room as he went, yet never lowering the pistol aimed at my chest. He grabbed my elbow, pulled me to him, and turned me around, pressing the pistol's barrel against my spine. He walked me onto the balcony, still looking for Nicholas. My hands were shaking so severely that the hot wax from the candle showered on them.

He led me back inside, instructing me to sit on the edge

of my bed. He kicked the wicker divider aside and sat directly across from me on the edge of the other bed. The aim of his weapon never wavered.

"Strange that Marks would leave you alone. Not a very fast learner, is he?"

I focused on my breathing, trying not to hyperventilate.

"He'll be back though, won't he? He will be back for you." His tone was matter of fact.

Captain Black sat on the bed and looked at me easily. He acted as if he were having tea with an old companion. Aside from the gleaming pistol pointed at me, there was little threat about the man. It seemed as though he was comfortable to wait in this holding position all night.

Deciding that I was not in any imminent danger of being shot, I tentatively asked, "What do you want with him?"

"To kill 'im."

He said it so good-naturedly that I was compelled to press the issue further.

"Why?"

The captain cocked his head, peering at me sideways.

"I guess the reason would be you, now wouldn't it? The mutiny. Losing my post. Losing my ship. And though it were Marks who saw it through, it was because of you. Can you imagine what that feels like, Miss Monroe? To lose everything at the hands of your closest friend for a bint he barely knows?"

A cold shiver slid up my back.

"Tell me something," he lilted. "Tell me about your father."

My father? If possible, my heart pounded faster. "How do you know about my father?"

"A little eavesdroppin' is all it takes and news travels faster than fire. I heard that Marks was askin' about some warlord in St. Kitts. And I think it has somethin' to do with you."

Though confused at his implications, I jumped at the opportunity to use my father's position as leverage. "That's right. My father is an admiral in the Royal Navy. He is hunting pirates, looking for me. He knows that you kidnapped me." I stuck out my chin.

"I'll bet he does." The captain smirked diabolically.

He stood abruptly, looking around the room once more. "Come here." He beckoned to me with the pistol.

I arose mechanically. The pistol found its way against my waist, directing me where Black wanted me.

He positioned me in front of the mirror and instructed me to place the candlestick on the table. I numbly obliged. Black exchanged his pistol for a dagger. My eyes involuntarily flitted to my throat. I could still see the small mark at the hollow of my neck where Wrack had tried to kill me with a similar blade.

Black grabbed my right hand. I tried to pull back, but he was too strong. He slashed my pointer finger with the tip of the dagger, then forced my hand to the mirror. A sticky stream of blood spilled down my finger and inside my wrist.

Using my finger like a writing quill, he penned a message with my blood.

HOW ABOUT A GAME OF BLACK JACK?

I stared unsteadily at the red letters, the smeared blood already drying into an ugly brown in some places.

The captain smiled menacingly. "It's rude to leave without a note."

Yanking my arm downward, he commanded me to kneel.

I dropped to the floor.

The blade of the dagger lifted against my chin, coaxing me to tilt my head back. With my neck extended, I felt critically vulnerable to Black's blade. The thin edge of steel settled below my jawbone. Black caressed my hair with his left hand.

Erratic gasps escaped my lips. I trembled with each one, convinced that these violent shivers would surely cause the knife to slit my throat. My lips quivered.

"Please," I breathed, feeling the blade's edge more acutely as I spoke.

"You like games?" he asked me.

I could hardly understand his words. My thudding heartbeat echoed in my ears and I was too distracted keeping my breathing under control. I didn't know what he meant and, as close to hysterics as I was, I could not think about it. All I knew was that playing a game was better than being dead.

"Yes," I trembled.

"Do ya think Marks likes games?"

What was I supposed to say? "Yes."

"I'd been thinkin' he'd fancy a treasure hunt."

The cool edge of the blade traced a slow line across my neck from one ear to the other. A trail of goose pimples sprung up in its wake. The sensation was so light that it would have tickled if it hadn't been so frightening.

Black grabbed a handful of my hair as if admiring it. Then swiftly, he pulled it taught, jerking my head to the side. I whimpered. Before I knew what happened, the tension released.

"Hold out yer hands."

I held my hands—palms up—before me.

A thick lock of glistening chestnut hair fell into them. I screamed, dropped the hair and grabbed my head, certain to find blood or a wound of some kind. My quivering fingers searched my scalp frantically. Everything was fine. Except the lock of hair that now hung only to my jaw.

Piece by piece...that's how he was going to do this. Piece by piece.

I fell forward, bracing myself with my hands. Tiny whimpers escaped my lips with every passing gasp.

On the edge of madness, I barely realized that Black was doing something behind me. I didn't dare look, but it sounded as though he was rummaging through my packages from the market.

"Pick up the hair." His voice was cold. No longer playful.

He dropped a square of brown paper and a piece of string in front of me. He had torn it from one of my packages.

"Wrap it."

The dirk nudged my back.

I clumsily laid the length of chestnut hair on the piece of paper, my hands fumbling with every move. I somehow managed to tie a crude knot around the wad of paper.

The captain grabbed it, then forced me up.

"Put on yer shoes."

I stuffed my feet into my new boots without lacing them.

Pressing the dirk against my side, Black steered me out of the room and down the stairs.

I was surprised when we entered the lobby. I thought Black would avoid such a public place. With the dirk positioned brazenly against me, I was certain someone in the lobby would do something, but to my complete vexation, no one noticed us.

I needed to scream, make a fuss.

"You're thinking of screaming," the captain smirked into my ear as he twisted the dirk into my side. I sucked in a breath. "It's no use in a place like this. No laws. No rules. No one who cares."

Captain Black approached the innkeeper and handed him the parcel.

"Give this to Mr. Nicholas Holladay when he returns. He rented the corner room on the second floor."

"Aye," the innkeeper said indifferently, failing to acknowledge the silent pleading in my eyes.

Captain Black pushed me out of the door into the humid night.

"We'll give good ol' Nick a little treasure hunt. He'll be findin' pieces of you on this island for a month."

CHAPTER FORTY-THREE

WE SNAKED THROUGH THE darkest alleys of Willemstad. Black never loosened his grip on me or removed the dirk from my side. I was incoherent with hysteria, unresponsive to the world around me, yanked around like a blubbering doll. Fear had such a complete hold on me that the threat of the dirk was superfluous. I would have followed wherever Black led, I would have done whatever he asked.

Periodically, Black would stop, shove me to my knees and saw off another lock of hair. He'd place it boldly upon a landmark—a street marker, a residential fence—where Nicholas would easily spot it.

I imagined Nicholas returning to the inn, perplexed by the package the innkeeper would give him. His face would twist as he untied the morbid gift and recognized the clump of hair. Then he would dash upstairs to our room, terrified of what he'd find on the other side of the door. Drawing his cutlass, Nicholas would burst into the room, bracing himself to find my lifeless body. In the heavy silence, he'd explore the room cautiously, his eyes landing on the sinister message on the mirror. Would he know it was my blood? He'd demand answers from the innkeeper—he wouldn't get anything useful. Then he'd search. He'd tear down the streets, checking the places he knew Black frequented. And finally, he would happen across a lock of my hair blowing in the night's breeze. I imagined the sick pit in Nicholas's stomach as he found each telltale piece, realizing that this was a trail...a game...

A treasure hunt, indeed.

And what would be the prize at the end?

As we passed through a darkened churchyard, Black sawed off another handful of hair. As he draped it on the wooden cross in the churchyard, I wondered how much hair I had left, how many more clues I could afford. After my hair ran out, what would be next?

Instead of continuing down the street as I expected, Black led me through the church's door. With more care than I thought him capable of, Black lifted the shell necklace from Liam from around my neck and hung it on the church's door latch.

Black pushed me into the church and shut the door behind us. This was the end, then. This was where all the clues led.

The altar was ablaze with more than a dozen candles. Grotesque shadows writhed on the walls. I blinked as my eyes adjusted. It was easy to see that this church had been out of commission for some time. It was almost entirely wooden and it had begun to rot. The planks of the floor were dull and rough. Derelict beams supported a rotting vaulted ceiling. A thick blanket of dust coated every surface and the pews were recklessly rearranged to fit whatever purpose they now served.

Black shoved me towards a pew at the front of the church, not bothering to secure me. Maybe he finally realized that I was too distraught to defy him. Or maybe he just knew that in this small and secure church I had nowhere to run.

He strode to the altar, his back to me.

"Can't say how long it will be now. Depends on when he returns. He'll follow the trail smartly enough. Not too thick for that. We will give it some time before we continue, though."

He spoke to two men sitting in the dark shadows next to the altar. I had failed to notice them before. They were playing cards and eyed me quizzically.

"Sure he'll come?" one of them asked in a heavy Spanish accent, looking at me skeptically as if to say I was not a worthy prize.

"I'd bet my life on it." Black winked jovially.

The two men went back to their card game, snickering to each other in hushed tones. Black absent-mindedly paced the church. No one paid attention to me. I hoped that if I sat still and quiet enough, I would somehow be forgotten.

The darkness pressed in. The silence was suffocating. I was too frightened to try anything brave. I was merely glad for my continued existence. But while time was a gift for me, it was against Nicholas. Every moment brought him closer to this ambush.

I wished I knew how long he had been gone. I hadn't the faintest idea when he'd left. Was it hours or minutes before I discovered Black? Would it be hours or minutes before he arrived here?

Black peered out the single window by the door, looking for Nicholas. Satisfied that he was not yet approaching, he paced back towards the front of the chapel and sat next to me on the pew staring straight ahead.

"Headed to St. Kitts then?" His tone was casual, conversational.

I stared at him blankly. After a moment, he looked at me for my answer. I continued to gawk.

"I've known Marks since he was just a lad. Scrappy little thing, he was." Was he actually reminiscing? "Always thought o' him like a brother."

It was impossible to wipe the blank stare off of my face. This man who planned to kill not only me but the man I loved was prattling on as if I cared what he said. Aggravating as it was, I couldn't help but be intrigued. This man knew Nicholas better than I. Maybe better than anyone. There were so many secrets, so much that Nicholas would never tell me. And Black knew all of it. Though disgusted at my own curiosity, I devoured every word he said.

"He was a fine sailor—and an even better pirate. A natural. Got himself a stomach for killin' and a mind for strategy." My face twisted with his words. I saw Nicholas through the captain's eyes—it was an image Nicholas had so desperately tried to keep from me. I pictured him skewering someone with his sword, fresh blood splattering his snow-white shirt, smiling with pleasure. "He elevated it to an art form," Black continued with fondness. "Can disembowel a man without killin' 'im. Torture 'im for days. No mercy. No emotion. See, that was my downfall. I get too emotional. Can't help but empathize a bit with those at the other end of me blade. But not Marks. His focus is rigid as steel. Keeps his eye on the target and sees it through to the end. That one, he don't give up. Somewhat stubborn. That's how I know he'll show tonight." He smiled at me wickedly.

I cringed.

Noticing my reaction, Black softened perceptibly. "Maybe you really do care for 'im. It's too bad. It's not like you really deserve this. You were a catalyst. Nothin' more. Marks though...Marks knew what he was doin', knew what betrayin' me means. This isn't as unexpected for him as it is for you. Don't pity him. I still think o' him like a brother—despite his back-stabbin' treachery. So, in light o' my unfounded affection, not to mention my insatiable greed for gold, I'll be granting 'im mercy tonight."

"Mercy?" I stammered, taken by surprise.

He nodded solemnly. "Mercy for you, too."

"You'll release us?"

Black barked out a laugh, a raw snort that reverberated on the wooden walls of the chapel. "Such naïveté! You are a charmin' lass, aren't you? He deserves to suffer. He took away everything I had. Everything that meant anything to me. My ship. My men. My future." He dropped each word hotly as if it burned his tongue to say them. "And I'm still here to live without it all. True justice would do the same for him—take away everything that means anything to 'im, and let 'im live without it. Easy enough to wrangle his ketch away, his gold and his friends, but that wouldn't have been enough. So there's you. You woulda been the final touch. Your pain, your torture, your death...takin' *you* away and lettin' 'im live— now that would be justice."

I sat stoically, strangely unaffected at this casual talk of my murder.

"And that was the plan until tonight." Black winked a red eye at me paternally. "When I finally tracked Marks down, I overheard 'im talkin' about a certain admiral in the Royal Navy who be missin' a daughter. I could only assume he meant you. And instead of killin' you and lettin' 'im live, I decided to mercifully kill Marks, and let you live."

258 | LARA HAYS

"What? How can you call death merciful? You just said he was like a brother to you!"

"There are many fates worse than death."

"And what do you plan for me?" I demanded rudely, no longer caring to pussyfoot around this demented murderer.

"I'll return you to St. Kitts."

I sat forward, "You will take me home?" My voice did not conceal my disbelief.

He shrugged. "I'm sure to get a right handsome sum of it all."

"A ransom?" My voice cracked. "You'll charge a ransom?"

The captain looked forward and shrugged nonchalantly. "Your father'll pay it."

"He will attack you."

"Not with you on board."

It was a vile plan, and I didn't believe a word of it. A generous ransom would not likely quell Black's desire for revenge against the witch who inspired a mutiny.

I realized then that Black was right about his mercy. Death was a far better option than living out one's life after everything precious is taken away. If Black thought he would be showing me mercy by sparing my life, he was wrong. Mercy would never force me to live without Nicholas.

"I do not want your mercy."

"What's that?"

"I do not want your mercy."

"Are ye askin'..." he trailed off. He looked at me quizzically, a playful glint in his eyes.

"Kill me. Please."

The captain's brows knitted together and he studied my face. I stared into Black's curious eyes, hoping he would be tempted enough to run me through with his sword. I did not want to live without Nicholas, knowing that his death was entirely my fault.

After a moment of silence the captain responded softly, "No. My mind's made up. Your ransom will get me back a sizeable part of what you caused me to lose."

"Please," I said again, a note of begging in my voice. "If you kill him, please kill me, too."

Black looked away from me. He would not answer me again.

"You will never get the ransom. I swear to you, if you kill Nicholas, I will be dead by sunrise." The words blurted out before I could truly comprehend my threat. Though I didn't know if I could really do such a thing—or if I even knew how—I meant it.

Black jerked his head back to me, his demonic eyes boring holes into mine. I lifted my chin and tightened my eyes, daring him to challenge my resolve.

"There be a ransom either way. A father would want to bury the body."

Black stood abruptly, irritated I thought, and stalked to the window of the church, peering out into the darkness.

"Mendoza, it's time," Black commanded sternly, still looking out the window. "Don't let her out of your sight. And see to it that she doesn't harm herself."

A monstrous bearded man picked himself off the floor and lumbered towards me. He was the largest man I had ever seen, with a bulging chest as broad as a door. Thick muscles wound around his arms like snakes. His black hair hung in matted braids and golden hoops dangled from his ears. When he smiled, golden teeth flashed against his swarthy lips. A massive paw grabbed my wrist and pulled me to my feet. I noticed that his hand was missing the last two fingers. My flesh crawled. Finally finding the nerve to fight, I struggled against the man's hold on me. His three-fingered grasp held my wrist like a shackle. He drew his cutlass and pointed it under my chin.

"Death is a luxury you'll not be havin' tonight, miss. But don't you worry, there are other things that can be done with this knife."

His black eyes widened wickedly. With grim calculation, he placed the cutlass back in its scabbard at his hip. He dragged me through the church and into the night.

CHAPTER FORTY-FOUR

"Where are you taking me?" I demanded.

"You best be quiet."

"No!" I insisted even louder. "Where are you taking me?"

Mendoza turned on me, the cutlass I didn't even see him draw scraping at the soft skin beneath my left eye. "I told you to be quiet."

Daring him to lose his temper and kill me, I said, "You will never get your ransom. I will make sure of that." I spat on his face.

In a swift movement, the butt of the cutlass landed in my stomach. I doubled over, wheezing for air.

"And I may not be as concerned about the ransom as ol' Black Jack is."

Mendoza turned and continued down the street with me in tow.

I continued to twist and struggle. With only three fingers, his grip was bound to slip at some point. But every time I yanked my arm, his grasp tightened, twisting my skin. I ignored the pain and fought his grip. If I could break free and run as fast as I could, then I could intercept Nicholas before he entered the church. This was my only chance to save him. I knew the path he would take. Each landmark had been seared into my memory as Black had draped mutilated locks of my hair on them. All I had to do was break free and run.

Mendoza lumbered along heavily. I could see the thickness of his legs and sense the stout strength in his binding muscles. But he walked slowly, unevenly with a well-hidden limp. Though he was strong, I was convinced he wouldn't be fast. I could outrun him. I just needed the chance.

"Nicholas has money," I rushed breathlessly, not really sure of what I was saying. "Lead me back to him and you'll have more than Black can promise you."

Mendoza didn't break his stride or even bother to look at me. "I thought I made it clear that I ain't interested in gold."

"What do you want, then? A pardon? You'll have it. My father—"

"You'll not be bribin' me, miss. Fact is, Marks did me wrong in another life. Ain't nothin' you can offer me that'll be better than what Black gives me tonight."

I pulled at my arm sharply, the friction from Mendoza's vice-like grip tearing my skin.

"What is it with you pirates? Why all this vengeance? Aren't you all supposed to be mesmerized by piles of gold?" I muttered to myself.

My question went unanswered.

I focused on the buildings and shapes we passed, trying to memorize all the details so I could easily retrace my steps and intercept Nicholas.

The buildings changed and the road widened into open plazas. Though hauntingly empty now, I remembered the lively crowds that polluted these plazas the previous day. We were nearing the docks. We were still too far away to see the turbulent waters of the ocean, but I could make out a number of masts stretching into the sky.

Mendoza was taking me to the harbor. Time was slipping away. Once on a ship, I would be so much easier to contain. It would be all but impossible to steal away and warn Nicholas. If I wanted to save both our lives, I needed to think fast, to act fast.

I stared at the passing buildings, desperately looking for something—for anything—to spark an idea. I had no inspiration, just a growing queasiness in my bones telling me I was too late.

Hopelessly trying to stall, I dug my heels into the ground and said, "Stop. I need to rest."

"There'll be time for that soon enough," was the heartless reply.

"No," I insisted, pulling against Mendoza's weight. "I need to stop now."

Mendoza stopped and looked at me suspiciously. As I scanned my surroundings again, my inspiration finally came.

With my free hand, I pointed to a clump of tall grasses growing between two buildings. "I need to relieve myself."

Mendoza looked where I pointed. "There will be time soon enough," he said again.

"I can't wait," I blurted. "I'm going to be sick."

He hesitated slightly. I took advantage of his indecision and started walking towards the grassy area. Just as I hoped, Mendoza followed, his grip still firm.

When I reached the area, I tugged my captive arm, thinking Mendoza would release it so I could do my business. His hold remained tight.

"Some privacy?" I let annoyance color my voice.

Still holding my wrist, Mendoza turned slightly and faced the street.

I noticed that the grass was actually a path extending between the two buildings and running behind them, creating a walkway among all the buildings. If I could escape, I could zigzag through all the shops and stores, emerging on another street altogether. I could be quick and nimble. And with Mendoza limping along behind me, I was sure to lose him.

Still perturbed that he would not let go of me, I fell to my knees and feigned gagging noises as if I were starting to retch. Mendoza cringed slightly, taking a step away from me. His arm was extended as far as possible while still keeping hold of my wrist. With my free hand, I quickly felt the surrounding ground for a weapon.

My searching hand felt out the rod-like shape of a small branch. My fingers curled tightly around the rough wood. Wielding it like a club, I swung the branch down with all my might on Mendoza's wrist, breaking his taut grasp. He did not even have time to make a sound as I simultaneously stood and swung the stick again in a fluid and graceful movement. The club landed squarely at the base of his skull with a sickening thud. Mendoza staggered back and fell. Not waiting to see if he lost consciousness, I sprinted through the grass between the shadows of the buildings.

CHAPTER FORTY-FIVE

ADRENALINE SURGED THROUGH ME, giving me strength I did not know I had. My feet carried me swiftly through the winding paths between buildings. I had more energy than grace. The faster I ran, the more I stumbled. I tripped on the soft rolls of earth beneath my feet, catching myself on the sides of buildings and fences I rushed past. My long nightdress snagged on the rough corners. Bits of lace probably tore off the hem, marking every turn I made. I was leaving an easy trail to follow, but I was more concerned with putting distance between Mendoza and myself than disguising my whereabouts.

A burning pain crossed my waist, telling me it was time to rest. I fought against the stitch, forcing my legs to keep pumping. My breath came out in shallow spurts. I crashed through the underbrush, weaving through the row of buildings, running away from the harbor.

The path ended in a jam of buildings. I could turn left and follow the road that Mendoza had dragged me down, but that seemed too obvious. I darted to the right only to be stopped by a six-foot high fence. Resolutely, I dropped my club, grabbed the top of the fence and hoisted myself up with all my strength, my feet slipping against the smooth wood. My arms shook under my weight and I dropped back into the grass.

I spun around, staring at my options. I could return the way I came, a direct path to the church. It was the easiest course of action; and the riskiest. I could try climbing the fence again. Or, I could backtrack down the grass alleyway, hoping to find an easier way to divert my course. As I eyed the grass path, my ears prickled at a distant sound. It was the swooshing sound of someone trampling through long grass.

I was being followed.

I needed to move!

Grasping the pointed tops of the fence planks, I thrust myself upwards again. My feet scrambled but finally found a hold. One at a time, I threw my arms over the fence, the pointy wood stabbing into my armpits. I inched upwards. When my waist was level with the top of the fence, I threw myself headfirst to the other side. I landed loudly on a pile of rubbish. A startled dog announced my position as I picked myself up and stumbled across the street.

No longer able to fight against the pain in my side, I slowed my pace to a steady jog. I tossed reckless glances over my shoulder, looking for a pursuing shadow. No one was behind me. After a few confusing turns, Mendoza would lose my trail, and then I would be free to search for Nicholas.

I loped passed three drunkards, keeping my distance from them. As soon as I had passed them, a booming voice broke through the darkness.

"Stop her! She's a thief!"

The voice did not startle me nearly as much as the

direction from which it hailed. Rather than being behind me, Mendoza's voice was directly in front of me.

I skidded to a halt and took several steps backwards. I couldn't see him but I knew he was there. I looked behind me only to see the three drunken men closing in. Mendoza definitely knew the exact thing to say for action.

I frantically searched for a way out. I dared not run forward. I had underestimated Mendoza's speed, but I was not foolish enough to underestimate his strength. I turned quickly, running at full speed towards the three men, in the direction of the docks. I tucked my head and barreled easily through the inebriated trio.

Mendoza's deep voice muttered a string of obscenities as I dashed away. I hugged the left side of the street where the shadows were the darkest, though there was not much point in being stealthy just yet.

The pain in my side sharpened. I couldn't ignore it much longer. Pinching my waist in between my thumb and fingers, I pushed on.

I saw an intersection ahead. I ran hard, veering towards the center of the street so Mendoza could easily see the direction I took. At the intersection, I cut sharply to the left, almost losing my balance. My legs numb, I sprinted hard, then dashed around the corner of a stone building and hid.

My instincts raged inside, telling me to run. It took all my willpower to stay hidden against the stone wall.

I was winded and my breathing was heavy and loud. I couldn't hold my breath for more than a few seconds at a time, but I kept trying so I could listen for Mendoza. In those quiet seconds, all I could hear was my thumping heart. I tried to muffle it with my hands, hoping it wasn't truly as deafening as it sounded. I was sure it would betray me.

The light padding of footfalls on dirt caught my attention. He was coming closer. My plan worked. I perched on the balls of my feet, ready for action.

I held my breath as the footsteps passed me. I counted my heartbeats, though they were almost too rapid to track. I reached one-hundred-and-ten before I dared to let myself take a controlled breath. I was so focused on standing still and listening to my heart that I had forgotten to listen for the directions the footsteps took. Holding my breath again, I opened my eyes and listened hard.

The silence grew to a deafening din. I couldn't even hear the ocean waves crashing in the distance or crickets chirping in the night. All was eerily still. Mendoza was gone.

Or, he was silently waiting for me to emerge.

The more I thought about it, the more I was convinced he was waiting for me, just around the corner. As soon as I ventured out, a burly arm would grab me and never let go.

I dared not move. I measured every breath, inhaling and exhaling with steady discipline. It took all my energy. My lungs were bursting, wanting to pant heavily.

He was waiting for me, I was certain. But, I realized, he was not positive I was here. If he were, I would be in his clutches now. No, he was standing frozen in the middle of the street, waiting for me to let down my guard enough to move.

This was a waiting game then. I would win. I would stay silent, stay still. After enough time, Mendoza would doubt himself and venture off to track me.

So I waited.

I distracted myself by counting heartbeats again, trying to identify rare sounds in the night—like the sound of a bird flapping its wings and the distant tolling of a bell.

The minutes moved like molasses. Every moment I spent here was a moment wasted. Nicholas could be on his way to the church now. He could be there any minute. He might have already...I didn't finish the thought.

I stared into the sky, expecting to see a lightening in the east signaling the sunrise. The air was still thick with night. How long had I been awake? It felt like forever, but the darkness told me there was still time before the dawn. Time was all I had. I hoped I still had enough.

Was Mendoza still waiting for me in the street? I had not heard anything for such a long time. I needed to move, to take action, but it was a huge risk. If I were caught now, there would be no mercy, no chance to warn Nicholas.

Just a little longer, I would wait just a little longer. I deliberated my next move, allowing myself to take action as soon as I had a clear plan. I could find my way back to the road the church was on and work backwards from there. That would be the best way to intercept Nicholas, but at the same time, it was also the most dangerous. Mendoza knew I had no regard for my own life—my sole reason of escape was to warn Nicholas of the danger at the church. Mendoza would be waiting there for me, planning to ambush me before I could catch Nicholas. I could not risk going near the church.

Instead, I could wind through town and cross Black's trail at an earlier point. There was a chance Nicholas hadn't even started searching for me yet. Maybe if I found my way back to the inn, I could stop him from ever embarking. That was my only choice, to pick my way through unfamiliar streets, hoping to find a location I had only been to once.

I inhaled deeply, trying to settle my nerves. Time was ticking away. I needed to move swiftly, but smartly. I peeked around the corner of the building. Just as I hoped, no one was there.

Cautiously, I tiptoed down the street, scrutinizing every shadow. I strained to hear any noise the night would reveal. I walked along the oceanfront until I reached another intersection, then turned left, hoping to travel parallel to the church street and eventually cut over. I was frustrated to see that the road curved unexpectedly to the right.

It was not long until I was lost.

I quickened my pace, fearing I had gone too far. I found a cross street that seemed to lead in the direction of the church street. I took it.

I was surprised by how empty the city was. In a pirate town where society's rules did not apply, I expected revelers to be carousing all through the night. It was a little unnerving, but I decided it was a lucky turn of events. If the streets had been full of strangers, I would not know whether I was being followed, and I might have a harder time navigating the town.

As I hurried down the street, I ducked under a low hanging sign before realizing I had been here earlier. With Black. The sign advertised a blacksmith shop. A horseshoe hung like the letter "U" from the bottom, letting the illiterate know the trade of the business. Black had threaded a piece of my hair through that horseshoe.

But the hair was gone.

Nicholas had found the trail.

CHAPTER FORTY-SIX

I SPRANG FORWARD, RUNNING for the church, praying there was still time.

I anticipated the next landmark and searched quickly for the bunch of hair. It, too, was gone. I ran harder, ignoring the two other markers. I sped down the road, turning briskly on the street where the church was located. In the darkness, I searched for any movement. Every beat of my heart sent out a prayer, pleading to see a lone figure in the darkness. As the outline of the church came into relief, I saw the door swing shut.

"Nicholas!" I screamed, not wanting to believe what I just saw.

It was too late. He had already entered the church. By only seconds, I was too late.

"No! Nicholas!" I yelled as loudly as I could, my screams scorching my throat. It didn't matter who heard me now. My reason for secrecy was gone.

I dashed to the church and hurtled myself against the door. It was bolted shut. "Nicholas, no! He'll kill you!"

"Tessa?" My heart skipped a beat at the sound of his

voice. He was alive. Nicholas sounded disbelieving and ecstatic at the same time.

"Nicholas, it's me. You need to get out of there! Black is going to kill you." I hoped my warnings weren't futile.

"Run away, Tessa. I will find you. Just get out of here!" Panic tinged his voice. The fight for his life had begun.

I threw myself at the door again, noticing it gave a little. I remembered how rotten the boards were. With enough pressure, the door would surely break down.

Muffled voices and the sounds of furniture scraping across the floor came from inside the church. I listened for the sounds of a fight—the clanking metal of swords, the thud of fists falling, or the dreaded boom of a pistol. But I only heard a small noise behind me.

It was Mendoza.

His hulking figure, perfectly silhouetted in the night, crept towards me. His presence annoyed me more than threatened me. Fighting for my own life at a time like this was just a distraction. I shifted my weight to my toes, preparing to flee. Mendoza's knees bent slightly in response. He was going to pounce. He couldn't outrun me, but if he threw himself at me, there was no way to escape the strength of his mass.

Quickly calculating his intentions, I jerked slightly, spurring Mendoza to take action. In that moment, he did just what I expected. The full force of his brawn slammed into me. His tackle launched us both into the church door, which caved in from the force, rotten wood splintering all around us.

We skidded across the floor, crashing into a pew. The crack of buckling wood followed us. The pew had rammed into a rotten support column. I screamed and threw my arms over my head as heavy beams broke from the ceiling and buried me.

I was falling fast and the world was spinning around

me. Sounds were distant, like the buzzing of a fly in the background. I couldn't be sure, but I thought I heard my name. I felt as though I was spinning, free-falling through the air. But I could feel the floor beneath my back and a crushing weight on top of me. My arms wrapped around a heavy square beam across my chest. I hugged it tightly, trying to stop the sensation of falling.

I opened my eyes. Though I could not see anything but blackness, I could sense the stack of wood on top of me, a large beam only inches from my face. It was enough to help me reorient myself. The spinning stopped. I was lying still, buried beneath the collapsed roof of the church.

I choked for air, realizing I had not been breathing. Though I opened my mouth and sucked in eagerly, the crushing pile of wood prevented the air from getting to my lungs. I tried again and again, desperately sucking air in through my mouth, yet still suffocating.

I struggled against the weight that pinned me to the floor. A heavy beam lay diagonally across my torso— from my left shoulder to my right hip. I couldn't feel my legs. I could move my arms, but my left arm was practically useless with my shoulder pinned so solidly against the floor. The beam crossed my right arm near my elbow, allowing me more motion. I managed to place my right palm under the beam, my arm bent at the elbow and wrist, coiled like a spring. Grunting with air I could not afford to waste, I pressed as hard as I could against the beam. It raised just enough for my lungs to expand. I inhaled deeply, but the air wasn't right. A fit of coughing overtook me and I dropped the beam back onto my chest.

"Tessa!" It was Nicholas. His voice was loud and demanding.

I tried to respond, but I couldn't stop coughing.

The muted sounds around me erupted into a loud din. It was as if I were in the middle of a waterfall, a rush of noise enveloping me. I heard angry voices but could not determine what was said.

The weight on me shifted and my view was no longer blocked by wooden boards. Brilliant orange spread across the hazy air above me. The sun must finally be rising, I thought. This night had lasted long enough. I wedged my arm under the beam on my chest and pressed it up again. Poisonous air burned my throat, making me cough, but I did not drop the beam. Again the weight on me shifted, and I made out the blurry shape of a figure standing over me.

The beam on top of me disappeared, and I fell back in exhaustion, coughing more and more with each breath I took. My eyes burned and tiny tears trickled from their corners.

The shape over me—I knew it to be Nicholas—latched his hands under my arms and pulled. My body shifted a few inches, but my lifeless legs seemed to anchor me down. Nicholas disappeared from my line of sight. Suddenly, I could feel my legs again. Hot pain rushed through them. Nicholas hooked his hands under my arms again and pulled me free from the remaining debris.

He tossed me over his shoulder and staggered for a few steps before collapsing onto the floor, spilling me in the process. Between the rasps of my own coughing, I heard him coughing too. I wiped away the moisture pouring from my eyes and tried to see what was going on. I squinted against the haze, seeing that the front half of the church had collapsed. Nicholas had pulled me from the rubble, but I could see a twisted arm tangled in with the beams. Mendoza. I turned my head to look at the back of the church, my eyes stinging instantly.

The church was on fire.

Angry orange flames licked at the walls and ceiling, cornering us against the slope of the collapsed roof.

Rolling black smoke undulated above us.

I struggled to my feet, desperate to run. My legs wouldn't work and I scrambled aimlessly on the floor. I gasped for breath only to inhale fumes. Nicholas grabbed my shoulder and yanked me down. His hand pressed against the back of my head, pushing my nose to the floor. The air was cleaner here, and I managed to take a few shallow breaths. I turned my head and glanced at him sideways. He held an arm across his face, using his sleeve as a filter. I copied him and buried my nose in my elbow as I slowly sat erect.

Our eyes locked. This was it. This was the end. He'd saved me and I'd saved him, only to die here in each other's arms, sealing our fate with fire. It was poetic, albeit tragic.

The fire popped and another beam plummeted from the ceiling. Nicholas grabbed me to his chest, shielding me from the spray of fiery cinders. Our eyes met again, fear and panic raging behind the stinging tears.

"I love you," I choked out.

Nicholas shook his head fiercely. "No," he said. "Not like this."

He rose to his feet, crouching low to avoid the black smoke. He hooked my left arm around his neck and supported my waist, helping me stand as well as I could. I ignored the searing pain in my legs and let him lead me several steps to a section of wall that was not on fire—yet. Roaring flames ate their way towards us. I cringed against the boiling heat.

Stooping low, Nicholas set me down and filled his lungs as best he could. With both arms protecting his face, he stood tall and faced away from the wall. He raised his knee, then shot his leg out behind him, kicking the wall like a mule. Despite the roar of the fire, I heard the boards groan. He kicked it again and his foot broke through the rotting wood. With a few more well-placed kicks, there was a hole big enough to fit through.

I felt a cool gust of wind on my face and drank in the fresh air, just to cough it out again. The breeze fueled the blaze and the fire danced closer. I was afraid it would consume our escape route before we could crawl out.

Nicholas roughly shoved me through the hole in the wall. I coughed deeply, expelling the smoke from my lungs and breathing in the sweet outside air. I was so absorbed with breathing that I barely noticed the surge of people surrounding me. They helped Nicholas through the small hole and dragged us away from hungry flames of the burning church.

Safe on the other side of the street, Nicholas and I sat, huddled together, with a crowd of spectators standing behind us. The fire brigade raced around the disaster, desperate to prevent the flames from spreading. The hazy sunrise was as vivid as the flames before us. The whole world was on fire.

Nicholas's arm found its way around me and I tucked my head under his chin. Our labored breathing grew even. We sat there for hours, just watching buildings burn.

CHAPTER FORTY-SEVEN

"OOH," I CRINGED AT the sound of the metal snipping. "Not too much."

"I have to make it even," Nicholas said.

The scissors snapped again.

After a solid twenty hours of sleep, a hot bath, and a full meal, it was time to cut my hair.

I smoothed my hand down the back of my head, feeling where my hair stopped short halfway down my neck.

"I told you to keep your hands away," Nicholas reprimanded impatiently.

I sullenly clasped my hands in my lap.

Though Black had hacked away most of my hair, some long strands had remained. Not now. I could see them curled gently on the floor beside my bed. I sighed at the sight.

"Maybe we should have gone to a barber," I lamented for the hundredth time.

"Come on, Tessa. I'm a carpenter. This is easy." His ability to saw lumber and hammer nails did not put me at ease in the slightest. "Besides, how would you get to a barber anyway?"

My legs spread before me like lumpy tree trunks. My right leg was massive with splints and bandages meant to hold my fractured bones stable. My left leg was in better shape, but my ankle had been turned. It, too, was thick with bandages.

We extended our stay at the inn, resting and healing. Aside from a few mild burns, Nicholas was fine. On the other hand, I was completely incapacitated. The collapsed ceiling had crushed my legs and bruised my ribs. It had also sliced open my scalp—an injury I had forgotten until this very moment when Nicholas accidentally scraped it with a comb.

"I'm sorry," he whispered quickly when I winced. He lifted my hair aside for a better look and fingered the gash tenderly.

"What did you find out earlier?"

Nicholas stiffened at my question, letting his hands fall from my head.

"Anything?" I prompted when he didn't answer.

While I was bathing with a maid's assistance earlier, Nicholas went for food and information. He hadn't reported his news yet.

He breathed heavily, then returned to cutting my hair. "The ashes have cooled and now they are going through the rubble."

I could tell from his tone that he wasn't telling me everything.

"What else?"

"They asked me what happened. I told them it was a brawl over a girl. That things got rough and we knocked over the candles on the altar."

Although that was true enough, Nicholas was holding back.

I awkwardly repositioned myself so I could look at him. "You are not telling me everything."

His lips pressed into a thin line and he stared intently at my hair. He was avoiding me. I stared harder at him. Finally, he met my eyes.

"They only found two bodies."

"Mendoza and Black," I confirmed.

"Tessa, there should have been three bodies."

I furrowed my brow, confused for a moment. Then I remembered. There *should have* been three—Mendoza, Black, and the man playing cards with Mendoza.

"Two men met you in the church?" I had not thought of it before because I assumed that Black would want to take on Nicholas independently.

He nodded once, so slightly I barely noticed it.

"Which two bodies did they find?"

"Can't say. They were charred beyond recognition."

"You told me you wounded Black. You said you stabbed him and knocked him down before you pulled me free. So the other man must have escaped while you were fighting."

"I hope you are right." He was grim.

After a moment of replaying the night in my mind, I asked, "How did you know Mendoza?"

"We knew each other once."

"He had a particular hatred for you. Why?"

Nicholas breathed heavily. He was debating if he should tell me. "He was quartermaster on the *Banshee*. I actually considered him a mentor of sorts. Rumors began that he was ready to defect. He'd fallen in love with a woman. He'd been sending his gold to her. He was a good leader. Valuable. I didn't want him to go. I convinced a few men to find this woman and steal the gold. If Mendoza's money disappeared, he'd have to stay on to earn more. We found her, and things went wrong. She was killed. And she was pregnant with his child. Mendoza blamed me. Tried to kill me. Probably would have if I hadn't cut off his fingers. When Black learned of it, he burned Mendoza's contract, gave him a handful of my gold, and dropped him in port."

I swallowed hard. Nicholas, the pirate. Not a misfit. Not a lost little boy. *A stomach for killing*, Black had said.

I saw Nicholas differently now. He took pleasure in killing. It was his craft. If I were smart, I would sever ties with him. But I knew I never would. I loved him. Knowing that I could so easily dismiss his darkness made me acknowledge my own.

"What about you? Did Black punish you?"

"I was locked in the brig for three days. Then, Black promoted me. Said I showed initiative without fear. That's how I became quartermaster."

Nicholas stared at me with his steely eyes, trying to read my response. I held his gaze, unwilling to let him see the emotions churning in my mind.

He expected me to say something. Gasp in horror or show disgust. At least reprimand him. Confused by my emotions, I sidestepped the conversation. "It seems odd that he was working with Black. Didn't he hate Black as much as you?"

"Perhaps the opportunity to exact revenge on me was enough for him to form a truce."

"But they are both dead now—Mendoza and Black. Do you have to worry about the third man? Does he have some kind of vendetta against you?"

"I'm not concerned about him at all."

"But you're still concerned, I can tell. What is it?"

Nicholas shifted. He hated telling me things that would worry me, but I knew he wouldn't hide anything from me if I asked directly. "The fire crew found weapons. Those don't burn. They found knives and swords. But they've not found Black's rapier."

"Oh."

"There is a lot of debris. It could be buried," he told me with a forlorn smile. His reassurance was hollow. "Besides, you are absolutely right. I ran him through and punched him out. I didn't see him get back up or escape. And nobody else saw him come out of the church either."

I nodded. I could tell Nicholas wasn't convinced.

"Are you worried that he'll come back for you?" I asked quietly.

He shook his head slightly.

"I'm not worried," I said confidently. "Even if he did make it out, he was badly hurt."

Nicholas pressed his lips into a tight line. Something was bothering him.

When he realized I was waiting for an explanation, he quietly whispered, "I hesitated."

I knitted my eyebrows together in confusion.

"I could have killed him but I hesitated." The confession darkened his smoky eyes.

I remembered the look of betrayal on Black's face when he saw Nicholas leading the mutiny. "You and he were close."

Nicholas shook his head, his sad eyes turning angry. "I should have finished the job. If he is still alive, it's my fault."

I couldn't keep up with Nicholas's emotions. Unsure of what he wanted to hear, I did my best to comfort him. "I do not think he's alive, but even if he is, we will never see him again. In a few days...or, uh, weeks—" I corrected myself when Nicholas looked meaningfully at my splinted leg, "—we will be on the *Freedom*, then in no time we will be safe in St. Kitts."

Nicholas raised the scissors and I faced forward again. He snipped steadily at my hair, brushing it onto the floor as he trimmed. "You're excited about St. Kitts, then?"

"Of course. Why wouldn't I be?"

"Last time we talked about it—before the fire—you were so anxious, so reluctant to believe your father was alive."

"Maybe I shouldn't let my hopes get so high, but I think you are correct. Like you said, if so many different sources are talking about him by name and telling the same story about his daughter's disappearance, then it has to be true. It can't be coincidence."

"I'm right more often than you think," Nicholas teased. I heard him set down the scissors on the nightstand then he walked around the bed and sat in front of me, careful not to jostle my legs. A perfect smile spread across his tanned face.

My hands flew to my hair, assessing the abrupt bob. I groaned. "I look like a boy."

Nicholas shook his head, but he still had a mischievous smirk on his face.

"Yes I do! Even your hair is longer than mine."

He carefully leaned in to me and brushed the side of my neck with his lips. "Short hair has its advantages." He pulled back and looked in my eyes. He knew I was still doubtful. His warm hand slid through my hair. "Trust me," he said huskily, "you do not look like a boy."

My face flushed hot. Nicholas continued to run his fingers through my newly shorn hair. He honestly seemed mesmerized by it.

"It looks all right?" I asked tentatively.

"Aye. I would have never expected...It's really quite fetching." He grinned again then touched his lips to my earlobe. I trembled with chills.

Nicholas stood and retrieved a dish of scones he had

purchased earlier. He set them on my lap and sat by me again.

"These are good," I said finishing one and starting on another.

I picked the scone apart, popping little morsels in my mouth. When I caught Nicholas watching me, I smiled flirtatiously.

"You are happy today," he noticed. "Especially for a girl with two broken legs and a shocking new hair cut."

"Hey. That's only one broken leg."

"Still, you are in a sprightly good humor."

I shrugged lightly. "It's just...everything is falling into place. We don't have to go to London. You won't have to work a torturous job in that sooty city. My father will award you a pardon. We can stay in the Caribbean. We can stay free."

"Is that what you were worried about?" Nicholas asked, sitting forward and tucking my hair behind my ear. "You were worried that going to London meant giving up our freedom?"

I nodded slowly. "Yes, I think that's it, though I didn't realize it until just now. I felt London was being forced upon me. And you do not belong there. You really don't. I know you would have made it work, but you belong here. In the sun and wind." I stared at him intently. His limpid eyes sparkled.

"And I can't say whether I belong in England anymore. I've changed so much. Look at me! I'm eating scones on a bed with a pirate!" I giggled.

"That's true," he smiled. "You are definitely not 'Miss Monroe' anymore. I can't even say it without laughing."

We both laughed.

I tugged at his shirt, signaling for him to come closer. Nicholas set the plate of scones aside and obliged, wrapping his solid arms around me. I nestled into his broad chest, inhaling his delicious smell.

"I'm not quite sure who I am anymore, or where I belong. But I think I might belong in the sun and wind, too." I looked into his face. "I think I might belong with you."

Our lips met, the kiss starting tenderly, softly. My blood rushed, warming me from the inside out. The hot breath from Nicholas's mouth mingled with mine and I found myself suddenly gasping for air. His hands moved to my face, cupping my cheeks gently. I melted completely into his touch, relaxing, and molding into him.

Nicholas pulled me into his arms and cradled me close, stroking my cheek and staring into my eyes.

"I think you might belong with me, too," he whispered.

* * * * *

A fortnight later, a fair wind filled the sails of the *Freedom* as Nicholas hauled in the anchor. I stood barefoot on the deck leaning against the railing to take the weight off my splinted leg. I closed my eyes and inhaled deeply, drinking in the feeling of the sun on my face and the wind in my wild hair. Nicholas made his way to the helm and said, "Onward ho! To St. Kitts!"

The ocean danced eagerly, pulling us away from Curaçao and into open waters.

Squinting into the horizon, I took a deep breath of sea air and sang a chantey into the wind.

The End

About the Author

Photograph by Jason Miller www.millcreekphoto.net.

Born and raised in Idaho Falls, Idaho, Lara is the youngest of five children. She had to be pretty dramatic to get any attention whatsoever. She has since learned to channel her theatrics into writing.

At age seventeen, Lara's poetry and a short story was published in an anthology of teen writers. For the past seven years, Lara has utilized her writing skills as a technical writer and creative copywriter.

Lara holds a degree in psychology from the University of Idaho. She lives with her husband, two daughters, two dogs, cat, and ghost cat. She is a blogger, adoption advocate, brownie lover, and Oreo hater.

She is the author of the young adult historical adventures *Oceanswept* and *Undertow* and is currently working on the final installment of the trilogy. To learn more about Lara and her books, visit larahays.com or follow her on at Facebook.com/LaraHaysAuthor.

PROLOGUE

I WONDERED WHAT HAUNTED his dreams. What creations of sleep could possibly terrorize my pirate warrior? I sat on the edge of Nicholas's bed in the blackness of midnight, humming softly as my fingers slowly swirled through his hair. I could still feel the dampness of sweat on his scalp.

The sea was tumultuous tonight. The sails were reefed but I could still hear them snapping in the wind a deck above us. The air was heavy and damp and smelled strongly of brine.

Nicholas seemed as restless as the weather. He moaned and writhed.

"Shh," I whispered, stroking his cheek to relax his tense jaw.

He never talked about the nightmares. Even when I asked. Although, once I thought I heard him cry out, "Mama."

I traced the shape of his lips with my fingertips. He

finally stilled, his breathing growing deep and steady. I bent over and kissed his cheek, then stood to leave.

His hand reached out and grabbed mine. "Stay with me?" he whispered, sliding to make room on the bed.

I took my place next to him. He buried his face in my hair. And we both slept.

CHAPTER ONE

I STOOD AT THE porthole in my cabin, hypnotized by the undulating waves of the ocean and the rocking motion of the boat. The Caribbean sun burned relentlessly, turning the waves into reflective mirrors. Down in my cabin, there was no breeze to break up the heat. The smell of the ship was strong on days like this—the smell of baking wood and a whiff of mildew. I had never thought much about the smell of wood before, but Nicholas did. He loved wood and whenever his hands touched a plank or a rail, it was with reverence. He talked about the way wood smelled, the way it spoke in creaks, the way it cried sap when it was fresh. I absentmindedly placed my palm on the bulkhead and let my fingers press against the smooth, unyielding wood, willing it to speak to me the way it spoke to him.

A soft rap sounded at my door. "Tessa?"

There were only the two of us on the ship. I smiled over my shoulder, inviting him in.

"There is a ship approaching us."

"Pirates?" I asked, unable to mask the fear in my voice.

Nicholas smiled broadly, his hands slung casually on his hips. "A ship from the British Royal Navy."

My eyes grew wide. "Oh no. Do they think *we're* pirates?"

Nicholas laughed. "I think your father has sailed out to meet you."

"Sailed out to meet me? How? Why?"

He looked at me shyly. "I sent a letter."

Back in Curaçao, when we heard rumors that my father had survived the hurricane that I thought had killed him, Nicholas encouraged me to write a letter and send it ahead of us since we had to wait a couple of weeks for my broken leg to get stronger. I refused to write it, too scared to hope my father was actually alive.

Nicholas looked only slightly contrite at his small act of defiance. "You did?" I eagerly looked out the porthole but saw only the familiar view of endless sea and sky.

"Portside," Nicholas clarified.

I grabbed my cane and took a few shuffling steps with my splinted leg—a souvenir from my last encounter with pirates. Nicholas scooped me into his arms and carried me out to the wide corridor—more of a foyer that spanned the width of the ship—and gently deposited me in front of a porthole that looked out over the other side of the ocean.

A giant, tri-masted ship flying Britain's colors crested on the waves about a half a league away.

Nicholas looked at me anxiously. "Are you excited? It will be no time at all until you see your father again."

I smiled uneasily, still staring at the ship on the horizon.

I felt Nicholas behind me, his arms circling my waist.

"You're nervous," he stated.

"I'm not nervous."

"What is it?"

His lips found a soft spot on the side of my neck.

"This happened so fast," I said truthfully.

A moment later, Nicholas prodded me again. "What is it really?" He turned me towards him, breaking the spell the window had on me.

Nicholas's striking looks still took my breath away. Vibrant grey eyes fringed with black lashes; full lips; tawny skin; thick, dark hair that fell in waves around a chiseled face; a strong chin with a dusting of dark stubble. Everything about him was rugged and untamed. I could hardly believe he found me as irresistible as I found him.

His eyes blazed with concern—he wasn't used to me being unsettled. "Everything has worked out perfectly. Your father is alive. He has come to welcome you home. He can grant me a pardon. I will no longer be a fugitive. Our life together can begin at last. You should be ecstatic."

"I know," I mumbled. I *should* have been ecstatic, but I was far from it. I was eager to be reunited with my father. For the past three months we had both thought the other dead—him, the victim of the hurricane that sank our ship during the crossing from England, and me, claimed and murdered by pirates.

A stray hair fell over my face and tickled my nose—a constant occurrence with my new chin-length style. Still watching me with apprehension, Nicholas brushed the lock behind my ear. Even that little action stoked a horde of unsettling questions.

How would I answer my father when he asked what happened to my hair? Would I tell him that it had been sawed off, handful by handful, by a revenge-crazed pirate captain? When he asked what had happened to me over the past three months, would I tell him that I had been tried and found guilty of witchcraft and murder, ignited a mutiny and barely escaped with my life, then worked as a scullery maid in a bordello? And how, exactly, would I explain the renounced pirate officer who had his arms around me?

I caught Nicholas's hand and pulled it to my face, kissing his palm. "I have become accustomed to my freedom here on the…*Freedom*," I smiled knowing we had named Nicholas's ketch well. "I am not sure how I will adjust back into a world of corsets and crumpets and chaperones."

I took Nicholas's face in my hands and kissed him on his lips. "I will have to learn to do without certain things."

Nicholas let out a full-bodied chortle. "I have certainly corrupted you!"

I blushed but didn't turn my gaze away from his. "Everything is going to change."

"Some things will change," Nicholas conceded softly. "But not everything. Not the way I feel about you."

"I know that."

"Are you afraid of what your father will think?"

"No," I answered quickly. Too quickly. I paused and gathered my thoughts. "The girl I was in England…the girl I became over the past few months…they seem like two different people. Today I have to reconcile them."

Nicholas lifted my chin and pecked me on the nose. "We've been renegades long enough, luv. It's time we let society civilize us a little."

I nodded nervously. "I suppose so."

"There is only one thing I need to do," he said.

I cocked my head. "And what would that be?"

He lifted my chin with his fingertips and, with a crooked smile, ran the tip of his nose along mine. I closed my eyes and tilted my face to his and he pressed his lips to mine. A familiar excitement blossomed in my stomach. I placed my hands on his arms to steady myself, feeling the swell of his biceps under his thin shirt. He cupped the back of my head with a hand and pulled me closer, his kiss growing from tender to fierce in an instant. I met his passion, pressing myself into him. He kissed me again and again, his lips urgent and hungry. I was overwhelmed, lost to an undertow I could not fight.

"Kisses like this will be in short supply for a while." Nicholas gave me a flirtatious smile and kissed the tip of my nose, but the truth of his statement hung heavy between us.

"Let's get our fill, then," I whispered, weaving my fingers into the hair at the nape of his neck and pulling him closer for another kiss.

An earsplitting roar tore through the stillness.

Nicholas stood alert, his eyes sharp as they swept around the room. "Cannon fire," he stated matter-of-factly. He sprang up the ladder to the main deck. I cursed my broken leg, wishing I could follow.

Through the porthole I saw that the British ship was on us. They had made excellent time. I took up my cane and hobbled to the base of the ladder.

"Nicholas?" I called. "Is everything all right?"

The staccato sound of boots was my only answer. Nicholas was barefoot. Someone else had boarded the ship.

"Hello?" I called. No one answered. "Nicholas? What's happening?" I paused and listened. I heard voices, but could not decipher what they said. More footfalls. "Nicholas?" Still no answer. Fear pooled in my stomach. "Nick!" I called.

Something was wrong.

In a panic, I tried to pull myself up the ladder.

"Down there!" an unfamiliar voice sounded from

above. After a scuffle of footsteps, two strange faces looked down at me from the main deck. Startled, I fell off the ladder, my splint catching on the rungs, and landed with a violent thump.

"Are you Miss Monroe?" one asked.

I nodded.

The men jumped down the hatch and crowded over me, peppering me with questions.

"Are you all right?"

"Are there any others?"

"What is the matter with your leg?"

"Are you hurt?"

I closed my eyes and threw up my hands, gesturing for the men to stop their ranting. They quieted immediately.

"Where is my father? Is he here?"

The older of the two sailors stepped forward and helped me to my feet. His face was pocked and lined. He wore a white wig that hid his natural hair color but his eyebrows were flaming orange. "Madam, I am Commander Ephraim Bidlack. This is Lieutenant Johnson." He jerked his head to the dark-haired sailor next to him. "Your father is not here. He is breaking through a pirate siege at Nevis. In fact, he knows nothing of your whereabouts."

"He did not issue the order to find me?"

Commander Bidlack continued his explanation. "When your captor's letter arrived, the admiral was gone. I read it in his stead and ordered instant pursuit. Your father would not have wanted us to waste a day."

My captor?

"Lieutenant? Are there any others?" a voice from the main deck called.

Johnson climbed partway up the ladder so he could talk to someone on the main deck. "No, sir. Just Miss Monroe."

"Is she well?"

"It appears she has an injured leg, but she is stable."

"Can she be moved?"

The man named Johnson peered down at me. "It would be difficult for her to board the other ship."

"Very good," the voice from upstairs said. "We have the pirate in custody and we will take him to the other vessel instead."

I looked frantically at the gentlemen with me. "What does he mean by that? He has the pirate in custody?"

"Don't worry," Johnson comforted, stepping off the ladder. "You are safe now."

"I was safe ten minutes ago," I insisted, my frustration finally exploding. "I demand you tell me what has been done to my escort."

The men exchanged a surprised look.

Commander Bidlack coolly said, "We understand him to be a pirate. He has been arrested."

"Release him! He is not a pirate, he is my rescuer."

Johnson knitted his brows together in confusion. "We received a threatening letter."

"You received no such thing!"

"Do you have the letter, sir?" Johnson asked Bidlack.

Commander Bidlack nodded and retrieved a folded piece of parchment from his coat. I recognized Nicholas's slanted writing—I'd seen it enough in the log books. I snatched the letter out of Bidlack's knotty fingers.

Dear Sir,

By way of introduction, I am a humble sailor who had the good fortune of meeting your daughter, a certain Miss Tessa Monroe, under circumstances of duress. I write to inform you that she is well. She is npresently in my custody in Willemstad, Curaçao, where she is recovering from an injury. As soon as her strength returns, I shall take her aboard my fishing ketch and sail to Basseterre, St. Kitts, to reunite the two of you and discuss further arrangements. I hope this news finds you well. I anxiously await our meeting.

Your Obliged,
N. Holladay

"This letter is not threatening," I hotly chided.

Bidlack pounded the letter with a finger. "This is practically a ransom note."

I quickly reread the letter, then looked back to Bidlack, confused.

Bidlack huffed and scowled.

"The man we apprehended upstairs," Johnson began, "is he not Nicholas Holladay?"

"Yes," I answered tentatively.

"And is he not the same man who is a pirate known by the name Marks?"

I groaned. "He answers to the name Nicholas Holladay. He has acted as my protector for the past twelve weeks and does not deserve to be treated as a criminal."

"Our sources were quite clear. He is the quartermaster of the pirate vessel *Banshee*," snapped Bidlack.

"He is the *former* quartermaster of the *Banshee*. He has renounced his *former* profession and is, in fact, wanted by that pirate crew for desertion."

"His letter professes custody over you," Johnson said, reading over my shoulder and pointing out the words. "The mention of your injury. Duress. Your return in exchange for further arrangements."

"You've made a lot of assumptions." I quickly folded the letter and returned it to Bidlack. "I am indebted to Mr. Holladay—a man who rescued me *from* pirates and nursed my injuries. He has brought me to St. Kitts at great personal sacrifice. *My father* is indebted to him."

Johnson softened, his warm brown eyes mystified. "All this can be sorted out. For now, he's already aboard the other ship. You'll see him back in St. Kitts."

I huffed dramatically and prayed for a swift wind.

Undertow is now available at all major online book sellers.

www.ingramcontent.com/pod-product-compliance
Lightning Source LLC
Chambersburg PA
CBHW022023240626

47154CB00007B/2228